Christmas in Brookside Falls

by

Lita Harris

Christmas in Brookside Falls

Cover Art by *Diana Carlile*

The Wild Rose Press, Inc.
PO Box 708
Adams Basin, NY 14410-0708
Visit us at www.thewildrosepress.com

Publishing History
First Edition, 2021
Trade Paperback ISBN 978-1-5092-3957-3
Digital ISBN 978-1-5092-3958-0

Published in the United States of America

A soft wave of hair barely revealed his eyes as he stepped out from behind the tree. His cashmere overcoat told her he wasn't from Brookside Falls. She caught her breath and steadied her voice. "Yes, I'm sure it's mine."

"But I want this tree." He tightened his grip around it.

"Too bad, it's mine." His green eyes twinkled from the moonlight. She moved in closer and staked her claim to the innocent evergreen embroiled in a custody battle in the church parking lot.

"It's mine and my aunt's tree, now give it back." Danny let go of her coat but continued to clutch her purse even harder.

The man knelt in front of Danny. "Oh, really? And how do you know this tree belongs to you?"

Kristen wanted to wipe the hank of hair from the stranger's eyes. The unkempt lock of rogue hair drove her crazy. "Can we say it's mine? I'm sure you'll find another suitable tree."

He stood. "Hmm, I'm not sure. I like this one."

"Yes, I do." She held onto the tree, motioning with her eyes to Danny so this pain-in-the-butt person would get the hint. The smirk of his crooked smile annoyed her, yet it was familiar.

He stretched out a hand. "Luke."

Dedication

My editor, Leanne Morgena, your guidance has made this book possible.

Emma Kaye, who is always available for a last-minute critique and understands the importance of chocolate.

Chapter One

"Isn't the snow beautiful?" Kristen brushed an unruly tuft of hair from her nephew's soulful eyes and pulled him closer. She cradled him in her arms against her chest and rocked him, the same way her late sister Carly protected her when they were kids. She vowed to care for Danny with every bit of strength she could muster.

She hoped the window seat in her old bedroom of her grandmother's house in the countryside of Brookside Falls, Pennsylvania provided the same comfort to Danny as when she was young. At seven years old, Danny was young to lose a parent.

"It's pretty. We never got any snow in Florida." Danny stretched an arm and drew circles in the frost on the window. A tear fell onto his cheek. "I wish Mommy could see this."

"Oh, but she can!" She hoisted him onto her lap, pushed aside the ivory, lace curtain, and watched light, dry snow cover the grass in the front yard.

Danny climbed off and knelt beside her.

She laid a hand over his and pressed the tip of his finger against the glass. The snow gave way to a starlit sky. "See, there she is. See that bright star?"

"Where?"

"Right there." She hugged him and pointed at the sky. "The one twinkling. It's the brightest star in the sky."

"Yeah, I see it. It's really her?"

"Yes, sweetie. Look for the brightest star, and it'll be your mom looking down with the same love as before." She hugged him tightly.

He didn't resist, a sign he was becoming comfortable with her.

She stifled tears, which desperately needed to be shed but did not want to add unnecessary worry. Her insides trembled. She stayed strong for both of them.

Danny watched his mother waste away the past year, and Kristen's heart broke every time she thought of him alone in Florida with Carly. Her sister would never burden family with her problems. The Andersons were taught to never show weakness. The ability to work through their own struggles was considered a badge of honor.

Thanksgiving came and went without mention of the holiday, and Kristen was damned if she would allow any more ugliness into his young world. Except for the occasional holiday dinner, she hadn't spent much time in Brookside Falls since she'd left town not long after graduating high school and obtained her cosmetology license.

Carly brought Danny to their grandmother's home, fondly referred to as Nana Keets for her love of parakeets, and insisted he live there to be with family. The sleepy town in northeastern Pennsylvania with its single-screen movie theatre, sporting goods store, and grass median down the center of Main Street was a stark contrast to the crowded, cement covered lawns of Florida.

Maybe it's what Carly wanted, a small town with

plenty of land for Danny to explore and a home that made one feel welcome.

But not Kristen. She wanted to raise her nephew at the Jersey Shore. It's not Florida, but the beach was something he was familiar with and was her home the last twelve years.

The small-town, former bed and breakfast her grandmother owned was the heart of the Anderson family. Maybe Carly knew what she was doing when she brought her son there. She would have to trust her sister—at least, for a little while.

"There she is again!" Danny yelled.

"Yep, that's her." She heaved him from the window seat. "Come on, let's go see what Nana is doing. I smell chocolate chip cookies." She held his hand to keep him from sliding down the winding banister. Because that's exactly what she did as a child, yet as an adult, she was charged with her nephew's care. Once she was confident he was safe to venture without incident, she relaxed her hold on Danny.

He wiggled his hand free and ran down the last flight of stairs, launched from the third step, and landed squarely on his feet. "You know what I like about Nana's house?"

"What?" Kristen met him at the bottom of the staircase.

"The birds. They're all over the house." He pointed at green, yellow, and blue stuffed parakeets lined up on curtain rods, peeking out from branches randomly stuck in vases throughout the inn. "Can I have one?"

His blue eyes melted her heart, but she wouldn't dare give him one of Nana's former pets—expertly hand-stuffed by Nana herself.

"They're not mine to give. You have to ask Nana."

Quick save, shrugging the responsibility. Her grandmother would never give up one of her treasured birds, no matter how hard Danny pleaded.

She followed the familiar aroma of freshly baked chocolate chip cookies into the kitchen. Kristen sneaked up behind her grandmother and playfully tugged her apron tie. "Are you finished baking?" She snatched two warm cookies from the plate on the counter, handing one to Danny and eating hers in one bite.

"Yes, finally done. Guests seem to like the chocolate chips the best. I like them because they're the easiest to make." Nana rubbed her hands in her faded, blue-checkered apron, her loose bun dangled at the back of her neck. "Danny, would you please take out the garbage and check on the cats while you're out there?"

He jumped off the chair and headed for the door.

"Wait. Put your jacket on." Nana picked it up off the chair and tossed it to Danny. She watched him button up and leave the room. "How's he doing?"

Kristen pulled out a chair from the kitchen table and put her third cookie back on the plate. She couldn't afford a new wardrobe, and a few weeks of her grandmother's cooking already showed on her thighs. "He's doing better. I'm keeping him busy and distracted the best I can."

She gave in and picked up another cookie. *Chocolate cures all.*

"He needs time to grieve. We all do." Nana stood with her back to the sink, arms across her chest.

In spite of the circumstances, her grandmother was happy to have family in the house. Her steely, eighty-year-old eyes glistened whenever Danny gobbled down one of her home-cooked meals. "I know. But I also believe Carly wouldn't want us to waste time mourning her. She'd want us to celebrate her life, especially knowing how fragile it is."

"What breaks my heart is his father doesn't care." Nana sat at the kitchen table.

"I know, Nana, but that was her business. Respect it."

The kitchen door flew open and banged against the wall.

Kristen spun in her chair.

"Hey. Do know how to fix a hole in the wall?" Nana put her hands on her hips and glared at Danny.

"No." He lowered his gaze.

"Well, stop banging doors. Is all I'll say." Nana turned to the sink and washed her hands.

Kristen stooped down to hug Danny. "Don't take off your coat. Grab your hat and gloves. We're going out to buy something special."

"More garbage bags for me to pick up leaves?" Danny pursed his lips.

"Nope, something a bit more fun. We're getting a Christmas tree and have to hurry if we want a good one before they're gone." Kristen rubbed her hands together, excited to do something fun.

"Yay! A real tree? Like the kind that grows in the yard?"

"Yes, a real one." Until that moment, Kristen didn't realize Danny never celebrated the holiday with a real Christmas tree. Carly said the real trees sold in Florida were cut down so far in advance, they dried out before the holiday. "We're buying the biggest tree we can fit in our house."

"Are you coming, Nana?" Danny yanked on his hat to cover his ears.

"Nope, my tree shopping days are over. I'll have the hot chocolate ready when you come home." Nana winked, removed the last batch of chocolate chip cookies from the cooling rack, and put them into a cardboard box decorated with poinsettias.

The cookie boxes brought Kristen back to holiday baking days when she was Danny's age. Her heart flooded with happiness at the memory.

"See ya, Nana. Off to buy a tree." Danny yanked down his hat to cover his ears. "Ready."

"So am I." Excited yet scared in her new responsibility as guardian, she opened the front door and welcomed what was next.

****

"Thanks, guys." Luke Baldwin handed the furniture movers a twenty-dollar bill and closed the door after they left. He plopped himself down in an overstuffed leather recliner, which stood in sharp contrast to the streamlined minimalist style of his new apartment. He was ready for change. Time away from New York City was welcome. Circumstances brought him back to his childhood town, and he needed time to adjust.

Buying a condo was a consideration, but the small borough of Haineswood didn't cater to that demographic. The choice was either an old apartment above a business in the center of town or the scarce two-family house. Single homes dominated the landscape of the neighboring town of Brookside Falls, so unless someone rented out a house, he was stuck above a storefront. The living arrangement was convenient since he rented the office space below and got a good deal on the two rents.

What to do first?

Not in the mood to connect with old friends in town, he ignored that option, not that he had many he cared to contact. Besides, they probably left Haineswood like he did when he went off to college. He worked hard to overcome his isolated world, yet he wasn't ready to embrace a new one.

He headed downstairs to organize his new office. A knock on the front door echoed throughout his nearly empty space. He walked across the room, each step reminding him to buy rugs to balance the acoustics of the room. He peered through the glass and sighed before he opened the front door.

"Hello there." Aunt Gladys shoved a large pot of orange and yellow chrysanthemums into Luke's arms.

"Thank you. Come in." He took the woodsy scented floral arrangement and set it on top of a bookshelf. "The movers left a few minutes ago."

"Were they as good as I said they would be?" Gladys followed him to the desk. She pushed her purse up her arm and scraped gloved hands together to remove a bit of dirt from the flowerpot.

He nodded. "Even better. And thank you for the welcome gift."

Gladys cupped her cheeks and shook her head. "Oh, honey those aren't for you. I didn't want to leave them in the car. It's cold out there."

"But…" He shook his head. Foolish of him to think his aunt would give him a housewarming present. Not like she made a huge commission on his deal. And he wasn't a horticulturist, but he was pretty sure chrysanthemums could survive forty-five degrees.

"You're in for a big change from New York." Gladys rubbed a small spot of dirt from the window behind his desk with the cuff of her faux fur coat sleeve.

"I'm ready for a break from the city." He harbored minimal doubts about the adjustment as an adult, but his aunt didn't need to know about his uncertainty. "I'm sure a lot has changed in Haineswood."

"Not around here, sweetheart. Maybe they've replaced a stolen stop sign but that's about it." Gladys took back her flowers. "Well, you have my number. Call if you need anything, especially if you decide to buy a house. This place is okay for a single person, but..."

"This single person is happy with his decision."

She shook her head. "Okay. See you around."

He closed the door behind her and was thankful the flowers weren't for him. At least, he wouldn't have to take care of them. His mother was enough for now.

The room was quiet. The lack of noise would take time to adjust. No more garbage trucks rolling down the city streets to collect trash at the crack of dawn. Or squealing brakes of dairy, newspaper, and bakery trucks making deliveries.

He scanned his sparse desk and pulled a pad from his briefcase. He jotted down the immediate supplies he needed for the office and apartment—window cleaner, paper towels, binder clips, pens, pads. Of course, he needed sketch pads and candles. He remembered a lot of electrical outages in the area when he was a kid. Then again, his mother missed paying the electric bill on occasion. Looking back, her dementia might have been developing, and he thought she was simply ignoring him. His heart sank at the thought of not recognizing her decline sooner.

He pulled out his cell phone and climbed the stairs to his apartment. "Hello? Is Nurse Proctor there? Luke Baldwin calling."

"One moment please."

An unfamiliar woman responded. Classical music filled the silence while he was on hold. He preferred dealing with the same nurse who was familiar with his mother's condition. He didn't have the patience to rehash the story each time a new person answered the phone.

"Hello?"

"Nurse Proctor, hi. How is she today?" He stood at the living room window, arms crossed, phone held in place by his chin and resting on his shoulder. He stared at the street below. The unusually warm air skirted leaves in piles along the edges of the building foundations. A squirrel ran across the wire from one telephone pole to another.

"Hello, Luke. Today is a better day. She recognized me and ate her oatmeal without protest. She even asked for apple bits. Orange juice, too. She wasn't a fan of the over-cooked, dried-out rye toast, but she managed to finish her meal."

Relieved his mom was having a good day, he took a deep breath then looked up at the sky and wished things were different. "I'm glad to hear this. She can become melancholy this time of year."

"Are you settled into your new location?" Nurse Proctor asked.

"Yes, thank you for taking such good care of her while I do this. Moving her to a new facility might not be the best choice but considering the situation, I'd like to have her living in a place where she can be outside more."

"I understand. We'll do what we can while you set her up in a place nearer to you. In the meantime, know she is well cared for at our facility. My grandmother spent her time here and loved it, because some of her friends were in the same wing. Being close to familiar people made the adjustment easier."

"I know, and your honesty was the reason I decided on your facility." His chest relaxed, and his breathing eased. "Thank you again. I'll keep checking on her, and you have my new office phone number, correct? Cell service can be spotty at times out here."

"I made sure all your information was updated before you left. Don't worry. She's fine."

He hung his head. Any other time would have been a bad idea to bring her back to Pennsylvania, but she didn't remember much of her past so the memories were lost. She loved her country town and never wanted to leave. But the gossip was devastating and merciless when she was younger. The decision to move away with Luke than subject him to whispers and stares of people who put their noses in other people's business was their best option.

But he wanted some answers also. He was strong enough to deal with the whispers. "Okay. Thank you. Please never hesitate to call if she has an episode. Bye."

He slid his phone into his jeans pocket and looked around the small living room. He would be fine. The situation was temporary. With so much uncertainty surrounding his mother, he could not make lifelong decisions until she settled into a permanent home.

The first thing on his agenda was to buy a Christmas tree. He transported the family box of ornaments himself, not worth taking a risk of the movers breaking a cherished memory. The few things from his grandparents and childhood rested in the broken-down box shuttled with each relocation.

He needed stability, and Haineswood would be his attempt to secure a foundation. As an architect, he traveled to most building sites so where he lived didn't matter. As long as he had a good Internet connection, he could work.

Years ago, he learned to live with less. The material stuff he accrued in the city meant nothing. To impress potential employers, girlfriends, and his buddies was foolish. People deserted him when his mother became ill. His stomach churned at the thought of time wasted on others who proved insincere.

But his life didn't end when he realized what was going on around him. The emptiness of his youth crept in as his surroundings faded into meaningless tokens of accumulation.

Once Jillian left him, he was on his own. If she couldn't support him through a family crisis, he was better off without her. Good thing he didn't make it to the jewelry store to pick out an engagement ring and surprise her.

A fresh start at life and new apartment required picking out a Christmas tree. He pulled on his coat and opened the door. For a moment he stood on the front stairs and sucked in a deep breath. *Yes. A new beginning.*

****

The trip from the Anderson house into town wasn't very far, but Kristen took her time driving to revisit her former town without traffic in her way. A few homes were decorated with lights, some entwined in boughs of evergreen wrapped around porch railings. Other strands hung from the roofline to imitate icicles.

"Isn't this pretty? What's your favorite? White or colored lights?" She glanced to the rearview mirror and caught Danny mesmerized by the display.

"The colored lights. Blue is my favorite."

"I agree but I think I favor red."

The darkness of the small-town street opened to the glow omitting from St. Theresa's parking lot. Strands of white lights strung in-between fresh cut evergreens illuminated the area. Three weeks before the holiday was too early to buy a tree, but she wanted Danny to experience a northern Christmas for as long as he could. Each holiday, trees sold earlier than the last year and consumers struggled to keep the fir alive through the holidays.

Danny threw off his seatbelt and jumped out of the car, racing to the tallest tree. He pulled down on the highest branch he could reach. "Can we get this one?"

"Slow down." She bent over to catch her breath. The tree must have been about twenty feet high. At least he showed enthusiasm, the most he had since his mother passed away. If this is what life would be like raising a seven-year-old, she had to get in shape. No more cookies. After the holiday she'd focus on eating healthy and be back on track. Once they moved to New Jersey, she would hit the beach and none of her grandmother's baking could sabotage her efforts.

"This one? Please?" He yanked the branch and the tree lurched forward.

She grabbed the trunk to steady the falling evergreen. "Uh, no. Though the tree is very nice, it's too big for the living room." She rubbed his head and squished his hat onto his forehead.

"But it's big. I want a big tree." He squeezed his eyes shut to fake cry.

She wasn't falling for that trick again. "Listen, I have a plan. You know the gigantic pine tree in front of the house?"

Still holding onto the branch, he nodded. "The one with the hoot owl?"

"Yes. We can decorate that tree with whatever you want. We'll load the branches with lights, balls, candy canes, anything you like. But we need a smaller tree for inside the house. One about this big." She stood on her toes and stretched a hand above her head. "Sound good?"

Danny wiped his nose with his glove. He slipped his other hand into hers and squeezed her fingers. "Okay."

She squeezed back and kissed the top of his hand, then kneeled beside him. "We'll be okay, kid." She pointed toward the sky. "There's your mom, like I told you she would be."

He tilted back his head and looked at the sky. "Mommy's star." His cheeks turned red from smiling.

"Mommy's star, she's always with us." Her eyes burned from tears fighting to escape. "Some nights she shines brighter than others. This is one of them. I guess she wants to help us find our tree."

A flick of her hand wiped away tears from her

eyes. She stood and guided him to a section of trees about eight feet high.

He took off his gloves and ran his hand down the branches. Danny pushed his nose deep into the tree and nearly buried his head. "I like this one."

Kristen stood back, arms crossed, head cocked to the side. "Hmm, let me see." She stood on her toes and stretched an arm above her head. "Are you sure you want this one?"

"Yep."

Danny grinned, full of excitement as she had never seen before. "All right, I think this one is yours. Hold this." She handed her purse to Danny who wasn't much bigger than the bag. "Humph, this tree is heavy. Are you sure it's not still in the ground?"

Danny knelt down and looked under the tree while clutching her purse. "Nope, not in the ground. Pull harder."

She yanked on the tree, and it sprang back, nearly pulling her arm out of her socket. "What the…" She walked around to the back of the evergreen where it rested against a slatted fence. "Hey, that's mine."

Danny sprang up and ran to her side, clutched her coat pocket, and dragged her purse.

"Are you sure this is your tree?"

A soft wave of hair barely revealed his eyes as he stepped out from behind the tree. His cashmere overcoat told her he wasn't from Brookside Falls. She caught her breath and steadied her voice. "Yes, I'm sure it's mine."

"But I want this tree." He tightened his grip around it.

"Too bad, it's mine." His green eyes twinkled from

the moonlight. She moved in closer and staked her claim to the innocent evergreen embroiled in a custody battle in the church parking lot.

"It's mine and my aunt's tree, now give it back." Danny let go of her coat but continued to clutch her purse even harder.

The man knelt in front of Danny. "Oh, really? And how do you know this tree belongs to you?"

Kristen wanted to wipe the hank of hair from the stranger's eyes. The unkempt lock of rogue hair drove her crazy. "Can we say it's mine? I'm sure you'll find another suitable tree."

He stood. "Hmm, I'm not sure. I like this one."

"It's mine." She held onto the tree, motioning with her eyes to Danny so this pain-in-the-butt person would get the hint. The smirk of his crooked smile annoyed her, yet it was familiar.

He stretched out a hand. "Luke."

"Nice to meet you, Luke, but I'm not letting go of this tree so you can rip it away." She narrowed her eyes, and with shoulders firm, she made a promise to Danny and this was his Christmas tree. His first real evergreen, and the first since his mother died. No one would take it from her.

"What about I give you a hundred percent ownership in this tree in exchange for your name?"

"It's Kristen. Now let go of my tree!" Danny yelled.

Eluding the stranger was impossible now. Her nephew gave her up in exchange for a prematurely cut tree.

"Truce." Luke released the evergreen and held up his hands.

"At least you play fair." Kristen took hold of the prized tree.

Danny dropped her purse on the ground, crawled under the tree, and grabbed the trunk.

"Unlike you." Luke laughed.

"Whatever. Don't you have to find a tree?"

Danny popped up from under the evergreen and dragged it away from Luke. The tree was his to take home.

A boy scout appeared from behind the row of trees. "Did you find what you want, ma'am?"

"Yes, thank you. How much for this one?" She pointed to Danny, wrestling to steady her new purchase.

"Sixty, and that price includes trimming the trunk, wrapping, and hauling it to your car."

She sighed and counted out three twenty-dollar bills with a five and handed over the money that should have been used elsewhere, but she made a promise. She didn't expect the tree to be so expensive. The most she decorated for the holidays was to take home a dried-out poinsettia plant from the beauty shop on Christmas Eve and hang a scratched-up gold ball she found in the shop's storage room.

Luke strolled behind them toward the prep area while the trunk was cut and tree run through the netting machine.

"Why are you following me?" Kristen stopped short.

"Still looking for a tree. Want to see what's over here." He stood chest to chest with her and looked out into the small forest in the church parking lot. "Nothing yet, but then again you are impeding my progress by blocking my way."

That chunk of hair in his eyes annoyed her even more. She clenched her fist to refrain from swiping at his forehead.

"Where to, ma'am?"

She spun to follow the voice behind her and motioned to her beat-up, small SUV.

The scout grabbed the tree by the trunk and hoisted it on top of the roof, expertly tying it down with twine on the carrier racks.

"Well, Luke. I hope you find the perfect tree. Good night."

"How about your phone number?" He waved a casual salute.

She walked away struggling with a gnawing feeling she knew him. But how?

Chapter Two

Luke walked away, his cheeks hurt from smiling. He had no intention of taking the tree from the kid. He wanted to meet Kristen. After being away from town for a little more than a decade, he didn't know many people in Haineswood anymore.

He walked through the parking lot and measured each potential tree against the height of his forehead. Stand, tree, and star couldn't be over eight feet. Once, he made a mistake and brought home an evergreen that scratched the paint off the ceiling as he dragged the too-tall tree through the room. His mother wasn't happy, but he made good on his promise to repaint the ceiling in time for the holiday.

Though he barely settled into his new place with nothing more than a small, round dining table with two chairs, and a couch, he was decorating for the holiday. The one memory of his childhood brought happiness.

He couldn't complain. His mother did her best to provide for him, but being a single parent in a small town wasn't easy. College provided his way out of the isolated existence that stifled him and his mother. She worked a lot, and he stayed in and studied.

He thought about the last time they spent Christmas together at his mom's house. She was too ill to get off the couch. He decorated her tree with her favorite gold bows and red glass balls. He feared it could be her last holiday to remember. No matter where he lived, he made it a point to always have a tree. The memory of their holiday made it special.

Since this would be his first tree in his new home, he didn't want anything too big, unsure how it would fit in the living room. He kidded with Kristen at the church lot to tease her. He smiled each time she tightened her lips to keep from laughing at his foolishness. His chest warmed while he had fun watching her blue eyes fill with frustration the more he chided her about not giving up the tree.

"Can I help you?"

A different scout sneaked up on him, breaking his concentration. "Looking for a Fraser Fir."

"We have trees. Not sure on all the different types." The boy scratched his head.

Luke laughed. The scout was probably eleven and didn't care what kind of trees they were selling. "I'll continue looking. Thanks."

"No problem, sir. Yell when you're ready."

Luke walked through the perfectly spaced rows of trees, from three feet to twenty. He wondered if he would ever have space for a large tree.

Nah. Too big.

He could put a small tree in his office and spruce up the place. No pun intended. He shook the trunk of a Douglas Fir and then ran his fingers down the branch, checking for dead needles. Not what he wanted but it was the traditional Christmas tree. No Frasers were available on the lot. "Douglas, you are coming home with me."

Change could be good. After all, he was starting over. He checked his phone. No messages. His hermit-like behavior was becoming too much even for him to accept.

"I'm ready." He yelled to the scout.

"Yes, sir. Ready to help."

"I'll take this one." He pulled the tree away from the makeshift wooden wall of two-by-fours it rested against.

"This is a nice one." The scout bounced the tree on the ground. "See, no dead needles."

"That's exactly what I'm looking for, one that doesn't drop needles." He wished such a tree existed. He shuddered at the thought of digging pine needles out of the faded, orange-yellow shag carpeting the last place his mother lived. During his college stint, his mom moved into an old, rundown apartment. He didn't know at the time she was sick and wanted to be near him.

The living quarters with its dingy, brown, scratched paneling and ripped window shades aged with road dirt made him shiver at the memory. Only good thoughts going forward—no looking back.

Kristen. A cute smile made her cheeks glow, and her eyes—so familiar but he couldn't place it. She possessed a fresh-faced, blonde-hair-beach-girl look though the closest beach was four hours away. "Bag it up please. How much?"

"Forty-five."

Luke shelled out three twenties. "Keep the change. Merry Christmas."

"Thank you, sir. Merry Christmas to you." The scout smiled and shoved the bills into his jacket pocket.

"Over there." Luke pointed to his compact car, "Think we can secure the tree to the roof?"

"No problem, sir. I can tie this down to get you home."

Home.

Was he?

Mixed emotions swirled through his being. The base of his neck tightened. He closed his eyes to ward off a headache. Coming back to Haineswood regurgitated unpleasant childhood memories he worked hard to bury, and he wasn't the type to dwell on the past. Yet, he was compelled to go back home. He opened his eyes and looked to the sky. *Everything will work out fine.*

"Thanks, kid." Luke helped hoist the tree onto the car roof while the scout whipped the rope into secure knots with the precision of a sailor.

"Thank you again, sir. Enjoy your holiday."

Celebrating the holiday was his plan, even if he was alone. Sure, he would visit his mother, but most days she didn't know who he was. His long-term plan to settle into Haineswood or preferably, Brookside Falls depended on if he could afford a house and bring her home. Even if she only remembered a glimpse of the lakes and town center, it was the place she loved most in the world.

He drove away, and the white lights of the parking lot faded from view. The star-like twinkle reminded him of Kristen's eyes. He would get to know her better. But first, he had to take his tree home so he could decorate and bring his mother home for Christmas.

****

"Please open the door." Kristen dragged the evergreen up the porch stairs and then stopped to catch her breath. "This is heavier than I expected."

Nana threw open the front door before Danny had a chance to turn the doorknob.

"How beautiful! It's been a while since we had a nice tree like this." Nana moved out of the way as they passed through the foyer and plopped the tree in the living room.

"I know, and this is the perfect year to put one up. With me and Danny staying with you, decorating will be easier, right kid?" She brushed her hands together to rid her palms of bark dust.

"You bet!" Danny jumped up and down. He tore off his jacket and threw it on the chair, his hat and gloves followed. "Mommy's star helped us find this tree, but we almost didn't get it because some man said it was his."

Nana turned to Kristen. "What's he talking about?"

"Oh, nothing. Some guy wanted our tree, and he gave me a little hassle about it. But we won." Kristen tossed her coat on the chair as she thought of his green eyes. He was cute but she didn't have time to be involved with anyone. Even if she wanted to she couldn't since she was going back to New Jersey after the holidays. Her boss was understanding, generous, and let her take time off from work. The salon could survive without her for a few weeks. Kristen grabbed the tree and dragged it to the corner of the living room her grandmother cleared out.

"You can see the tree through the window from there." Nana moved a stand with three of her stuffed parakeets to the side of the fireplace. "Don't want this in the way."

Kristen and her sister were always freaked out by their grandmother's fetish for memorializing her birds.

But time brought understanding. The birds were all Nana had to stay busy except for her and Danny, and they wouldn't be staying in Brookside Falls.

"Come here, kid." She sat on the window seat and held her arms open wide.

Danny jumped into them and hugged her.

She plopped him down beside her hip. "Turn around. Do you see Mommy's star?"

"Yep, right there." He pointed to the sky.

"Thanks, sis. Thanks for helping us find the perfect tree. Love you." She blew a kiss to the sky. Her heart swelled with so much love she thought her chest would burst open. A flash surged through her mind of the last time she saw her sister alive. She finally was at peace. "Okay, let's decorate. But first, we have to bring down the decorations from the attic."

She held his hand and led him up three flights of stairs. Years had passed since she ventured up there. The creaky floor and dusty furniture scared her to death. She embraced her obligation to protect her nephew. *Show no fear.*

She turned the doorknob, then pushed open the creaky attic door. Dim light from a single bulb barely illuminated the room, but the area didn't seem so frightening now, though still dusty and dark. Discarded chairs were stacked in one corner—her grandmother meant to have the broken furniture fixed while the inn was open but lost interest when her husband passed away.

Trunks sat in the middle of the floor, filled with unused linens, a reminder of memories of a once beautiful inn. She and Carly used to stay at the inn during the summers when school was out. But then one night changed their lives forever. "The decorations should be in those boxes."

Danny made his way to the pile of boxes, flaked from age and neglect. He picked up a small box and shook it.

"No, no, no!" Kristen leapt across the room. "Those ornaments are glass. Don't shake them."

"Sorry." He froze in place. His small hands gripped the package.

"Give me, sweetie." She took the decrepit box and placed it on the floor.

He knelt beside her.

She pulled open the flaps, and his eyes filled with wonder.

Flecks of glitter flew into the air as she lifted an ornament nestled in crumpled tissue paper. "This one is my favorite."

She held a clear, dark purple glass ball toward the light bulb. "You can see through it when the light hits it just right."

Danny reached out to touch the ornament but quickly put his hands behind his back. "It's scratched. The yellow and green stripes are broken."

"Maybe so, but it's what makes it special. Some things are irreplaceable so you love them no matter what condition they're in." She hugged him tightly, feeling more like a mother than an aunt. "Come on, you take the tree stand, and I'll get the rest."

She turned off the light and closed the attic door—and its memories—behind her. An image of Luke standing in the church parking lot with his hands in his overcoat popped into her head, and she smiled. Something about him bugged her, but she couldn't figure it out.

****

The quick stop at Wally's Five-and-Dime store turned into an hour ordeal. Luke forgot how friendly people were in his new neighborhood and could spend an entire afternoon asking how every member in his family was doing. Not that he minded, but he wasn't used to the willingness of others to spend their time conversing with him.

Life in the city kept him active, mostly with his head down looking at his phone while faceless people rushed past him. The slower pace and casual interaction would take some getting used to after being away from small-town living for so long.

Armed with boxes of new ornaments, glass balls, and strings of lights, he pursed his lips, unable to decide between white or multi-color bulbs for the tree. He smiled and piled on three boxes of each. He would decide later where he would hang them.

He stood in line, arms loaded with decorations, and scanned the store. Not much changed since he was last there as a teen. A red, laminate soda counter edged with chrome remained with matching swivel chairs. Every once in a while, his mother brought him to Wally's for a cream soda and french fries. The few times he had some pocket change, he would wander through the store, especially the toy selection. Most times he held onto his money in case he needed cash to help his mother.

Those moments seemed distant but stung, which is why he thought moving back to Haineswood could be challenging.

"Are you ready, dear?"

The cashier peered over her glasses attached to a black, beaded chain around her neck. For a minute, he thought she was the same woman from his youth.

It's possible.

With his purchases on the counter, he shook his arms to relieve a tingling sensation and regained feeling in his hands. "Good evening."

"I see you're getting ready for the holidays." The cashier keyed in each item to the register. "New to town?"

Luke sighed quietly. Now wasn't the time to go into his history. He hoped most people didn't remember him and his mother. The scandal was the talk of the town for years, and he did his best to ignore the gossip. He didn't have any interest then and definitely now that he was grown. "Yes, just arrived. Getting a few things for my place."

News travels fast in a small town. Small talk was the most he would offer. Conversation was expected, and he didn't want to offend the locals.

Ring.

Without lifting her gaze from the register, the cashier pointed toward the sign above her head.

NO CELL PHONES.

He hit the button to silence the offending ring. "Sorry. Habit."

"It's a bad one. I suggest you try and break it."

Yes, she was the same lady from his childhood. Back then she would yell at kids for running in the store.

"Is the counter open?" He pointed toward the empty stools.

"Yep. Shirley's probably in the kitchen."

"Thank you." He nodded and gathered his purchases.

"Just yell for her so she'll know you're there. Have a good day."

No one was seated at the counter, yet the faded, *Please Wait Here for an Available Seat* sign was still posted on the cash register. Obviously, the rule did not apply any longer, so he sat and placed his stash at his feet on the foot bench.

Tattered menus from the sixties stood in an aluminum holder bolted to the counter. Faded glossy images of sandwiches and burgers egged on his hunger. He caught a glimpse of Shirley from the side of his eye. Flame red hair piled high in a messy French twist made her hard to miss.

"Hi. What can I get you?" Shirley whipped out a green order pad and pulled a pen from her hair.

"Turkey club on white toast with a cream soda."

"Good choice. The turkey is about the only fresh meat we have. Well, the burgers are okay because they're frozen."

He winced and thought maybe he shouldn't risk eating there. She must have sensed his concern because she smiled.

"Honey, I'm only kidding. Our food is fresh. Just because the place hasn't changed its décor since the mid-twentieth century doesn't mean our food is old. Be right back with your soda. Fries and coleslaw okay with your club?"

"Yes. Thank you." He nodded and glanced at his phone. Almost five o'clock, he guessed that was the reason for the empty counter. Wally's Five-and-Dime didn't strike him as the place to go for dinner. However, he was fine with eating alone. Years of slipping into a restaurant for a quick bite in-between job site runs rid his fear of dining alone.

Scratched red balls hung from tattered gold garland, draped along the mirrored wall behind the counter, looked cheesy. But he liked decorations, one of the few pleasurable memories of his childhood.

Being fatherless in the small town made him and his mother a target for hateful gossip. The rumor of him being the love child of a local, beloved townsman made him a topic of conversation. But his thick skin grew stronger throughout his time in New York so he was prepared for anything, should the subject present itself.

"Here you go, dear. Enjoy." Shirley placed his food and drink on the counter and walked away.

He grabbed the half-sour pickle and bit into it with a snap. *Hmm.* Wally's lunch counter didn't disappoint. The fresh, crispy pickle was as he remembered. Maybe nostalgia interfered with reality, but for a moment he was brought back in time. The noise of the city was gone. He had to get his business up and running. Time would help him get established, and his clients were loyal and quick to refer his services so he expected a comfortable start.

The turkey club caught his attention, with its three slices of toasted white bread—something he hadn't eaten in years—turkey, lettuce, tomato, mayonnaise, and bacon. Tiny plastic swords held the quarters together. He bit into it with gusto, each bite satisfied his hunger. Wally's could easily become his favorite eating haunt.

Shirley stood at the end of the counter, wiping it down.

Luke put a twenty-dollar bill on the counter. "Thank you. Have a nice evening. The sandwich was great."

He checked his phone for messages. A few missed calls from his half-sister Deborah. He wasn't prepared to have a conversation with her yet. Once he got himself in order, they would have time to spend together. He mentally prepared to deal with her. They weren't raised together, but during the past five years, he made attempts to forge a better relationship by calling her more often than he had in the past.

"Hey, you look familiar. You from around here?" Shirley cocked her head and squinted her eyes.

He stood to leave and then gathered his packages. "Sort of."

Shirley leaned on the counter and looked closer. "You're Amanda's kid?"

Hearing his mother's name uttered from someone who knew her startled him. He wouldn't expect anyone to remember her. *What did she know?*

Chapter Three

Kristen and Danny carefully made their way down the stairs and carried the fragile boxes and tree stand to the living room.

The first floor smelled of freshly made popcorn, which Nana strung for garland to hang on the tree. Readily available popcorn was a huge problem when her keets were alive. Often, the birds would perch on the Christmas tree and eat the popcorn faster than it could be hung.

The stand weighed nearly as much as Danny, but he was determined and positioned it in the correct spot.

Kristen plopped the tree into the stand on the first attempt and stood back to check if she needed to reposition the evergreen.

"It's crooked, Aunt Kristen."

"Yep, it is. Now to straighten the tree." She knelt and placed a hand on his back, taking him onto the floor with her. "Do you see those little screws?"

"Uh, huh."

"You have to turn them until they are tight against the tree while I hold it straight. Once done, we're good to go and can finish decorating. Ready?"

"You bet." Danny wriggled under the tree on his belly to tighten the screws. "How's that?"

The tree stiffened in her grip. "Come out here and see for yourself."

They both stood back, assessing the tree's vertical stance.

"Good?" His face glowed.

He was eager and excited to please her. She tousled his hair. "It's perfect and is what we want. You're the official tree stand person. Now, for the most important job of decorating a tree. Putting the star at the top." She handed her nephew a silver, tinsel-covered star and hoisted him up to the tip of the tree.

He fumbled with the top branch as he pushed the lit star onto the top of the tree.

As she thought of how she and Carly would take turns putting the same star on the tree, a wave of sadness swept through her. Now, her sister's son would be that person. This first year without her sister was painful, but she was grateful she and her nephew would carry on the tradition.

Sad moments surfaced without warning. Danny's smile eased the pain.

"It looks beautiful. All these years and the star still shines." Nana set down a tray of chocolate chip cookies on the coffee table.

"Ssssh, don't jinx it, Nana. Carly called it the eternal star because the lights never burned out." She didn't mean to sound sad. The last thing she wanted was to put a damper on the evening.

Nana picked up the pile of coats from the chair. "What's this? Luke Baldwin's business card?"

"What?" Kristen took the card from her grandmother. "The nerve of him."

"Found it right here on the chair. Must have fallen out of your coat pocket." Nana hung the coats in the hall closet. "Stop throwing your stuff on the furniture.

Both of you."

"He's the man who wanted our tree, but we got it." Danny pumped his arms over his head.

"I didn't even see him do this." Kristen stared at the information in her hand. *How did he do this?* It had to be when she stopped short and he bumped against her at the church lot.

She slid the card in her back jeans pocket then opened a box of decorations. She admitted the attention was exciting. Her last relationship lasted nine months, and that was five years ago. Her friends and family blamed her unreasonably high standards. The truth was she was afraid to let anyone get close.

A high school boyfriend left her for her best friend, and she never recovered from the rejection. The safety of a wall around her heart kept her emotions in check.

"The card says he's an architect. He might be a good contact to have." Nana winked. "You never know when you'll need one."

"Why?" Kristen unrolled a strand of lights along the living room floor and plugged them into the socket. Success, each green, blue, red, and gold bulb glowed with life.

"He must have a reason to give you his card." Nana pulled out another strand of lights.

"Probably wants to drum up business." Kristen expertly draped the strand of lights on the tree, placing each bulb on its own branch and stuffing the wires toward the trunk so they couldn't be seen.

"Or maybe he had another reason." Nana handed her niece the second strand of lights. "Who knows why someone comes into your life."

"Whatever, let's finish the tree so we can have

dinner. I don't like Danny eating so late, even if tonight is special." One of the first changes she put into action was a routine eating schedule. Take-out at ten at night was not the way to raise a child. She couldn't let her bad habits become his.

She quickly finished stringing the tree with lights and let Danny hang most of the ornaments—except for her favorite ball. He wouldn't touch it, and she was the only one who ever placed it on the tree, always in the same spot on top, below the star.

Danny leaned in as Kristen picked a speck of glitter from the tip of his nose. "Nana will be finding glitter and pine needles for months after the tree is down. She picked him up and hugged him. And realized how big he was as she carried him over to the chair and held him on her lap to admire their handy work.

"What do you think?" She set him down and walked over to the fireplace, balled up some newspaper, and tossed it into the firebox. "We did a terrific job considering we threw it together so quickly."

"It's pretty and smells nice. It smells like we're outside." He wrinkled his nose.

"It will smell even stronger when the fire is burning." She added kindling and placed one log on top of it then set fire to the newspaper. A vision of Carly stoking the fireplace flooded her thoughts. The holiday conjured up memories of Kristen's past and filled her with heaviness and sadness. In a few months her life changed from independent hairstylist living at the Jersey Shore to responsible guardian grieving in the mountains of Pennsylvania.

She shook her head to clear her thoughts. The inn stirred up memories. Only time would heal the family.

"Our tree never smelled like this in Florida, and we didn't have those stringy silver things hanging on the tree."

Kristen laughed. "It's tinsel. I know it's old-fashioned but I prefer it. I like the way it catches the light when it sways from the tips of the tree."

"Pretty." Danny snuggled closer, resting his head against her chest, his breathing synchronized with hers. "I miss Mommy."

"I know, sweetie. I know."

"Dinner's ready." Nana yelled from the kitchen. "Set the table in the dining room."

"Dining room?" Kristen questioned. They never ate in the dining room unless they had company for dinner or guests were staying at the inn. Whatever, she took the dishes from the hutch to set the table.

Danny brought a pitcher of homemade ginger ale to the table while Nana carried out a platter of roast chicken. "Kristen, would you get the potatoes and carrots please? Oh, and the mushroom gravy."

The kitchen was a disaster—gravy on the stove, potatoes on the wall, carrot peelings on the floor. Her grandmother was a great but messy cook. She balanced the mushroom gravy and mashed potatoes on her forearm, the candied carrots in her hand. Years of waitressing came in handy. "Nana…" She opened the door with her hip and nearly dropped the bowls of food.

"Well, we meet again."

****

Luke smiled and walked up to Kristen and then took the gravy boat from her shaky hand.

"He's joining us for dinner. I told him he can stay, but he can't take our tree." Danny took the carrots.

She stood frozen in the doorway, her eyebrows knitted together. "Why are you here?"

"I was invited." Luke took a seat at the dining room table.

"Nana, you know him?" She brought the food to the table and set it down.

"Sort of." Nana passed the potatoes to Luke. "I thought, why not add a beauty parlor to the inn? Isn't it a wonderful idea?"

"And who will run it?" Kristen pursed her lips.

"You, dear. You'll need something to do for an income."

Kristen sucked in her stomach, and her chest tightened. Her plan was to go back to New Jersey, not stay in Brookside Falls. She enjoyed the countryside of Pennsylvania, but it didn't have the excitement of the city. Plays and concerts in New York, the ocean. *Oh, the ocean!* Many days were spent walking along the Jersey Shore. The ocean connected and grounded her soul. She wanted Danny to experience the same happiness she achieved.

"I can't run a salon." She threw a spoonful of potatoes on her plate and turned to Luke. "And how does that involve you?"

"Didn't you read my business card?" Luke piled carrots onto his plate. He waved the plate under his nose. "Hmm, smells good. Something different about them."

"Brandy. Nothing like a good spike of brandy in the carrots during winter." Nana spread a napkin across her lap.

Luke looked at Kristen and then Danny.

"She does it all the time. She rubbed brandy on our

gums when we were teething as babies." Kristen shrugged, who was she to tell her grandmother she was wrong?

Silence filled the air until a loud pop from the fireplace startled everyone. Luke cleared his throat, "So, my Aunt Gladys tells me you want to build a hair salon on the premises."

"Yes, for Kristen. She's the one you need to speak with." Nana stabbed a piece of roast chicken on her plate.

Kristen shook her head, her mouth full of potatoes. She didn't want the responsibility of running a salon. She liked to come and go as she pleased. Staff! The last thing she wanted was to have people work for her. All their personal issues brought into work. No, she didn't want to be in charge. She liked to cut and color hair and keep to herself.

"It would be a nice feature." Luke put down his fork. "This building has good bones. I checked the blueprints, I wanted to make sure the town would permit an additional building and allow a beauty parlor to operate on the property. And they will approve both."

"Smart man, huh?" Nana nodded.

Kristen dropped her head, gathered up another forkful of potatoes, and dipped it in her carrots. "You need more brandy in these."

She worried about her decision to come back to Brookside Falls. Caring for Danny wasn't a problem, Carly left enough money from bank accounts and an insurance policy to keep him fed and clothed. Kristen never anticipated Nana would expect her to stay permanently. She definitely didn't want her grandmother to go into debt with the cost of new construction for something she didn't want to run.

"The salon is a good feature. It would add to the resale value. Even if a new owner didn't want to run a salon, it could always be leased to someone who does." Luke finished his meal and pushed away his plate.

"I like the idea whether Kristen wants to take it on or not." Nana cleared the table and took the dirty dishes into the kitchen.

"Danny, why don't you go check the bird feeders outside? I'm sure they need more seed."

"Okay." He ran to the closet, grabbed his coat, and slammed the door on the way out.

She would have to work on his manners. He couldn't misbehave with guests at the inn. Kristen turned to Luke. "Listen, I don't know how much you know and it really isn't your business but I have no intention of staying here."

"Oh, I think your grandmother thinks otherwise." Luke laughed and stretched his arms over his head.

Something about his movement intrigued Kristen. She couldn't place him. Luke was familiar yet she had the impression they never met before. "Are you from here?"

"Sort of." He leaned onto his closed fists, elbows on the table.

"Hmm." She poured another glass of ginger ale.

"I was asked to come here for business, and your grandmother was nice enough to make dinner."

She leaned back and crossed her arms. "Well, I don't want to own a business, run a business, or be involved in a business. I planned on staying a short time so Danny would have some stability through the holidays, and then we would go back to Jersey."

"You live in Jersey?" He cocked his head.

"Yes, why?"

"Aunt Kristen!" Danny ran into the dining room. "Look what I found!" He stood near the table with his hands cupped in front of him.

"What did you find?"

"A hamster!" He jumped up and down, nearly crushing the furry body in his grip.

Kristen looked at Luke. "I don't…"

Danny opened his hand as a whip-like tail thrashed about.

"It's a mouse!" Kristen jumped up on her chair and frantically brushed her chest with her hands.

The mouse ran under the hutch. She stamped her feet on the seat of the chair, scared half to death. "Get it! Get it!" she screamed.

"My hamster's gone."

"Not really. Your 'hamster' is hiding in a wall somewhere. He'll come out when it's dark." Luke laughed.

She composed herself and slowly stepped down from the chair, watching for any furry-tailed rodent crossing her path. "God, I hate those things."

"But you're okay with hamsters?" Luke smiled.

"Hamsters are different." She remained standing, on alert for the errant rodent.

"How so?"

"They just are."

Danny stretched his arm through the carved-out section of the hutch, hunting for his newfound pet. "I want him."

"It's not a hamster, it's a field mouse, and you

can't have it as a pet." Kristen pulled him up from the floor. "We'll buy you a real hamster, but you have to promise me you will keep it in a cage." Kristen feared Nana might extend her taxidermy talents to rodents.

"Don't worry, Danny. I'm sure you will see the mouse, err, hamster again." Luke cleaned crumbs from the table.

"I need a home for him." Danny removed a shoebox from the bottom of the coat closet. "This will work."

"No, don't." Kristen gasped and lunged toward him. Too late. He opened the box to reveal green, yellow, and blue parakeets.

"Cool." Danny stared at the glassy-eyed birds.

Kristen took away the box. She knew better than to open any shoebox that wasn't hers, because the box was sure to contain Nana's birds. Fortunately, live birds no longer lived in the house.

"Quite the talent your grandmother has." Luke smiled.

"I know she's odd, but she's harmless." She sighed, relieved Nana didn't catch Danny with the box. "She simply loved her birds so much she could never let them go. She used to bury them in the yard until I dug one up and brought it into the house."

"So, you're responsible for her obsession?" Luke walked over to the tree and slid his fingers down a strand of tinsel. "I didn't think anyone used this stuff anymore."

"Well, I do." Kristen put the box of stuffed keets in the closet. "Shower time."

"Am I in trouble?" Danny's voice tremored.

She kneeled then wrapped her arms around his

shoulders and kissed him on his forehead. "Of course, not, sweetie. Nana is protective of her beloved birds. Don't take anything without asking. Okay?"

"Got it."

Danny took off to shower. He was a good kid. Carly had been lucky—especially since she'd brought him up alone. She never told anyone who his father was, but Kristen did know Danny was conceived in Brookside one summer when the family got together sometime soon after their grandfather died. Funny how the inn was the place for healing broken hearts and shattered dreams. As quickly as relatives rushed to move away from Brookside Falls, the family home was the place they sought comfort.

"Your grandmother's busy, and it's getting late. I'll call her tomorrow." Luke put on his jacket. "Enjoy your evening."

"I haven't discussed the salon with her." She caught a whiff of his scent. Nice, not of cologne but a real man scent. She moved closer as he walked to the door to leave.

He brushed the lock of hair from his eyes and lowered his face. "I'll call anyway."

She closed the door then pushed aside the lace curtain covering the sidelight.

He looked back and smiled.

Her pulse quickened. *How soon would he call?*

****

The next morning, Kristen shoved her hands under her arms as she waited for her car to warm up. Cold weather essentials, like gloves, would have helped—if only she remembered to pack them. Visions of Luke crept into her head, and the memory of his scent still invaded her nose. Yes, he was cute, handsome even—at certain angles. Part of her was eager to spend time together. Who was he? What was his story? She shook her head. No time for her personal life.

She had to focus on taking care of Danny. The poor kid had been through so much, watching his mother waste away as cancer ravaged her body. Danny playing nurse and cleaning…she didn't even want to think about his life while he took care of his mother. By the time Carly reached out, it had been too late. Kristen could never recapture the lost moments and vowed she wouldn't have any with Danny. She didn't know what to expect being a guardian, but she would do her best to raise a child. She didn't have time to get involved with someone, especially a long-distance relationship.

She watched Danny and Nana in the rearview mirror as they approached the car. Her grandmother had a slight tilt when she walked. Nana always seemed younger than her eighty years, but her age was beginning to show. Danny opened the door and helped his great-grandma into the front passenger seat. He was growing up to be a perfect gentleman.

"I know you two waited for the car to heat up. Nice family. You let me sit in the cold all alone." Kristen winked at Danny.

"Oh, stop complaining and get one of those electric starter things." Nana plopped her carpet bag across her lap.

Danny jumped into the back in his booster seat and strapped himself in with the seatbelt. "Where are we going?"

"I need to buy you a pair of gloves. We're not going any place special. I thought we would spend time

41

out of the house. Maybe take a walk through town later."

"Weren't you complaining about the cold?" Nana motioned toward the window.

"We're going to the mall first." Kristen drove down the long driveway. The inn was the only house in town with cobblestone. At one time, nearly the entire town had cobblestone roads to the houses so a horse carriage could drive right up to the front door to unload passengers. She loved the old time feel of a prior lifestyle woven throughout the property, even though the driveway was rough driving atop the uneven surface.

Traffic was light. The mall was nearly empty, which was good because she wanted to be in and out since she had a full day planned.

White lights dotted the balcony of the second level of the mall. A sixty-foot Christmas tree stood in the center, fully decorated with balls and candy canes. Presents of various sizes covered in red or green foil wrapping paper lay at the base. Gifts were topped with velvet bows that cascaded down the sides of the boxes.

Kristen ushered Danny along and stopped in front of the pet store.

Nana made a beeline for the birdcages.

"Damn," Kristen muttered. She hadn't even thought about her grandmother adding to the bird collection. She sighed and brought her nephew over to the hamster village. She removed his hat and combed his hair with her fingers. "You can have one, and it must stay in its cage at all times."

"Really?" His face lit up and he clasped his hands together.

"Yep. But you have to go by the rules. We don't want it running around loose in the house and getting lost."

He pressed his hands and face against the glass and observed the rodents play. "That one."

"Which one? The light brown teddy bear hamster or the darker brown one with white on his chest."

"The one with the white spot on its butt."

"Can I help you?" A clerk approached them.

"Yes, we'll take the dark brown hamster." She nodded toward the clerk.

"The one with the big white butt." Danny smiled.

The clerk laughed, placed the hamster in a box, and handed it to Danny.

He hugged it tightly against his coat as if he would never let it go. Kristen gathered hamster essentials—cage, food, and bedding. Then, Nana walked toward her with a small brown box. Kristen didn't even have to ask, she was positive a parakeet would be added to the collection. "I thought you were never purchasing another bird." She pulled out her wallet.

"You're correct. I said I was never getting another bird, but I never said I wasn't buying two birds. One blue, one green. Two budgies for the lobby desk."

"Put them on the counter. Consider it a grand re-opening present." She lived with her grandmother long enough to know what battle to fight.

"Love you, dear."

"Don't expect me to clean the cage. It's bad enough I have to keep after a seven-year-old."

Danny sat on the floor of the pet store with the boxed hamster resting on his knees as he poked a finger into the breathing holes.

He never owned a pet. They'd moved around too much was what his mother used to tell him. Then when they finally settled into a place, she got sick and was too ill to care for anything else.

"Okay, ready?" Kristen gathered her purchases. "Change of plans. We have to stop home first. It's too cold to leave the birds and hamster in the car."

"That's a good idea. I don't want them to freeze to death." Danny wrapped his arms around the box.

She felt a shift within to happy and content. Was she being sucked into staying in Brookside Falls?

Chapter Four

Luke's apartment wasn't so bare with the Christmas tree standing in the middle of the living room floor. He even lined the front window with white lights, saving the multicolored lights for the tree. A few more ornaments and balls would have filled in the bare spots better, but tinsel took care of the deficiencies. He thought back to the garland adorning the mirror at Wally's Five-and-Dime, but he wanted to shake things up so he bought tinsel. He was surprised to see Kristen used it on her tree as well, because not many people did.

The last Christmas he spent with Jillian was miserable. She informed him she couldn't deal with his mother's illness, and he knew then he could not stay with her. He pushed aside the memory of his ex and focused on a mirrored snowflake. He twirled the ornament so the light reflected and danced against the wall and then hung the decoration on the tree.

Jillian. He dodged a bullet. How he took two years to see how selfish she was astounded him. He wasn't sure if he could trust anyone after his experience with her. The three years they knew each other before they started dating should have let him know enough about her agenda.

He was never much good at reading women. Jillian was proof of his inability to judge. Kristen, however…nah. He did find himself thinking about her. He liked her spunk and could tell her love for Danny was sincere.

Funny how life takes a turn.

Luke hadn't anticipated taking care of his mother any more than Kristen planned on taking care of a kid. He hit redial on his phone.

"Hello, Luke. Settled in?"

Gladys' shrill voice on the phone cut through him like ice. Why didn't she realize not to scream into a phone? "As well as I expect to be. Did you set up an appointment for me to visit the assisted living center?"

"Yes, can you make it tomorrow at two?"

He glanced at his phone calendar. A conference call at noon. "Sure, I can make it. The place is on Main Street in Jackson Corners?"

"Not really, it's off of Main on Trumball Drive. You can't miss it. Go into town and make a right at the drugstore, and it's a few feet down. It's the only building on the block."

"Thank you, Gladys. I know I've been relying on you for more than a real estate agent."

"Don't worry, sweetheart. I don't mind. Plus, the sooner you bring your mom out here, the sooner we can get you into a house." Gladys laughed.

"Of course." He smiled. She went out of her way for her clients and built a strong reputation. That's why he hired her, not because she was his aunt but he liked her work ethic.

"See you at two?"

"Yes, I'll meet you there. I have to run right now. I have something to take care of."

"Me too, sweetie. See you tomorrow."

He rearranged a few strands of tinsel and was done for the day. No more decorating though it did keep his mind on Kristen. He couldn't forget the determination in her eyes when she thought he wouldn't give her the tree.

But he had a surprise in store that she couldn't argue. He strolled downstairs to his office. He did like the convenience of being so close to work. He could literally roll out of bed fifteen minutes before he needed to be there. Not that anyone would be banging on his door at nine in the morning since most of his work was referral based, but he wanted to come off as professional as possible, especially being a new business in town.

With Internet access and his phone installed, he was set to go. Video conferencing would allow him to spend less time on the road. He sat in his swivel chair and swayed side-to-side. It felt right. Gladys really came through for him with the office location. The rental hadn't even hit the open market and she secured it.

He pulled up the West Haven Assisted Living website. He wanted an apartment style arrangement for his mother so she would feel at home during her rare moments of lucidity. The grounds were well-maintained. A Colonial-style center building accompanied by wings, where the resident units were located, looked welcoming. And the facility was close to home.

Deborah lived nearby, in Jackson Corners, and he put off seeing her. As hard as he tried, he could not feel close to his half-sister. Something wasn't right about their relationship. He understood she didn't fault him for their father's infidelity. But they couldn't connect even though they tried harder after Brian's unexpected death.

Luke was in college when Deborah called with the news. He did his best to be understanding when she cried over the death of her brother, but Luke never got along with his half-brother, in spite of their sister's relentless attempts to hold them together as family.

Brian never accepted Luke. Period. And Luke understood. When he found out his brother was gone, he barely shed a tear. He chalked up his lack of emotion to not being raised with his half-siblings. How can you feel like siblings when you were strangers?

Hmm.

Odd. Logic was not applying to Kristen. Each time he envisioned her face, he could swear they met before. Then again, he met so many women over the years, and she resembled a lot of blonde-haired, blue-eyed females, still, he enjoyed her company. Spunky she was. Different from the businesswomen he worked with in the city, often career driven and too busy for an impromptu date. He yearned for a laid-back existence. At least for a little while.

The last year had been draining. Gladys secured a new home for his mother. He was happy with the facility and checked another item off his to-do list. His next goal was focused on his business.

The first thing on his agenda was to reach out to prior clients and inform them of his new company for referrals. The few jobs in process were winding up, and he needed to generate a positive cash flow. He planned and structured his finances to carry him through the transition, but he didn't want to exhaust his savings.

Would his business plan work?

****

On the ride home, Kristen realized she might have taken on more responsibility than she was capable of managing. She missed Jersey, her friends, and even the job she thought she hated. But she made a promise to Carly, and she always kept her word. Yes, she might wait until spring to go back home. She could help her grandmother through the winter since the inn would be open for its first season. That way Kristen would have an idea of how things would go and what was required to run the place. Also, she liked the idea of creating events to lure people to the inn. Plus, Luke interested her.

A woman waved to them as Kristen drove onto the driveway.

"Who is that?" She turned into the parking spot and off the engine.

"Gladys." Nana buried her budgies beneath her coat to keep them warm.

Kristen didn't really know Gladys, who'd only become friends with her grandmother after the death of her husband.

The woman danced in place, clutching her coat closed as the wind kicked up.

"Come in. Gotta get these budgies in the house." Nana bustled toward the porch.

Gladys ran up the stairs and opened the front door into the foyer.

Coats and boots were cast off and thrown in every direction.

"Beth, you have to keep after this place because...you are sold out!" Gladys threw up her hands.

Beth? Kristen never heard anyone call her grandmother by her real name. It sounded odd.

Danny stepped over his coat. His attention was taken by his new furry friend.

Nana strolled into the lobby then retrieved an empty cage from behind the counter and released the birds into their new home. "There you go. Welcome to The Inn."

"Beth, did you hear me? You're sold out! It's wonderful! Now I'll earn my commission." Gladys laughed and straightened the bird cage, moving it closer to the end of the counter.

"Hi." Kristen extended a hand to Gladys. "What do you mean sold out?"

"From Christmas Eve through New Year's Day. Every room has been booked. We even have a few on a waiting list." Gladys rubbed her hands together. "We have to get moving with your ideas, Beth, if you want to make this event a success. You have one shot at a first impression."

Kristen glanced around the room, but she couldn't figure out why the inn would be appealing. The inn was a simple family home nestled in the rolling hills of northeast Pennsylvania with a few small shops. "Yes, why would it be such a draw? This town isn't even on most maps." She crossed her arms and stared down Gladys.

"Um, it might have something to do with advertising. Today, with the Internet, you can reach so many people." Gladys backed away.

"What advertising?" Kristen narrowed her stare.

"Okay, but remember I discussed my marketing

strategy with your grandmother first." Gladys pulled a flyer from her briefcase.

Kristen flinched. "What? Are you freakin' kidding me? You can't advertise something like this!" She waved the flyer over her head.

Nana held out her hand. "Calm down. It doesn't say we are haunted, just rumored to be."

"You're advertising an evening with the ghost of Christmas Past." Kristen shook her head. Dead, stuffed birds, and escaped mice in the house. *What else lurked within the walls of the old building?* Well, according to legend, ghosts were but...oh well.

Gladys cleared her throat. "The way I see it is, people really don't want to see a ghost, but do want to know there is the possibility of seeing one. How can anyone prove there isn't a ghost here? This house is certainly old enough. You can practically hear the horse hooves pounding on the cobblestone as we stand on these grounds."

"It's lying. We know the truth." Kristen picked up her coat and shoved it in the closet.

"Do we really? How do we know nothing lives here?" Nana chuckled. "I think it's genius."

"It's marketing to a possibility. A very real possibility. We never say an experience is guaranteed. But whatever, people are buying into it. Either the perceived reality or the atmosphere." Gladys winked as she buttoned her coat.

"Unbelievable." Kristen closed the door behind Gladys. "I need time to collect myself." She walked up the stairs to her room. Danny was off in his room, too busy with his hamster to know what was going on. Kristen curled up on the window seat, watching the cardinals feast on the black oil sunflower seeds in the feeder below. As she pulled her sweater tighter against her chest, she sighed. She could almost feel Carly beside her. She could use her now. Her life had been so hectic since her sister passed. She hadn't time to think about herself—which was unusual because for many years she was all she had to worry about. She never had a serious relationship. Always too busy to commit to anyone. She was starting to feel lonely. All alone with Nana and Danny to rely on her. She even felt responsible for the hamster, budgies, and a rogue mouse in the house.

"Carly, if you can hear me, please let me know once in a while if I'm doing okay." A knock on the door startled her.

"Luke is here," Nana yelled through the door. "I need you downstairs."

A slow smile crossed her lips. "Are you telling me something, sis?" Kristen ran her fingers through her hair, fluffing it out just enough to be attractive but not enough to, well, seem like she was coming onto him. She wasn't even sure if she was interested, but why pass up the possibility?

Kristen walked softly down the stairs and found Luke sitting at the dining room table. She hesitated at the landing to capture as much of him without his knowing. A people watcher by nature, she could tell a lot about people before they opened their mouth. "Good afternoon. Care for something to drink?" Kristen stopped at the bottom of the stairs.

"No thanks, your grandmother gave me coffee." He pointed toward the steaming hot mug in front of him on the table.

So much for her people-watching skills. At least she didn't have to make a pot of coffee.

He motioned to the counter. "I see your grandmother got some more birds."

"Yes, I hope they live a long and healthy life before she permanently mounts them on one of the curtain rods."

"Or in the chandelier." He pointed to the lighting fixture above.

She looked up and gasped. "I can't believe her. I never expected them up there."

"They seem to be in different locations every time I come here. It gives me the feeling they're still alive. Creepy, but harmless."

"How many times have you been here?" She sat across the table, one leg tucked under her, the other leg swinging under the table as she leaned on her fists, elbows firmly on the table.

"This is my third time. The first was when I came to town and rented a room for a night until my apartment was ready. This is a nice place but a little too girlie for me."

"Really? Too girlie?"

"Yes, the room on the second floor at the top of the stairs on the right. Too many flowers. But at least no birds."

No, there weren't. She was sure because the bedroom was hers. The room Luke stayed in...and slept in her bed. She sighed and her heart raced at the thought of him lying between the sheets.

Yeah, he was getting to her. But did he feel the same?

"Um, are you ready? I have some other projects to

work on." He sipped his coffee.

He didn't slurp his drink, and she appreciated that. *Nothing worse than a guy who makes noise when he eats or drinks.*

"More projects? How many could there be in a town like this?" She inched closer across the table. "Why bother with something as unimportant as this little beauty salon?"

"I didn't say it was unimportant or I wouldn't be here. But I do have to move on this project. Your grandmother reached out months ago, but she wanted to wait until you were here."

Kristen reeled in her unexpected interest in Luke to focus on his reason for being here. "I never discussed staying in Brookside Falls, and I can't commit to taking on this project, but I'll help set up the salon. She seems hell-bent on adding a shop, and I'd rather see it done right. If she can hire someone else to run it, she'll gain extra income. Do you have experience in designing a salon?"

"The salon is where you come in. I will lay out the building. I need to know what you want in it." Luke opened a sketch pad in front of him on the table.

"Three stations, three sinks, hookup for a washer and dryer, and small lobby area. Nothing extravagant." She sat back on the chair, leg still swinging under the table, arms folded across her chest.

"You don't want to think about it?" He finished his coffee.

"Nope, that's all that's needed. I know what I want, and once I make up my mind, well, it's done. No need to keep rehashing something." She leaned across the table again. "Don't you agree?"

He sat back. "My experience has been, a woman takes more time to make a decision."

"I'm not any woman," she snapped and sat upright.

Where did that change of mood come from? She was never so forward. The ease and confidence wafting around him sucked her in like no other. She didn't know him but wanted to. Was it his confidence? Could be. Was it his chiseled good looks? Most definitely, but she would never be taken in by something so superficial. Okay, well, maybe a bit—but only for a little while. Once, she dated someone purely based on looks. The experience was excruciating. She learned quickly that being involved with someone because of their physical appearance did not carry a relationship. A partner had to bring substance to a relationship for her to consider getting involved. She insisted on strength, thoughtfulness, and caring. From what she witnessed watching Luke's interactions with others, she felt confident he was worth the gamble.

"I'll make note of what you want and get back to you. Give me a day or two." He packed up his sketchpad and stood to leave. "Thank your grandmother for the hospitality."

Kristen was taken aback by his abrupt departure. What had she done? She thought she'd handled things well. Did she read him wrong? Whatever. She strolled into the kitchen and found her grandmother bustling about. Kristen grabbed a peanut butter cookie and stood with her back to the kitchen counter. "Luke left."

"Did you work on the plans?" Nana wiped her hands on her apron and sat at the table. "Where's Danny?"

"Still in his room. I told Luke what the shop needs,

and he left." She snapped her fingers. "Just like that. Said he would have something in a day or two. Where's he from?"

"You didn't ask him?" Nana took a cookie, as well.

"Not really. There's something about him I can't figure out." Kristen stood at the window, arms crossed, tapping her index finger on her elbow. "Looks like snow."

She leaned over the slow cooker and sampled the beef stew cooking for hours on the kitchen counter. Her grandmother's house always smelled like food. Her apartment never did except for reheated takeout.

"Gladys said he's her nephew…and a little shy. I told her what I wanted to do, and he showed up. I liked him so that was enough for me."

"Weird."

"Why? And stop eating my stew. There won't be enough for dinner if you keep picking at it."

She put the spoon in the sink then wiped her mouth with a paper towel. "I don't know but it's bugging me."

"Maybe your angst is a little more than just the shop. I think you like him." Nana smiled and pointed toward Kristen.

Kristen pursed her lips. "Don't be silly. I can't figure him out. That's all."

"What's to figure out? Either you like him or you don't. Either he is simply someone helping us with the plans or he's something more. You decide." Nana laughed and set the table.

Kristen stepped out of the kitchen and stopped at the foot of the stairway. "Danny! Dinner!" She stepped out onto the porch to clear her head. Chilly air brought shivers down her spine, but she needed something to make her feel alive. She thought it could have been Luke. The way he acted when he left made her unsure. Maybe she read him wrong. Heck, she didn't even know if he had a girlfriend…or a wife. Why should she assume he was available?

A burst of cold wind blew through her sweater. *Brrr!* Chilled to the bone, she went back inside to gorge on beef stew to warm her insides. After all, he did say a day or two. That would give her enough time to plan her next move.

Chapter Five

Day two and still nothing. Not a word. Kristen sat at the kitchen table sipping coffee. The past two days she wondered about Luke. One in the afternoon and he still hadn't called. She walked into the lobby for a change of pace. "Nana, I'll be back in a few. Can Danny stay with you?"

Nana popped up from behind the lobby counter, tapping her hand over her heart. "Jeez, you scared me. I thought you were in the kitchen. "Sure, I'll watch him and put him to work."

"Thank you." She threw her arms around her grandmother. "I love you so much. Be right back. Do you need anything?"

"No, I'm good."

She drove into town, the first time she'd wandered out on her own since arriving at the inn. Not having Danny with her felt weird, but she needed some time alone. No mall on this trip. She headed toward the center of town, what the locals called Haineswood.

As a child she'd thought town was so far away, but it wasn't. She probably could have walked if she'd wanted to—well, if she was desperate to work off a few pounds, and today wasn't the day. Too much to do. Plans needed to be finalized, and that reminded her of the address on his card. She pulled up in front of his office. She didn't see his car parked on the street, but he could be parked anywhere.

Main Street looked smaller than she remembered. Niche shops and attorney offices replaced most stores she frequented as a child. She peeked into the storefront of Luke's office. No one there. She hadn't traveled five miles to be discouraged so she tried the door. A bell rang above her head. Soft music played from a radio at the back of the room. Not much furniture, but how much furniture did an architect need? A desk, telephone, and a chair, perhaps?

She stepped farther into the office and bent over his desk, craning her neck to read the papers strewn across the top. With her keys, she reached down and pushed a paper from the top of the pile.

"Can I help you?"

Her stomach lurched, startled from the voice behind her. "I, uh, well, I …"

"What? Have a subpoena to search through my private paperwork?" He sat at his desk, pushed the papers into one pile, and placed a book on top.

"Is the information contained in those papers private when out in the open for anyone to see?"

"Someone like you?"

"Maybe. Could have been anybody. Besides you told me yourself my grandmother's project was the only one you had going on in this town." She stood with her arms crossed, her back straight, defiant, defending her nosiness.

"This is a different town than where you live. Remember?"

He was right. She lived over the town line. Brookside Falls was different from Haineswood. "Technicality. Anyone who is from here thinks it's the same place."

"As you say, 'whatever'. Are you here to go over the plans?" He swiveled in his chair.

"Yes, you said a day or two. This is day two."

"It is, and the day's not over. Are you always this impatient?" He leaned back in his chair and took a drink of coffee.

"Not usually." She sat in the chair in front of his desk. "I was in town and figured I would stop by."

"The plans aren't ready." He hit speaker on his desk phone and checked his voice mail messages.

"What do you mean they're not ready?" She recoiled in fear the shop would not open in time for the inn's grand opening. He had plenty of time to complete the plans, and she was in in a time crunch getting ready for guests and Christmas.

"They're not."

"When will they be ready?

"When they are." He stood and put on his jacket. "I'm getting lunch. Want to come?"

Considering it more of a demand than an offer, she followed him. Maybe he was taking her to the quaint café down the street or the new Asian fusion restaurant. She zipped her jacket, only to have him walk into the deli two doors over. "Are you kidding? You asked me to lunch at a deli?" She wrinkled her lips and read the menu. Mayonnaise smothered loaves of bread with fattening cold cuts—not her idea of a healthy lunch.

"I asked if you wanted to come. I never said I was taking you to lunch." He grabbed a ginger ale and a bag of kettle chips.

She figured he must be a regular because the counter clerk began making Luke's sandwich the minute he walked into the store. A man of exact words. He was much nicer when her grandmother was around. She searched the menu on the wall and wrinkled her nose. The healthiest thing she could find was a turkey wrap with lettuce, tomato, and no mayo. One thing she missed about Jersey was the food. Haineswood catered to heavier meals and so did her grandmother.

"Make sure you get it to go, unless you're eating it here. I'm going back to the office."

"Make mine for here." She pulled off her jacket, threw it on the back of a chair, and took a seat while she waited for her meal.

"Thanks, Leo." Luke put money on the counter then waved as he left the deli. "See you soon."

Her ears got hot, and her breathing stalled for a second. She found Luke frustrating. Maybe the problem with their relationship was her, she wasn't sure what she wanted and she might be a tad over-sensitive given all that changed in her life.

Out the window, she noticed shopkeepers clear the sidewalk of snow and ice. Signs filled merchant windows offering shoppers hot coffee or tea while they browsed inside the stores. A police officer on horseback trotted up the center of Main Street.

She pushed aside her annoyance for Luke as she thought of the times spent with her parents and sister in the town center. Summer brought about walks with her family along Main Street and a belly full of homemade ice cream. The farmers' market was a favorite place for her mother to visit. Founders Day was a time of carnival games, petting zoos, and balloon animals.

All the memories of what she enjoyed during her childhood, such as visits to Brookside Falls, brought her focus to her nephew. Danny was adjusting to living at the inn, but Kristen would have to check on enrolling him in school. She couldn't keep him out much longer, but since she hadn't planned on staying in Brookside Falls, she hadn't put much thought into his education. The plan was to manage through the holidays with as much cheer as she could muster on short notice. The real world would have to wait a few weeks to invade her forced bliss.

Kristen and Carly lived through a huge adjustment when they permanently moved to their grandparents' house. Maybe living in Brookside Falls would be a better place for Danny. Nana planned for the family to remain together, but near the ocean was where Kristen wanted to be. Although, what did she have in New Jersey but the shore?

Her turkey wrap, devoured, she crumpled her napkin then pulled on her jacket. She tossed her trash and walked out the door. Her heart wanted her to go back into Luke's office but no—too much to think about. She took a few steps toward his building. Her mind had other things planned, so she continued walking.

****

West Haven Assisted Living contained everything Luke wanted—washer and dryer, daily housekeeper service, but most of all, 24-hour onsite medical assistance. The facility even had a saltwater pool should his mother want to go swimming. Gladys did good.

He headed out to his mother's current residence to prepare her for her move to West Haven. The anticipated, bumper-to-bumper traffic to New Jersey was lighter than expected. He opted to take Route 611.

The tree-lined winding road along the Delaware River was a more relaxing drive. The sun was strong for late November which gave him an idea. He jumped onto Route 80 east and then headed south on the Garden State Parkway.

Pockets of the Atlantic Ocean appeared on his left. Boats dry docked for the season rested in their lifts. Summer homes were boarded up to protect them from a potential nor'easter. Mother Nature had not been kind to the New Jersey shoreline the past few years.

Hours later, he pulled into Shoreline Nursing Home. *Today's it.* Things would work out. He threw the car in Park and headed into the building.

A familiar staffer waved from the reception desk. "Hello, Luke."

"Is she ready?"

"I'll check. I believe Shawna is on duty."

"Thanks." He hated going into his mother's room. The staff was professional and attentive. The resident rooms were clean but possessed a clinical hospital feel to Shoreline, and he didn't want to subject his mother to that environment. His mom was too young to be losing her cognitive abilities, but apparently, dementia doesn't care who it affected.

"Hi, Luke." Shawna walked alongside his mom. "Mandy, look who's here to take you for a ride."

Amanda's face lit up.

She recognizes me. He missed her more so when she experienced an episode and struggled with remembering simple things like where she was. "Thank you, Shawna. You've been amazing. I can't thank you enough."

"Our doctor has been in touch with the staff at

West Haven. She's ready to leave here and move into her new apartment. We've even arranged to have her belongings shipped."

"Again. Thank you. Ready, Mom?" He slipped his arm through his mother's and guided her out to the car. Her silence was an indication she was unsure of her surroundings. He opened the car door. "You're moving up by me. I think you'll like the place. It's not by the ocean but a nice lake with ducks and benches on the grounds, so you can get plenty of time outside."

"Ducks," his mother said.

"All buckled in? We have one stop before we head north." He secured himself in his seat and turned on the ignition. He studied her out the side of his eye. Her breathing looked relaxed—a good sign. He wasn't sure how she would handle the four-hour drive, but he remained positive.

The sky opened as he left the nursing home and its forest-like setting. Traffic was on his side. The road was a clear shot through town to the beach.

"Too cold." Amanda clutched her jacket.

"Nah, come on, Mom. How about a little stroll on the beach before we leave? I don't know when I'll be here again. I thought it would be nice to grab a shell off the sand as a memento for your new home."

Her eyes glistened as he spoke of the shore. The ocean was her favorite place to be—well it had been. He remembered how excited she was when they left Pennsylvania and moved down the Jersey shore. Houses and apartments were affordable then. He was lucky if he could find a non-heated bungalow five blocks from the beach for under a million.

He made a promise. If his business took off and he

earned enough disposable income, he would buy a shore house.

"I like the sand."

"I know you do, Mom. Come on. So what if it's almost winter? We're here."

She nodded.

He embraced those lucid moments, though fleeting. He opened the door and helped her out of the car to the beach.

She kicked off her shoes and sunk her toes into the sand—wiggling each digit up and down so the particles of sand slipped between the spaces.

He studied her eyes, knit together, as she struggled to remember. He hoped the beach and standing at the edge of the ocean would help spark a memory for her. "Come on." He took her hand and guided her along the water's edge to protect her from the waves breaking on the shore.

Mom stopped short and bent over. "How nice." She picked up a nearly perfect scallop shell the size of her hand.

"That will make a nice holder for something. Are you keeping it?"

She nodded. "I want to go home."

"Of course." He held her by the elbow and walked back to the car. The ride home would be quiet. She would fall asleep once on the road.

Mom settled in her seat and crossed her hands over her purse on her lap.

"Mom, do you mind if I put on some music? It's a long drive."

"Luke. It's so good to see you." Amanda leaned over and kissed him. She clutched the scallop shell

65

against her heart.

"It's good to see you too, Mom. Enjoy the drive." His heart swelled when she remembered him. Watching her deteriorate was horrible, but maybe living in a different place would be good for her. Maybe she would remember more about Brookside Falls because of her childhood. He didn't want to doubt any possibility. Another doctor might even have a different take on her condition. Even though she had been cared for well at Shoreline Nursing Home, the facility was a large institution, and he never thought his mother got much personal care.

West Haven was more of a home environment; most importantly, the spot was close to his work and home so he could get to her faster if an emergency arose. Things were tough when he was living in the city and she was down the shore. The traffic alone could add half a day of traveling.

Yep, from here on in life would be smooth sailing. Mom would be settled in, and he could take time for himself and figure out what he wanted to do besides work. "Ready to leave, Mom? We have a long ride."

She nodded.

He smiled as he pulled onto the Garden State Parkway and hit the gas, eager to drive back to Brookside Falls because Kristen was at the end of the drive.

****

A week passed and Kristen hadn't heard from Luke. No way would the shop be up and running in time for the Christmas event. She wanted to call him. Lack of communication annoyed her, but maybe she annoyed him. When he caught her rifling through papers on his desk, he hadn't seemed too pleased.

With Christmas less than three weeks away, the inn needed to be decorated with more than a tree to prepare for a night with the ghost of Christmas past. Not much was available in town so she drove to Jackson Corners, a small town a few miles away built entirely on tourism and specialty shops. She found a parking spot on the street and welcomed the brisk air while she perused the main district. She walked the entire shopping district before filling her arms with purchases and lugging them around.

Strands of Christmas lights lined the street. She would have to come back at night to see them in their holiday splendor. She sensed as though she walked into a different dimension. Soft holiday music wafted from the stores into the street. The scent of hot chocolate and peppermint permeated the air, giving the sense of being encased in a North Pole village. She needed a distraction. A different environment, a different place to wander around, something fun to free her thoughts of the seriousness of the new world dropped in her lap.

She took in a deep breath, and her chest relaxed. She stepped into Jackson Corners Antiques. Although not much of an antique fan, but there must be an interesting knickknack she could buy for the inn. Nana's stuffed parakeets overtook the place, and something was needed to change the tone from crazy bird lady to awesome inn keeper.

Depression glass bowls lined a curio cabinet near the entrance. Rusty kitchen utensils were on display in crocks once commonly used for making brandied fruit. A special item had to be hidden amongst the clusters of random decorations. A black tapestry with a deer drinking from a lake lined with weeping willow trees hung on the back wall. *Perfect.* It would fit across the face of the lobby desk. Even if Nana didn't like it, Kristen did, so the hanging would make its home somewhere at the inn. She made her purchase and brought it back to the car, grateful for a parking spot so close to the store.

With the tapestry stowed, she continued her shopping spree. The town now looked more commercial than she remembered. She wanted something unique. Most of the merchandise could be found online or in the mall—until she walked up to the Artisan Guild. Chimes rang overhead as she opened the door. Sandalwood incense hung heavy in the air as if it had been burning for days. Plates, mugs, and vases occupied most of the shelf space. Not what she was looking for so she turned to leave.

"Can I help you?" A short woman wearing an alpaca shawl greeted her.

At first, Kristen thought the clerk was older because of the shawl and hastily set bun on her head. But upon a closer examination she could see the woman was maybe ten years older. "Hi. I'm not sure what I'm looking for." She turned and hitched her purse higher up on her shoulder.

"What will the item be used for? Functional? Decorative?"

"Decorative. Something festive for a holiday. Christmas themed." She glanced around the showroom. "I'm not sure if you have anything like that."

The clerk wagged her finger. "Follow me. You might be pleasantly surprised."

Kristen followed her lead, taking care not to brush

against the delicate and massive handmade pieces randomly placed throughout the store. She was led into a room in the back of the store. "Wow, I never would have known this stuff was back here." She put her purse on the floor, afraid it would swing into something and smash it.

"Follow me." The woman pointed to a doorway at the back of the store. "This is our Christmas room. We find it easier to keep the stock stored back here since most people only buy this stuff once a year. It's a lot easier than sprinkling it throughout the everyday pieces. Browse. Take your time. Enjoy."

Tight spaces made her nervous, especially tight spaces with fragile pieces. Plenty of holly-shaped candy dishes lined a shelf. *We could use a few of these.* She picked four and held them against her chest to protect them.

Standing still, she scanned the store instead of moving around and risk breaking a delicate knickknack. She couldn't afford to pay for something she didn't want to buy. Across the room, staring with bright blue eyes, stood a Christmas gnome. He wasn't any taller than three feet. Everyone has a Santa Claus, why not be different? The gnome was moving to The Brookside Falls Inn. The dull finish gave it a warm feel, almost lifelike, especially since his eyes followed her. "Hello?" No answer. She shuffled to the doorway. "Hello?"

The clerk poked out her head from behind a freestanding pantry. "Yes?"

"I'm taking the gnome."

The clerk hurried to Kristen. "Which one?"

"What? The one staring at me." She refused to release her grip on the candy dishes.

"Here, let me take those." The woman relieved Kristen of the pottery and placed them on the table. "Not comfortable around fragile things?"

"Petrified. I was clumsy as a kid and at times it still scares me." Her chest relaxed and breathing eased.

"Not a problem, we get that quite often in here. Pottery is much more durable than you think it is. I know, I've dropped enough dishes in my life." The clerk laughed as she made her way through the maze of Christmas pottery. Stopping at the back of the cluttered room, she pointed to the gnome staring at Kristen.

His green vest and red hat fit her Christmas theme. Kristen nodded, he was the right one.

"We have his two friends." The clerk held two gnomes barely a foot and a half tall.

"There's a family?" Kristen quickly calculated where she would use an entire family of gnomes.

"Yep, they travel in packs."

"Well, then I'll have to buy all three." She gingerly picked up her purse and waited for the woman to gather the gnome family from the crowded room.

With the magical family accounted and paid for, she took them out to the car one at a time, saving the largest for last. "Thank you for your help. You have a lovely shop here. I wish more stores that focused on local art existed in this area."

The clerk sighed. "There used to be, but people moved away, and the new shop owners found the cheapest way to run their businesses so the inventory is not what it used to be. Thank you for coming, and please tell your friends."

Kristen struggled outside with her three-foot-high find with eyes that seemed to follow her no matter how she turned. As cute as the gnome was, the last thing she needed was to fill the inn with impulse purchases that would clutter the place.

Was compulsive buying hereditary?

Chapter Six

"Can I help you with that?" Luke placed his hand on the car door. He was surprised and happy to run into Kristen. "Strange to see you here."

Kristen turned and smiled.

He opened her car door and took the gnome. "Odd little fellow."

"I like odd. Why are you here?" She grabbed a blanket from the back seat of the car and made a bed for her passenger.

"Shopping. It's a nice day to get out of the office. Have you had a chance to review the plans yet?" He closed the door and leaned against the car, hoping she wasn't in a rush.

"What? She pulled her eyebrows together. "You haven't given them to me yet."

Confused and flustered, he ran a hand through his hair. "Not to you but I dropped them off at the house later that day after you stopped at my office."

She shrugged. "Nope. I never got them. When did you leave them?"

"Around five."

"Nana!" Kristen sighed. "I took Danny out for pizza that night, but my grandmother never said anything about the plans."

"Stop at my office. I have another set of plans on file."

"Does this mean if you ask me to lunch again, I eat alone?" She smiled.

"Only if you want to." He grinned. She scrunched her nose, and stared at him, like she was reading his mind. He witnessed that look from Jillian many times, who told him how difficult he was to figure out. That he was a hard man to read his lack of being forthcoming frustrated her. He didn't think he was complicated.

He closed Kristen's door as she turned on the car and motioned for her to roll down the window. "Go on, I'll meet you at my office." He waited until she drove away and then ducked into the same shop Kristen left. "Deborah!" he yelled.

"It's so good to see you." She hugged him, hanging from his neck. "It seems like it's been ages."

"Two years. I should have gotten back here more frequently but work kept me busy. Honestly, if it wasn't for the job I'm doing as a favor for Aunt Gladys, I probably wouldn't be here now." He wasn't ready to tell her he moved to Haineswood. Their relationship remained fractured, and his mother contributed to some of the discord by keeping them apart. He didn't want to deal with his sister's onslaught of questions.

He found an old chair by the counter and took a seat. "I'm staying for a few. I have an appointment in Brookside Falls, but I want to make plans for dinner. Are you free tonight?"

Deborah nodded. "Of course, I am. I'll always make time for my little brother. Me and you?"

"We'll include Aunt Gladys next time, closer to the holiday. In the meantime, I need an umbrella stand for my office. Do you have any?"

Deborah pointed toward a tall narrow crock. "I use

these at home. Toss some wood blocks in the bottom so the umbrellas don't bang the pottery, and you're done."

"Good, I'll take one." He looked at the price. "I'll cover dinner. Call it even."

"You're taking my best one. They're hard to get," she yelled as he strode over to the door.

"I'll cover two dinners, then. I'll pick you up around six?"

"See you then." Deborah waved him away. "Luke?"

"Yes?" He stopped and turned to face her. Her smile was sincere, so he could tell she was happy to see him.

She moved her lips to say something but quickly shut her mouth and waved a hand. "Never mind. I can tell you later over dinner."

"I have a few if it's something important." What could she possibly be up to?

****

"Hi." Kristen hid a smile and warmed her gloved hands by rubbing them together. She rose from the bench in front of his office as Luke approached the stairs.

"Sorry, I'm late. I ran into someone." Keys jingled as he rushed up the stairs.

"In Jackson Corners?" She crossed her arms.

"Yes." He opened the door and stepped back. "Have a seat. I'll be right back."

She sat in the chair and took advantage of the warm office. Danny was off with Nana and her friend so he was okay. Kristen was amazed how much Danny adored his great-grandmother—maybe because he lost his mom at such a young age. Danny was lucky to have

Nana in his life.

Kristen refrained from peeking through Luke's papers again. He wasn't giving her much to work with, but she tried to put together as much about him as she could. Her fingers finally warmed. She tapped her fingertips on the table—she was tempted to snoop but held back. The light on the phone blinked as a call came through. *Hmm, he keeps the sound off.* So, he doesn't like to be disturbed.

The door opened, and a gust of cold air rushed through the office. He put a brown bag on the table. "Warm enough for you?"

"Not too bad."

"Maybe this will help." He handed her a cup of hot chocolate. "If nothing else, you can hold it to keep your hands warm."

Wrapping her fingers around the hot beverage, she breathed in the aroma. Warmth cascaded though her body. "Ah, I love this time of year, I could drink hot chocolate every day. Thank you. Do I owe you anything?"

"No." He smiled, offered a sandwich wrapped in waxed paper, and sat across the desk. "So, your grandmother never showed you the plans?"

"Nope." She opened the sandwich, turkey wrap with lettuce, tomato, and no mayo. He paid attention to detail. "Thank you." A slight smile warmed her cheeks. She had no need to question his motives or gush over the fact he took notice of her lunch choice. "Maybe one day I can convince you to try the Asian fusion place across the street."

He nodded. "I want to go there but not alone."

She squelched her excitement in anticipation of an

offer.

"So, I'm going tonight."

She imagined him sitting in the restaurant with a date, and that caused her heart to sink a smidge. Hell, she didn't know anything about his personal life and felt awkward interrogating him. So unlike her but his indifference made him so appealing, and she found herself doing things she wouldn't normally do, like suggesting they go out to eat together.

He quickly ate his ham and cheese sandwich and washed it down with a cream soda.

She pushed aside her hot chocolate and ate half the bland turkey wrap, packed the rest, then placed the leftover sandwich in her purse. "Can we go over the plans now? I need to get back soon."

He collected a piece of paper from the printer, walked around to her side of the desk, then sat in the chair. "I finalized the location of the salon with your grandmother weeks ago. Your grandmother wanted a separate building, but I talked her out of the idea. There's the extra room at the back of the house not being used for anything. It must have been a carriage house or maids' quarters. There's no sense building another structure." He shifted closer.

An opportunity opened and she leaned in—near enough to catch his scent which she found inviting, but not too close to make him uncomfortable.

"The other benefit is people won't have to leave the building to enter the salon, if you add a doorway from the side wall of the lobby." He leaned in as he used his pencil to note where the changes would be made. "This mark indicates the new doorway where you will enter the salon from the lobby. Placing the door in this location will utilize wasted space and make for a seamless yet private connection between the two businesses."

"Perfect. What about the salon layout?" She relaxed her shoulders and rested her chin in her hand. She was within whispering distance.

"That's where you come in. I have what you asked for." He moved the pencil to highlight the layout. "Three stations, three sinks, and three dryer seats with a closed-off area for a washer and dryer. There's enough room to make this work. You don't need much space for a desk. Your products can be displayed on shelves between the workstations, and towels can be stored over the sinks. I think the layout will work. Even if you don't stay, this arrangement is functional for anyone else who comes in after you."

She leaned back and crossed her legs, folding her arms across her chest. He really did listen, which was nice. She'd never known anyone to pay attention to her with the level of detail he expressed. "I like it. How will it be done in time for Christmas?"

"The permits have been approved, so we can start the renovation. The fact we're not creating another building saves us a lot of time plus it's a salon. The work is mainly cosmetic, plumbing, and updating the electrical. We don't have much time, but we can get the job done if there are no unexpected obstacles."

She flipped back her hair and then clapped her hands. "When do we start? Tomorrow? I have to pick out workstations and sinks."

"Do you plan on choosing standard setups or something exclusive?" He leaned back in the chair and spread his legs as he stretched them in front of him.

"Standard. I could never allow my grandmother to spend a ridiculous amount of money." Even though she didn't want to leave, she rose from the chair. Danny was waiting, and she didn't want him to feel like she would use any excuse to leave the house. "I'll do some research and get the information to you tomorrow. I don't want to make you late for your dinner." Eager to pry, she had to know if he was seeing anyone, but he didn't offer any clues so she didn't push it.

"Thanks. The sooner I have the information, the faster we can get this done." He cleaned the trash from lunch and tossed it into the wastebasket under his desk. He walked her to the door and placed his hand low on her back.

"I'll make this a priority." She slowly put on her jacket, pretending she'd misplaced her glove and stalling for time because she didn't want to leave. Luke noticed her. He paid attention and the feeling of being recognized soothed her inner uncertainty. "Ah, here it is." She pulled her glove out of her pocket. "Well, later."

"Uh, huh, bye." He held the door.

"Nothing else?" She ducked under his arm to pass through the door.

"No."

"You're sure?" She stared dead into his eyes.

He lowered his head, his mouth nearing hers. "No, I need nothing else."

As she walked away, she smiled and looked over her shoulder. "Somehow, I don't believe you."

****

Luke smirked as he watched her get into her car. She was a breath of fresh air, and he liked being around her. *Idiot!* What was wrong with him? He acted like a jerk and missed a perfect opportunity to ask her on a date. Had Jillian hurt him so badly he was ruined for dating anyone else?

But Kristen wasn't just another woman. She was funny, smart, and displayed a generous heart. He could tell from the way she loved and protected her nephew. She was a good person taking on the role of a mother when she could have said no.

He was being overly cautious and needed to move beyond Jillian. From the kindness he saw in Kristen, she was not a soulless person. No comparison could be made between the two women. He learned he didn't have time for inconsiderate people. He witnessed neglected mothers in the nursing home, abandoned by their children, and wanted someone in his life who understood the importance of family.

Kristen could be that person.

He reached for his cell phone in his pants pocket to call her and hesitated. *Not now.* She's a client. He would have to put aside his pursuit of Kristen until the project was completed. He had to focus on work, not his love life.

But he couldn't stop thinking about her.

The office door opened behind him as he walked to his desk.

"Good afternoon, sweetie."

Gladys.

For a moment, all the air had been sucked out of the room. He liked her, but the one thing he hadn't anticipated was how often she would pop over. "Coffee?" He extended a cup.

"No thanks. I stopped in to see how you are

managing." Gladys scanned the room. "You need some decorations in here. It's as sterile as a doctor's office."

"I have lights." He pointed to the window, proud of his light-hanging skills. A lot of talent was needed to string a perfect straight line.

"Yes, they're lovely. But you need something on the walls and maybe a potted plant. A tree in the corner." Gladys walked around the room pointing to an empty space.

"I don't want anything I have to take care of or dust. Too much clutter makes me anxious." He wasn't being funny—he got antsy when he was in a cramped room. Like his sister's store. He couldn't understand how she could work in chaos all day.

"Suit yourself. A few plants will make the office feel more inviting and welcoming to clients."

"Again, thanks for the suggestions but no. But I do want to thank you again for settling my mother at West Haven. It's a very nice place. Much better than where she was."

"Oh, no problem, sweetie." Gladys pursed her lips. "She really shouldn't have been in Shoreline."

He guided Gladys to his desk. "I know, but it was the only place that had an opening. I couldn't leave her alone since she almost burned down her apartment."

"It's a shame. So young. What's she? Sixty-five?" Gladys took a seat.

"Sixty-three. I know. I can't believe I didn't see it coming. I thought she was overworked and preoccupied, and that's why she was forgetting. At times, she's lucid, and you wouldn't know something was wrong." He poured himself a cup of coffee and joined Gladys at the desk.

"Well, you've done right by her. Many people would shove their parent in a home and never give them a second thought." Gladys smiled. "You're a good son to your mom. Always have been."

Gladys was the only Baldwin who recognized Luke as a full-fledged member of the family. She disregarded the circumstances surrounding the scandal and never cared what people thought. Luke knew she thought ill of his father who barely engaged with his illegitimate son. She understood Luke was the product of his father's indiscretion and not the reason. "I think I made the right decision to bring her back here. I know she loved this area, no matter how difficult life was for her at one time. She missed the mountains and fresh air. I guess once you know a place as home, nothing else can be a substitute."

He kind of believed that himself. He enjoyed the city but disliked the constant barrage of crowded streets and noise. Even in the solace of his apartment, he could hear sirens at all hours of the day and night. Though he was in Haineswood only a few days, he enjoyed the slower pace and quiet at night.

"I think she'll do wonderfully at West Haven. They have a caring staff and that's what you need. People who are willing to help her through her illness and not simply take the money you pay them each month." Gladys stood, wandered around the office, stopped at the coffee station, and poured herself a cup of coffee. "Nice setup."

"The coffee maker was a must. I can do without furniture or breakfast, but I can't live without coffee." He leaned back in his chair, his mug cradled with both hands. Steam rose from the cup and his nose filled with the familiar scent of his daily fuel.

Gladys sat again. "I noticed Kristen Anderson was here."

He narrowed his eyes, anticipating his aunt's next move.

"Pretty girl, she is." Gladys peered over the rim of her coffee mug and stared into his eyes.

He nodded. *Not taking the bait.*

"She's in quite a spot also with her family. Never thought she'd be taking care of a child, but she took to it like a fish takes to water."

Luke turned to the fax machine and pulled off a proposal. He didn't think he would need a fax machine, but he had one client who refused to use email. Sometimes you have to do what works no matter how antiquated the process might be. "I'd love to continue talking, but I have work to do." He waved the fax in the air, hoping she would take the hint.

"Think about it. You're new in town. You two are about the same age. You both have family obligations you took on willingly."

Gladys winked, like she was all knowing and knew what was best for him. He rose from his desk and gently took the mug from her hand and placed it on the desk. "Thank you but I'm fine. I've gotten through the first thirty-five years pretty much on my own. I think I can manage the rest of my life without interference."

"Okay. But I think you're missing an opportunity. You know as well as I do, opportunity is what moves you through life." Gladys buttoned her coat and left.

She was right.

Chapter Seven

Kristen made it home in half the time. Her mind focused on Luke. "Oh, he's so frustrating." She turned into the driveway of the inn, past an old weeping willow tree. When she was a child, she would wrap her arms around a cluster of branches and swing with abandon. That was a long time ago, she thought as she pulled into her parking spot.

Danny ran to the car.

She could always count on her nephew to make her happy. She climbed out and squatted down with open arms. Danny's smile pushed aside her uncertainty about Luke. "Hey, sweetie."

"We missed you, Aunt Kristen. Nana is the best. You ought to see what she got for me." He grabbed the cuff of her jacket.

"Can it wait?" She looked down, and the excitement in his eyes told her otherwise.

He jumped up and down. "No."

"Okay, I guess it can't wait." She surrendered to Danny's enthusiasm as he dragged her up the stairs, through the lobby, and up the staircase to his room. The door slammed into the wall, nearly knocking a hole in the plaster.

"This." He stood in front of a small aquarium which housed a brown snake coiled on a rock in the corner of the tank.

Kristen shuddered. Her skin crawled as she clawed her forearm and backed away.

"Watch out. My turtle." Danny rushed behind her.

"Nana bought you these reptiles?"

"Yes."

"Did you ask for more animals?" She stood frozen.

"No. We went to the pet store to buy food for my hamster, and she asked me if I wanted them."

"There aren't any spiders in this room, are there?"

"No, don't be silly Aunt Kristen. Spiders shouldn't live in a house."

She backed into the doorway. Reptiles must be how children made sure their parents or guardians never set foot into kid territory. Outside of the dinner table, she would never see her nephew again. His room would become a cave of reptiles and rodents as he lived in squalor, because she would never step foot in the room to clean it. Ever. He was on his own. She decided she would never have children of her own. One seven-year-old boy was enough.

Nana! If she bought Danny a snake and a turtle, what did she buy for herself? Kristen ran down the stairs and counted. Two birds chirped away in the cage on the lobby counter. She listened. *Chirp.* Sure enough, more budgies were in the house. "Nana!" Kristen swung open the kitchen door. Nothing. The basement—she wasn't going down there.

"Nana! Come here!" She followed the distant chirp. A new floor cage stood next to the fireplace in the living room. How had she missed it? Two newly-acquired, peach-faced lovebirds rubbed their heads together, with their eyes closed, and enjoyed their new home.

"Aren't they the most precious things?" Nana tiptoed into the living room.

"You can't be filling the house with birds again. I know you love your feathered friends, but I thought you conquered this obsession." Kristen ran her fingers through her hair, remembering how out-of-control her grandmother was in the past with her love for budgies. At one point, she possessed fifty-five live parakeets throughout the house.

"The intervention didn't take. What can I say? Some people knit, I raise parakeets." Nana extended her finger to the lovebirds.

"Yes, but now you are branching out into different breeds." She pointed toward the snuggling lovebirds. She breathed deeply to compose herself and vehemently block out the vision of the snake a floor above her. The turtle she could deal with, not the best pet choice but she was okay with it as long as it stayed in its tank. The hamster was pushing it, but the snake definitely crossed the line. "I met with Luke, and he said he gave you the plans." Kristen focused on business to get her mind off the growing menagerie.

"Oh, yes, he did, I forgot. He's such a nice man. You should date him." Nana walked over to the lobby counter.

"Yeah, whatever. Where are the plans?" Kristen desperately wanted a gin and tonic, even though she rarely drank.

"They're somewhere—somewhere over here." Nana rummaged through loose papers on and around the desk.

Kristen leaned on the counter next to the bird cage. She poked a finger into the cage to pet the bird. There it was—her brand-new, salon floor plan lining the bottom of the cage. She rolled her eyes and sighed. From the looks of the paper, the budgies didn't approve of the plan.

"Nana, never mind." Kristen shook her head and walked out onto the porch. She sat on the top stair and wrapped her arms around her knees. Even the cold porch floor against her butt didn't matter. She became more entrenched in Brookside Falls than she expected, and she couldn't ask Danny to leave his pets. She didn't have room in her apartment for cages and aquariums.

She propped her chin on her fist, her elbow on her knee. Maybe she was meant to stay in Brookside Falls. Danny was settling in deep so she would have to do something about school. Carly had been gone for a few months, and he was doing well with his home schooling, but he needed to attend a regular learning environment. For that reason, Kristen wanted to take him back to New Jersey. However, he forged such a strong relationship with Nana. She was afraid to force him to go through another loss in his young life.

Decisions.

A cardinal landed on the porch rail and cocked his head toward Kristen.

"Could that be you, Carly?"

The bird bobbed his head.

"Hello, bird. It's a beautiful day, isn't it?" She would make it through the holidays and then make her decision. The three-hour drive was too much to do on a regular basis, and going back and forth could make Danny more unsettled than leaving his home in Florida.

"Carly, wherever you are, I hope I do you proud. You have a good kid here, in spite of his incessant need for slimy pets." She stood and brushed the seat of her pants. A wave of confidence ensconced her body. *What to do next?*

****

West Haven was welcoming. Granite stone paved the way from the main street to the parking lot. He felt awful using a private service to transport his mother to her new home, but he wasn't sure he could focus on the long drive with her in the car.

His first attempt to relocate his mother to her new home was unsuccessful. Five miles out on their way to Pennsylvania, his mother demanded to be brought back to Shawna. Frustrated, he took the next exit and drove back to Shoreline. He would arrange for transport when she was more agreeable. He planned ahead for such a setback and paid for an extra month at Shoreline.

She was due to arrive at West Haven any minute. He timed his visit so he would be there—waiting.

Gladys informed him, his mother agreed to leave the New Jersey home without hesitation and settle into her new surroundings.

Finished setting up his office and apartment, he could have an uninterrupted afternoon—maybe even an early dinner. He walked up the front steps. Wooden high-back rocking chairs lined the front porch, and a cast iron fire chimney stood at the far end. A nice touch for cool autumn nights. Once he bought his own home, he would definitely build a fire pit. Nothing relaxed him more than chugging a beer and staring at flames dancing in the wind, which he couldn't do at his current residence.

"Good afternoon. Can I help you?"

A stunning redhead greeted him at the reception

desk. "Hi. Luke Baldwin. My mother, Amanda Baldwin, should be arriving any minute." He leaned on the counter and looked behind the desk. *Looks clean.* He liked order, and cleanliness was important. His obsession made living with him difficult. Maybe that's one of the reasons Jillian left him.

It didn't matter. She could never deal with his mother, and he couldn't live with someone so selfish. What if it had been Jillian's parent who needed care? He never would have deserted her.

"I have your information right here. The driver checked in about fifteen minutes ago. The transport team will be arriving shortly. My name is Trish."

She flaunted her chest closer to his face, with her finger resting on her name tag on a too low-cut neckline. Uncomfortable with her approach, he backed up. "Thanks, Trish. I'll wait on the porch." He kindly nodded and breathed a sigh of relief as he opened the door. He was sure Trish was hitting on him. He wasn't confident he had a charming effect on women, but she couldn't have been any bolder. He was put off by pushy woman.

He liked—Kristen. Simple, no nonsense, and authentic. Whenever he thought of her, he smiled, which was a lot. The stubborn streak fueled her determination, and he found that attractive.

But how did she feel about him?

Kristen was difficult to read. At times he thought he had the perfect opening to ask her out for dinner, but then doubt would hold him back. Maybe she had too much going on and wasn't in the mood to take on another relationship.

He didn't want to appear too eager. They both

lived in a small town, and people were quick to come to conclusions. If their date didn't work out, running into each other would be awkward.

What the hell?

Where's my thinking? Too much time alone. He needed something besides work to keep him busy. But what? Could be the breakup with Jillian was too fresh. He remembered back to the night of the church parking lot when Kristen challenged him for the tree. The look she gave him—nothing got between that tree and her nephew's happiness. He had never seen a person exude such love at another person.

He smiled and pulled his coat collar to cover his ears. The sun was setting and night air creeping in. He'd forgotten how the nights got cooler earlier than back in Jersey. Jackson Corners lacked the concrete landscape that covered much of his former neighborhood.

Headlights turned into the driveway. He shoved his hands into his jean pockets. He yearned for a cigarette, but hadn't lit one in five years and wasn't about to give into his nerves. His mother should be fine. Benches were scattered throughout the grounds from what he could see.

Gladys made sure West Haven had all the amenities he requested—a pool, trails, and bingo. He wasn't sure if his mother was a fan of the game but it would be an activity to keep her busy and help her meet people.

Since scaling back his work pace, he could visit her more often. He never knew if the old mom would be waiting when he arrived. Maybe her deterioration wouldn't seem so drastic if he was around her more.

A white van pulled up to the front door.

He could see her through the window.

She smiled.

Good sign.

An aide got out and opened the rear door.

Luke leaned into the back and held his mother's hand. "Hi, Mom."

Amanda smiled back. "This was a long ride. Will it take this long every time I come to see you?"

He shook his head. "No, this is your new home. Remember, Aunt Gladys told you about it?"

She stepped out of the vehicle and stared at the front entrance. "Hmm, this is the place that has bingo?"

He laughed. "Yes, it does. Twice a day."

"I hate the game. It's for old people. I'm not old." She crossed her arms.

She's right. Her memory fading at such a young age angered him. The best he could do was to keep her stimulated and not tucked away in some nursing home because he was afraid she would set the place on fire. "You don't have to play. It's one of the activities offered. You'll like it here. It's like having your own apartment, but you'll have staff to help. Someone will clean for you."

"I like that."

"I thought you would." He guided her up the stairs as the van pulled away. "It's like a hotel in New York City. You have a reception area and a lobby where you can read a book by the fireplace if you don't want to stay in your apartment. Plus, Aunt Gladys will be by a lot to visit."

Of that, he was sure. He was making the right decision. Coming back to Brookside would be good for both of them. He would learn how to live instead of fighting through his day to make another dollar. He put a lot of planning into this—

Kristen!

He gasped and remembered why she seemed so familiar.

****

"Aunt Kristen, look what I found." Danny held a red diary.

"Where did you find this?" A chill ran down Kristen's spine as she took the book that held the secrets of her sister.

"In the window seat in my room. There's a bunch of stuff in there. I know how you like to read so I brought it to you. Are you mad?"

Danny looked at her with loving eyes. "No, no, sweetie. Not at all. I'm glad you gave this to me. I've been looking for it. Thank you." She ran the tip of her index finger in the *C.A.* scratched into the imitation brass name plate. "I have something, too." She walked to the car and handed her nephew one of the small gnomes.

His nose wrinkled. "What's this? It looks funny."

"It's a decoration for the house. Don't you think it's cute?" She reached into the car to empty out the other small gnome and holly dishes. "Can you handle these because I have an even bigger surprise?"

"Ah huh. Got it." He stood with a gnome under each armpit and the holly dishes stuffed in the chest of his coat.

"Here it is." Kristen backed out of the car and revealed the three-foot gnome in his splendid green vest and red Santa hat. She planted it on the ground beside the front porch. "What do you think?"

"It's okay. What is it?" He stood, balancing the smaller gnomes under his arms.

"It's a gnome. Not cool? I think it's very cool." She took a step back to admire the new addition. The odd-looking thing with its crooked hat caught her attention because she was drawn to imperfections. The gnome wasn't perfect, and she liked that. She gathered the rest of the brood and placed them near the taller figure. "How about here? Better?"

"I guess for being a gnome. Can we go in now? I'm hungry." Danny ran up the porch stairs.

True craftsmanship was wasted on him. She followed Danny into the house. Her stomach, slightly growling.

He handed over the candy dishes.

She placed them on the coffee and end tables, pleased with her new purchase.

"Those are nice." He hung his coat in the hall closet.

"Those you like? Those get your attention?" She would have to spend more time with him and teach him the finer things in life.

He ran to the corner and turned on the Christmas tree lights. "This, I like. Especially the angel."

"I do, too."

"Can we have one every year?"

He slipped his hand into hers.

"Of course. We will always have a real Christmas tree." She scooped him up and buried her face in his chest, hugging him as tight as she could. She never expected to feel so strongly for a child. Her life was meant to be marriage and child free. Funny, what life throws your way.

"Food's ready," Nana yelled from the dining room.

"No special company tonight?" Kristen walked into the room, and then silently counted the plates stacked next to a large pot of chicken soup. Of course, Luke wouldn't show up for dinner, because he had a date. "So, what did you two do today, besides shop for snakes and turtles?"

"We also considered a frog but thought that might be too much." Nana smiled.

"So, a snake and turtle are not too much to take care of?" Kristen ripped the end from a warm loaf of homemade Italian bread.

"Too much to carry." Nana winked at Danny.

Kristen shook her head and wanted to crawl under the chair. "I don't understand why you spend money on reptiles. Danny can go in the back by the creek like his mother did." She tried so hard to protect him, and one way was to not talk about his mother in front of him. Not yet, at least.

His shoulders sagged as if a weight were on them. A seven-year-old should not have to bear the anguish of losing his only parent.

He pushed his bowl away. "I miss her."

Kristen pulled him from his chair and plopped him on her lap. "I know, sweetie. We all do. Your mom was a wonderful person. I know it's hard. I miss my mom, too. But we have each other. You, me, and Nana, together forever."

She held out her right pinky and curled it around his. "Together forever!" they yelled in unison. She scooped him from his chair and carried him to the bay window in the living room. "And includes who?"

Danny pulled back the curtain and pointed to the sky. Snow wafted to the ground and dusted the gnomes. "Mommy!"

Nana rested a hand on his shoulder.

"Yes, honey. And anytime you want to talk about your mom, let me know." She gently squeezed both of his shoulders and kissed him on the head. Kristen thought it best to keep Carly's spirit alive. Not talking about her might have been the worst thing for Danny. As the youngest, she never had to be responsible for anything.

With the dishes done, she rushed to the girlie room—as Luke referred to it. She lit her lilac candle on the nightstand, sat on the bed, and then fluffed pillows piled behind her back to settle in. She opened the cover of the diary, then slammed it shut. Was she intruding? Carly would be annoyed if she were around. But she wasn't. Carly's secrets, likes, dreams, and desires might be written in the pages. Things Kristen couldn't answer or know about her sister unless she read the journal.

She looked toward the ceiling. "Sorry, Sis. I didn't snoop then but I am now. Get as mad as you want." She opened the book again, head down, gaze darting around the room waiting for her ghostly sister to disapprove.

Nothing.

She continued. The first page began when Carly was sixteen. Typical boring passages of a cheerleader—school wins and losses, proms. Things Kristen had never done. Always the outsider, she could never be a joiner like her sister. Flip, flip, flip. Kristen didn't find anything interesting until—

"What?" Kristen muttered. The entry date was smeared but based on the content, Carly lost her virginity to Brian that day. Kristen calculated that her sister was sixteen. She never would have guessed. Carly came across as the type who would wait for marriage. Then again, she did have Danny out of wedlock years later. The announcement of his birth shocked Nana, but she never spoke of it once Danny was born. It didn't matter. His presence filled the house with love, and the circumstances simply didn't matter.

She flipped through the rest of the diary and found a letter stuck to the inside of the back cover, the word copy written in red in the top right corner. The address scribbled on the back was for Brian Reeves at an address in Oregon. Her stomach tightened as she dug deeper into Carly's secrets.

Dear Brian,

Danny was born today. I know you're unsure where he fits into your life, but you have to know he's here. I'll send a picture as soon as I can. Right now, he's scrunched up like a cabbage, and I want you to look into his eyes. I also know us getting together was nothing more than that. I'll be in touch.

Carly

Kristen bolted upright. Danny's father. She had a name—Brian Reeves. *Think, think, think.* Nothing. Damn! She couldn't remember anyone by that name. The five-year difference between Kristen and Carly mattered now. Except for grade school, they never attended the same school or had the same friends. There had to be some clue somewhere.

Wait, the date of the letter was fifteen years after the diary entry. How could she not know for so long that her sister was involved with someone?

She ran to Carly's old room on the third floor and

flung open the door, knocking over the coatrack behind it. She turned on the light and sneezed. Her nose itched from the dust. Obviously, Nana didn't make it up here much, and it looked the same as when Carly stayed here. The green and brown patchwork quilt covered the twin bed. Pictures of their parents hung over the maple headboard. A lone lamp stood on the nightstand.

Kristen opened the window seat stuffed with papers, books, and sweatshirts. She rifled through the contents, found a Brookside Falls yearbook, and then sat cross-legged on the floor. She never owned a yearbook of her own. Yes, being anti-social as she was, those things weren't important. She thumbed through the seniors landing on the Rs.

Brian Reeves

Captain of the bowling team.

Ambition—to live in the Rocky Mountains when not surfing.

He was an ambitious fellow. Kristen studied the picture. He did resemble Danny. Hard to tell, though, since Danny looked so much like his mother.

She rested her back against the wall of the window seat. The black-and-white picture didn't give away much. Cheap school didn't spring for color pictures. She closed the yearbook and let her head fall back. "Oh Carly, why didn't you tell anyone?"

Sadness engulfed her as she fingered the faded yearbook. She had a name. How difficult could finding Brian be? Her immediate need was to run downstairs and tell Nana, but she couldn't. Why hadn't Carly let the family know about Danny's father? Her nephew had a right to know who his father was, didn't he?

She curled into a ball and clutched the yearbook to

her chest. Maybe it's another Brian Reeves…doubtful. The chance of another guy in Brookside Falls with the same name during those years was unlikely. She stretched back her neck, looked at the ceiling, and concentrated to remember someone named Brian Reeves. She looked at the picture again. Nothing. He wasn't familiar at all.

She placed the yearbook back into the window seat for safekeeping. She wondered how many more secrets were hidden away in the nooks and crannies of the old house. Investigation would have to wait for another day.

Chapter Eight

Luke's mother transitioned well into the new living arrangement. Of course, she had only been at West Haven a short time, and something could go wrong. But his gut told him it would work out.

Gladys was true to form and showed within an hour of Amanda's arrival. Luke was grateful he could count on his aunt. He was busy at work early in the morning. He had taken enough time from his desk and needed to finish some sketches.

He had to start work on Kristen's shop, and doing so provided the perfect opportunity to be around her. The exact detail of meeting her alluded him, but he felt a familiar twinge the night at the tree lot. They met before—but where?

He leaned back in his high-back leather chair and closed his eyes. Coffee wasn't kicking in, and his lids were heavy. Falling asleep would be easy, but he needed to finish his work.

Five minutes.

He took in a slow, steady, deep breath, placed his hands on his head, and relaxed his shoulders to ease the tension in his chest. A trick he learned years ago from Jillian. Little did he know at that time she was the reason for most of his stress.

Silence filled the room except for the low-wattage hum of the computer tower. If he listened closer, he could hear doves cooing in the flower box outside his front window. Doves were so much cooler than pigeons. He struggled to meditate. *Focus. Breathe.*

A subtle vision of a young blonde, about fifteen years old, filled his head. She was wearing a gauzy white shirt walking toward him. Carnival music filled the air. He could smell cinnamon-fried apple rings and maple cotton candy peppered with the burned rubber tires of the demolition derby.

But it was the laughter of the girl walking toward him he remembered most—

Ring-Ring.

He let out a sigh, his concentration broken by the office phone. He stretched out his arms to the side and glanced at his watch. Nine a.m. "Hello, Baldwin Architects." He was so original with his business name. He anguished for weeks to come up with something different and modern. In the end, he decided on personality and function.

"Luke?"

The sound of her voice made him freeze. "Jillian?"

"Ah, yeah."

He cleared his head. His spine tightened as he sat straight. The last few moments of calm—gone—never to return. "What?"

"You don't have to be so rude," Jillian snapped.

"Not being rude. I have nothing to say. We're done. You made that clear. If anything, I'm confused why you would be calling, especially my office number." He could hear a slight breath on the other end of the call. The last thing he wanted was to get into a conversation with Jill. He wanted to hang up, but he was raised to be polite no matter how upset he was.

"I lost your cell number," she said softly.

"Okay." He spun around to his coffee pot. Empty.

"I—I…"

"What? I'm working. What do you want?" he said in the kindest tone he could muster.

Jillian cleared her throat. "Do you remember the dog we looked at a year ago?"

He vaguely remembered the conversation. They were passing through north Jersey and stopped at a breeder for Golden Retrievers. Pure impulse, nothing planned and adopting a dog was never discussed again. "What about it?" He flexed his free hand to relieve tension.

"I filled out an application, and the breeder called me last night."

"What does that have to do with me?"

"I put down your name as a co-applicant."

Typical Jillian. Always easier to ask for forgiveness than permission. "Well good luck becoming a dog owner. I have nothing to do with this." Silence again. Jillian was predictable. She was looking for a way back into his life. He was done. Nothing could convince him to forgive her selfish behavior.

"I thought since you were a part of this decision, you might want to have a chance to look at the litter."

"Nope. You made the decision, not me. This call is done, and honestly, I couldn't think of a reason for you to ever call me again. Have a good life and good luck." He hung up the phone. This wasn't how his morning was supposed to start. His first business call and it was from an ex he didn't want to be bothered with. She realized she was on her own. No more taking months off between modeling gigs and him supporting her. Not that he minded but once he started to feel used, he grew to resent her lack of contribution.

Money wasn't really the problem. Jillian would spend all day watching soap operas and talk shows and wouldn't even make a simple dinner while he worked twelve-hour days.

Life was easier being alone. He checked his calendar. No conference call until noon. He couldn't wait for the shopping mall project in Jersey to be completed so he wouldn't have to go back and forth. He did as much as he could via teleconference.

Fortunately, he banked his money so he could take his time building a new business in Haineswood, which was less demanding and chaotic than living and working in the city. He would be lucky to secure a two-story structure, never mind a ten-story project, with elevators and waterfalls.

A simple life was his goal, and someone like Jillian would stir up negative energy and make him crazy. At least he knew where to get a room if he lost his mind.

Tap-Tap.

Aunt Gladys.

He grabbed his coat and flung it over his shoulder, approaching the door to fend off his aunt. "Sorry, not a good time."

"But…"

"Did something happen?" He slipped his arms into his coat sleeves.

"No, I want to tell…"

"Can this wait? I have the perfect idea. My mother was too tired to go to dinner the other night, so why don't you come with us later this week? We can make it early so it doesn't take up your night."

Gladys cocked her head. "That's perfect. I'll even pick up your mom and bring her with me. Where to?"

"Surprise me. Send a text. I'll meet you there." He placed an arm around her shoulder, herded her outside, and helped her into the car.

Coffee.

He yanked his collar around his ears and headed toward the diner for the largest cup of coffee sold. Maybe he would run into Kristen.

****

The next morning brought a sense of permanence and closure for Kristen. She poured a cup of coffee, then gazed out the window over the kitchen sink. A white-breasted nuthatch and downy woodpecker fed at the cage of suet hanging off the back-porch railing.

So much happened since she'd come to stay at her grandmother's house, and she was spending too much time inside. Helping her grandmother get the inn ready for her Christmas guests had been a non-stop whirlwind. Fortunately, Gladys took care of managing the guest reservations. One less thing for Kristen to do—she was grateful. Hauling out the linens, washing them, and making the beds was more exercise than she had done in a year.

She spent time learning how to be more than an aunt to Danny and a wrangler of rogue reptiles and rodents. Carly's secret was safe with her for now, but she struggled with the decision to tell Nana about Danny's father. She had to find out more before she unloaded the news to the family. What concerned her the most was why her sister kept Brian's identity a secret. She would have to find out why. Carly must have had a good reason for not telling her.

Time away from the inn was inviting, and a trip into Haineswood for breakfast with Danny was needed and necessary. Christmas music from the radio filled the car as she drove into town. Danny wasn't much company in the morning—a trait he definitely inherited from his mother. Kristen was not much of a morning person herself, but her sister had been even worse and could be cranky all day if someone spoke before she was ready to have a conversation. The memory brought happiness and made her smile.

Funny how the annoying moments became endearing when someone was gone. She smiled and glanced at Danny who sat with his hands shoved in his coat pockets. His hat almost completely covered his eyes, and his jacket collar pulled up to his ears.

She parked in front of the deli and didn't see Luke's car by his office. It's not like she was looking for him, but she was in his neighborhood, so if she happened to run into him, well, she wouldn't mind seeing him. She opted for the diner across the street. For a small town, there were plenty of places to eat located on one block.

The diner was nearly empty except for one elderly man seated at the end of the counter. She purposely arrived after the morning breakfast rush to have a quiet meal. "Pancakes?" Kristen pushed her jacket against the wall as she slid into the booth.

Danny nodded, knelt on the seat, and then pushed buttons on the tabletop jukebox. "What's this? All it's playing is Christmas music."

"I don't think the jukebox works anymore. I'm sure the music is coming from the speakers in the ceiling. And what's wrong with Christmas music?"

"Nothing, I guess." Danny traced a finger in the maze printed on the paper placemat in front of him.

"It's only for a few more weeks and then you won't have to listen to it for another year."

A server came over to the table. "What can I get for you?"

"He'll have a short stack of pancakes and milk. I'll have a vegetable, egg white omelet, and a cup of chamomile tea. Thanks."

"Um, we don't have chamomile tea." The server tapped her pencil on her pad.

"Okay, hot water, then. I have my own bag." She always carried a few tea bags in her purse for moments like this. Tea drinkers definitely were not catered to in the dining world, and she made it a point to give tea drinkers a second cup when she was a server. This little bit of attention brought in extra tips.

Danny plopped his elbows on the table and rested his hands on his fists, still kneeling on the bench. He bounced his feet against the back of the booth. "I'm bored."

"Sit back. Breakfast will be here soon and then we have to stop by the school." Kristen tapped his nose.

"School?" He sat back and crossed his arms across his chest.

"Yes, school."

The server put down a cup of hot water and milk.

"You didn't think you would be out of school forever, did you?"

"No." He swigged his drink and smiled with a milk mustache. "Do I look funny?"

"Yes, you do. Wipe your mouth." She handed Danny a napkin. The kid made her smile except when he let his snake loose in the house.

"Pancakes and omelet. Enjoy." The server smiled as she put their food on the table and left them to eat their meal.

Danny poured way too much syrup on his pancakes but Kristen ignored it. They didn't eat out often so she let him have some fun. She would have to learn how to make healthy meals at home. Oh sure, Nana would cook, but Kristen didn't want to rely on her grandmother to feed them every day. Kristen couldn't cook well, and she was much better at cleaning than caring to learn how to roast a turkey.

When the diner door opened, the bell rang, and a gust of cold air tunneled down along the booth.

"Luke!" Danny yelled with a mouth full of pancake as syrup ran down his hand and wrist.

Kristen turned around. Her gaze locked with his. An annoying lock of hair hung in his face, but his eyes distracted her from his wayward hairstyle.

"Morning, Dawn. The usual." He walked over to the table. "Good morning."

Kristen's morning got better by the minute. She needed to get out of the inn more often and expand her social circle. It would be easier once the holidays were over and Danny was in school.

Danny scooted over to make room.

Luke joined them. "Your aunt must think you're special to take you to breakfast at a fancy place like this."

Danny swirled a chunk of pancake in the syrup on his plate and then shoved it into his mouth and nodded. "Yep."

"Yes, he is special. We're off to register him for

school after breakfast." Kristen glanced at Luke. "No more home schooling."

"So that means you're staying?" Luke smiled.

"Yes, I am. I can always go back to Jersey during school breaks and the summer. Not sure what I'll do about my apartment. Maybe I'll sublet it for a few months. This is the best place for him to be right now. For many reasons." She leaned closer to Luke and rested her chin in her hand.

"It's a nice town. This is a good place for a kid to grow up." Luke leaned back and stretched his arm across the top of the booth.

"Luke, your order's ready." The server waved a brown bag in the air.

Kristen sat back. "I sent the furniture plans. Did you get them?"

He stood then grabbed his food from the deli counter. "Yes, and everything will be here on time. The carpenters will be at the inn tomorrow. Don't worry. We'll have it done before Christmas Eve. Maybe even a few days before. See ya."

A gust of air fell from her lips. She wanted to ask him about his date. She wanted to spend an entire meal with him without talking about construction, permits, and time lines. She wanted to know him—not the architect. But she couldn't *wait* for him to ask *her* for a date.

****

Luke left the diner in a better mood than when he walked in. He wasn't expecting to run into Kristen but was glad he did. Doing so made a nice start to his day. He almost had the courage to ask her to dinner, but he didn't want to intrude on her time with Danny

With his mother settled in and his aunt Gladys agreeing to stop in and visit her, he took the opportunity to drive to New Jersey. He left early so he could turn the trip in a day. Only a few boxes were left in his storage unit to grab then he could close out the account. With the commuter traffic clear, he could be back on the road before late afternoon and still have the evening free.

He hopped onto Route 80 east and rolled down the window, embracing the warmer than usual fall day, and cranked up the radio. Incessantly scanning the channels, he landed on a classic rock station, songs from his childhood. The current music scene wasn't one he could tolerate. Overproduced, no-talent singers didn't hold his interest.

His phone rang, and the radio volume kicked out.

"Hello?"

"Hi."

"Kristen?" He looked for a rest stop.

"Earlier, I forgot to ask you something about the plans."

Business call. What else was he expecting? Besides being really lousy at letting Kristen know he wanted to take her on a date, he probably left out an important detail because she distracted him. "Shoot. What's up?" The rest stop was closed. *Drive on.* He didn't expect it to be a long, involved call anyway.

"Did you include a lock on the door between the inn and the shop?"

Kristen sounded unsure. *An odd question.* Why would she be concerned about something so early in the project? "It's not something I remember off-hand but if it's not on the plans, it can be installed without a problem."

She hesitated. "Okay."

"Is there a problem?"

"There has to be a lock. I'll have chemical stuff in there, and I don't want guests walking into the shop when it's not open for business."

"Sure. I'll take care of it." He couldn't understand the urgency, but she was the client and he wasn't going to pass an opinion.

"Thanks. I guess that's all," she said.

"Unless there's something else."

"Um, nope. That's it."

"I'll be going."

"Okay then. Bye."

The radio resumed playing an 80s hair band, whose name he couldn't recall, rocking out to the sound of motorcycles in the foreground of one of their hits.

He couldn't begin to figure out what the call from Kristen was really about. Was she really particular, or was it an excuse to call him? He liked to think it was an excuse, but he knew better than to make sense of a situation when a woman told him something that didn't make sense.

He barreled down the back of a tractor-trailer and stepped on the gas to drive around the impeding vehicle. A few weeks out of the city and he was lacking in his defensive driving skills.

The phone rang again.

"Ah, you remembered something else?" He smiled.

"You can say that."

He cringed from the voice at the other end of the call. "What, Jillian?"

"Can you soften your tone?" she snapped.

"Not being rude. I'm on the road. What's up?"

"I'm getting the dog."

"What does that have to do with me?"

"I need my box marked Jillian's Junk Drawer."

For a moment, he thought he had thrown it out. Too bad if he did. He didn't owe her anything. "I'll check."

"I'd appreciate it. Buffy's old collar is in there, and I want it for the new dog."

"Whatever. I'll check when I have time. Gotta go." Maybe Jillian was right. He might be a tad rude, but no one got under his skin like she did. But he didn't have to put up with her anymore for the sake of the relationship.

The two lanes opened to four, and he sailed down the interstate, uninterrupted except for 80s tunes.

He pushed Jillian out of his head and thought of Kristen. Luke had to be thoughtful in his approach to ask her out. Because of Danny, he needed to maintain a delicate balance. He never dated a woman who had a child so he was unsure of the rules. His awkwardness put off people sometimes, but he did his best to smooth any unintentional insults or rude demeanor, though he was aware this was hard to do with his ex.

He jumped onto 78 east and then parkway south. Another half an hour existed to take in his tunes.

A self-storage facility came up fast, and he nearly missed the exit. It would be his last trip. He drove down the ramp and pulled into the industrial park. The lockbox accepted his code, and the clanky gate slid to the side as he drove through the opening.

He pulled next to a door and spun the combination, opening the lock. As it slid into the overhead track, the door rattled.

The stench of old cardboard and dampness made him wince at the thought of loading his car with stuff he planned to throw away. Most of it belonged to his mother, and he would let her go through the containers. Poor planning on his part—he should have done it before the junk was boxed and a small ransom paid each month to the storage company to keep belongings damp.

He placed his fists on his hips and gently kicked a box on the bottom of the pile to scare away any critter that might be nesting amongst the Baldwin memories. He shuffled boxes around and thought about throwing them out—but—he couldn't. Not to his mother's stuff. He popped open the trunk and strategically arranged the boxes like a puzzle.

The collection of random items was in better condition than he expected. The top boxes weren't damp, or musty, and would survive the trip home. But not the large one on the bottom. He opened it and found two beach chairs from when he and Jillian visited Myrtle Beach. He held a chair by the top-back-rail and flipped it open. The same he did with the second one and put them in front of the door to the neighboring unit with a sign.

ENJOY

Yep, he wanted nothing from her. He closed the door on the empty unit with the surety he was shutting the door to his former life.

Chapter Nine

The bang of workmen's hammers and scream of a buzz saw woke up Kristen early the past two days. If the carpenters kept that pace, the inn would definitely be finished on time. She was excited about the grand re-opening soon.

Danny wouldn't start school until after the New Year. Nana had been playing Christmas music for days. Kristen dug out decorations and placed them throughout the house, her favorite being the wreath on the door. She found the old frame buried away in the attic, and she and Danny gathered fresh pine branches from trees in the yard and made the wreath themselves. Pinecones from the woods and a homemade popcorn garland with cranberries finished it off.

She hadn't seen Luke since they ran into each other at the diner, and she found herself thinking about him often. New linens and cleaning the guest rooms took precedence over her love life right then anyway. She wanted to hire someone to help with the housekeeping, but her grandmother thought spending money for a week of cleaning was unnecessary. She was right. Why spend the money when breakfast and a night-time snack were offered? Six rooms were easy to maintain.

Kristen stayed in her bedroom to again relax with her sister's diary. Carly led a pretty boring life by Kristen's standards. Well, except for Danny. His birth was completely unexpected. But now she had a name and was eager to find his father.

What if his father was a horrible person? What if he was married with a family and the family didn't know about Danny? What if his father wanted him? Kristen placed a hand over her mouth as tears rolled down her cheeks. What if *she* lost Danny to someone else?

She shoved the ragged diary under her mattress. As far as she knew, her grandmother was unaware of the journal. The weight of discovering Brian Reeves' connection to Danny frightened her. She needed some time alone to process her newfound information.

Danny was busy watching the carpenters, and Nana would not leave the house while strangers were in her home. She ran downstairs and threw on her jacket. "Nana, I'm running out. Can Danny stay with you?"

"Sure, I can use his help cleaning the birdcages. Okay with you, Danny?" she yelled over to where he stood in the new doorway.

He nodded.

Kristen wished the New Year would hurry so he could make some friends at school. How much fun could it be for him hanging out with his thirty-something aunt and eighty-year-old great-grandmother? "Thanks." She rushed out of the house and headed into town.

She needed to see Luke and drove fast, but not enough to grab the attention of a traffic cop. She pulled up to his office. A quick glance in the rearview mirror and she finger-combed her hair then freshened her lipstick. She was ready.

She turned the knob of his office door, but it didn't

open. A sign on the door read, *Closed until tomorrow.* Tomorrow! She wanted to see him. He never mentioned he wouldn't be in the office. She went into the deli next door. "Hi, hot chocolate, please." She brushed a foot against the floor. "Hey, you know Luke from next door?"

"Yeah," the kid behind the counter responded.

"Do you know why he's closed today?" She reached out for her drink and placed three dollars on the counter.

"Something about going to New Jersey for a few days." The kid took the money.

"Jersey? Hmm, thanks." She waved away the change. "Keep it." She went back to her car and held her hot chocolate, barely sipping, then placed her drink in the cup holder. *A date. Jersey.* She started the car and wondered why would he be in New Jersey? Traffic out of town was light and she enjoyed revisiting the drive to Jackson Corners. Not much had changed, except for one or two new houses.

She arrived at the pottery store sooner than she expected, though she was oblivious to the time while lost in thought. Rarely was she distracted by someone. But she couldn't figure out why she was drawn to Luke. The overhead bell announced her arrival. "Good morning," Kristen called out.

The same woman greeted her from behind the counter. "Morning to you. How are those gnomes doing?"

"Great. They fit in perfectly with the inn." She unzipped her jacket then extended a hand across the counter. "My name is Kristen."

"Deborah. What inn?"

"Over in Brookside Falls. My grandparents ran it as an inn until my grandfather died."

"What's the name of the inn?" Deborah stepped back with her hands resting on her waist.

"Brookside Falls Inn. Being the only one at the time, that's what my family decided on. Not very original but it fits."

Deborah closed the register drawer and stepped from behind the counter onto the sales floor. "I see."

"We're having a trial run and have rented rooms for the holiday week. My grandmother thinks the inn can survive." She crossed her arms across her chest and shifted her weight back. "Of course, we can't know for sure how successful we'll be, but we'll see how it goes. My nephew is enjoying exploring the grounds."

Deborah straightened a cluster of finger bowls on the table. "How old is he? Maybe we have something he would like better than the gnomes."

"He's seven. I'm afraid he's at an age where he would break much of what you have here."

"Hmm, you never know. We have handmade wooden toys as well. The simplest things yet a lot of the kids like them." Deborah waved Kristen toward the back corner of the store. "Isn't the inn under renovation?"

"Sort of." Kristen picked up a wooden yo-yo, slipping her finger in the loop, and watched the wooden circle climb up and down the string. "The inn itself is fine. We're adding a small hair salon so I have something to do out here but mainly as a perk for our guests. My grandmother thinks it will be a nice service to provide."

"I thought I heard something about a salon. You

114

know, small town gossip, you can't keep any secrets in this county. I wish you luck. Take your time and browse." Deborah waddled behind the counter.

Kristen felt free to wander around without being forced to make small talk. The yo-yo was a good choice and would make a nice stocking stuffer. She browsed through the tables, taking care not to bang into anything. A small, heart-shaped jewel pot encrusted with gem dust on the lid caught her attention. The gemstones changed color when held to the light and she was fascinated by the intricate detail. Money could not be wasted on trinkets, so she put it down and decided to buy only the toy for Danny.

She walked over to the counter. "This is all for today. You have so much here I could spend all day looking, but I have to hurry back and check on the carpenters."

"That'll be ten dollars and fifty cents." Deborah wrapped the yo-yo in tissue paper and a box. "I hope your nephew enjoys this."

Kristen laughed. "Unless I keep it for myself. I've never seen one like this. The detail of the lightning bugs and the grass is amazing."

"Yes, the artist was a true craftsman. I hope to see you soon." She handed the bag to Kristen.

She caught a glimpse of a picture tucked against the register. "Handsome guy."

Deborah sighed. "Yes. He was."

****

Traffic had been light as Luke predicted, and he could squeeze in some last-minute sight-seeing before leaving Jersey. He wouldn't have another reason to be there unless a project came along that required him on site. He jumped back onto to the Garden State Parkway and headed south.

He could grab a hot dog for lunch down the shore and get in a last of the season stroll along the ocean. A trip to Wildwood would have been ideal, but he didn't have the time. He favored the beach after Labor Day. The tourists were gone, and on a nice fall day, he enjoyed the quiet and ability to be on the sand without getting hit with a football. There could still be shells to collect along the coastline.

The shore would be the one thing he would miss by living in Haineswood. The mountain lakes didn't hold the same allure the ocean did.

Thirty minutes later, he pulled into the empty parking lot at Sandy Hook.

A gray-haired man and a woman with oversized sunglasses biked along the path.

Luke grabbed a beat-up, navy-blue sweatshirt from the backseat and kicked off his shoes as he walked onto the sand. His toes curled from the coolness of the ground and took him by surprise. The tide must have gone out shortly before he got there, leaving the sand damp.

He stood at the water's edge and shaded his eyes with a hand, staring out over the horizon. His life was missing something. As much as he thought he could do it on his own—he didn't want to. The undertow pulled him deeper into the sand, as the sea water swirled around his ankles. He took a step back to regain his balance.

His stomach growled, and he zeroed in to find the hotdog he promised himself. Nothing tasted better than food down on the shore. Something about the salt air enhanced the flavor or experience of whatever you ate.

I miss it already.

He turned on his heel and headed back to the car. Two more cars were in the lot when he returned. They had Jersey license plates so they weren't tourists looking for directions.

The dream of owning a shore house eluded him. He wanted an office built like a lighthouse. Spiral stairs with his desk at the very top so he could see over the waves and watch the ships sail in and out of the New York harbor.

In the summer, he could enjoy the small private planes flying along the coastline with advertisements trailing behind the aircraft. Maybe he'd have the name of his company on one of the banners. Of course, he couldn't expect clients to climb the winding staircase so he would arrange for client-friendly seating like a semi-circular couch hugging the curved walls. His desk presentation still sitting in sight of the crashing waves.

Missing his favorite part of the east coast, he sighed. *There's another time for this.* He got into his car and drove out past the old barracks and ammunition shelters. In a few months, his favorite area wouldn't be so inviting as carloads of people from north Jersey, New York, and Pennsylvania piled into the small area, claiming any bare inch of beach.

On the way out in search of a chili dog, he stopped at the legendary Spy House. Often touted as the most haunted building in America, but in all the years he spent down the shore, he never stopped by to see it. He pulled into the vacant lot and caught sight of a hot dog joint across the street but closed for the season. His curiosity heightened and he walked over to the white clapboard house and peeked into the windows.

Hmm. Nothing but dust.

He strolled around the building and looked up to the second floor. A few of his friends told him how they would see an old lady in colonial dress watching them out the window. He didn't see a thing. Maybe the weather was too cold for spirits. Did ghosts go to Florida for the winter also like the snowbirds of New Jersey?

Still hungry and getting cranky, he headed out onto Route 36 in search of another hot dog joint. He turned on the radio, and 80s music blasted the car. As he caught every red light along the highway, he tapped his fingers on the steering wheel.

His thoughts turned to Kristen. He liked her and wanted to ask her out on a date soon. He didn't know what to make of her obligation to Danny. Cute kid but this was a tricky situation.

He was determined to eat a chili dog with raw onions and fresh out of the hot grease french fries, but his prospects didn't seem hopeful. Most of the businesses, except for the chain stores, were closed for the season.

Heck with it. He took the exit for the Garden State Parkway north and would entertain his hunger with stale BBQ chips and flat root beer he had left over from his trip. He didn't know when he would be down again, but he was content having spent a little time satisfying his Jersey desire. He raised the volume on the radio and pressed the gas pedal harder, testing his Jersey driving skills of still being able to outwit the state troopers. What he didn't account for was the traffic as he headed north.

****

Kristen arrived home to find Danny crawling under the Christmas tree. "What's up?"

"Bird," Danny muttered from deep beneath the pine branches.

"What?" Kristen's eyebrows knitted together. At least the snake hadn't gotten loose.

"The green budgie escaped and flew into the window and slid behind the tree." Nana wrung her hands together.

"Is it dead?" Kristen anticipated another stuffed bird perched on a curtain rod.

"Got it," Danny yelled. He wriggled out from under the tree on his belly then rolled onto his back with the bird safely cupped in his hands. "Here you go, Nana."

She scooped the traumatized budgie with her apron and waddled back to the cage. "That little bugger flew out of the cage. I think he thought he had friends on the outside." Nana sat in the chair next to the tree.

She looked pale. "Are you okay?" Kristen put the back of a palm against her grandmother's forehead. No fever.

"I'm fine. Just flustered from the excitement. I should've kept my word and not bought any more birds." She laughed.

"I know. It's like a sickness with you. An obsession like I've never seen before." She placed a hand-crocheted afghan across her grandmother's legs.

"Thank you, dear. I feel like it's going to snow. My knees are achy." She rested her head against the back of the chair.

"Yes, the weatherman said we should get a dusting.

Are you getting overwhelmed with reopening the inn? It must be a lot of work for you." Kristen sat on the floor and curled up against the chair as she rested her head on her grandmother's knee.

Nana sighed. "Not a lot of work. I'm actually excited. You and Danny are doing most of the work."

"And Gladys." Kristen looked to her grandmother.

"Yes, and Gladys. She's the one who started this. It's been quiet here for so many years. I even asked your grandfather if he could make an appearance on Christmas Eve."

Kristen raised her head. "You see Pop-Pop?"

"He still looks after the place." Nana yawned and closed her eyes.

"Has he always been here?" Her breath caught. One time after his funeral, she thought her Pop-Pop visited during the night but figured her longing to see him once more was nothing more than wishful thinking.

"No, recently." Nana nodded off to sleep.

Kristen gently patted her grandmother's knee and quietly walked away. She heard of people seeing deceased loved ones as they were near the end of their lives. Her stomach tightened. She couldn't bear to lose her grandmother, too. This past year held too many changes and too many emotions to process. How had she become the caregiver? She didn't like the role. She lay down on the couch and watched her grandmother. Her breathing seemed fine.

The phone rang, and she jumped across the room to answer the call so the ringtone didn't wake her grandmother. "Hello," she whispered.

"Kristen?"

"Yes, Luke?" Her tiredness disappeared as she

smiled widely.

"Hi. I wanted to check on the carpenters. I've been calling Tom's cell phone, but he's not answering. Are they there?"

"Yes. Where are you?" Damn, she didn't want to come across as clingy.

"On my way back. I ran down to Jersey to take care of some business. The three-hour drive can be a pain sometimes, but I won't have to do it anymore."

"What time will you be back?" She cringed. She'd done it again. She wasn't good at the 'semi-dating' thing, if that's even what was going on between them.

"Around five."

She tucked the phone under her chin, deciding to go for it. After all, what did she have to lose? "How about dinner at six?"

No answer.

Had she gone too far? "Luke?"

Still no answer.

"Luke?"

"Sorry. Dropped the phone. Passed a cop."

"You don't use hands-free?"

"I do, but sometimes the system doesn't connect. I keep meaning to get it checked. I haven't the time. What did you say?"

She sighed. Maybe it was a sign she read him wrong. "Nothing, really. The furniture is arriving tomorrow."

"Good. Hey, how about dinner tonight?"

Stunned, she nearly dropped the phone. He asked her on a date? Had her positive thinking kicked in? She had been fooled by him before, so she played it casual. "Sure. The Asian fusion place?"

"Sounds good. Meet me there at six."

Then he ended the call. Maybe he passed another cop—either way the conversation was over. *Meet him there!* She sighed. It wasn't a date. But she had a reason to eat out and have adult conversation. Not that she would settle, but she still couldn't figure out what his deal was. One minute he seemed interested and the next he'd back away. He probably had a girlfriend, anyway. How could he not? Those green eyes. How could a woman resist? Oh, this woman could. His flippant and disconnected manner—yeah that was enough to put off any woman. But why was she falling for him? *Hard to get?* Maybe. Enough guessing. She had to get ready for dinner. Her enthusiasm for Luke gave way to guilt about Danny.

He stood in the lobby doorway watching the workmen.

She worried she wouldn't be enough for him. Would she be a good enough guardian? Could she provide enough love and strength to support him as he grew up? A lump filled her throat, she straightened her back, and walked over to Danny. "Doesn't the room look good? She rested her hand on her nephew's shoulder.

"I want to be a carpenter."

"Why?"

"So, I can pound on walls with a hammer."

She laughed. "You say that now. You'll change your mind a thousand times before you settle on a career. Take your time and enjoy being a kid."

New walls brightened the room, and a twinge of hope filled her heart. Initially, she doubted Luke but he was right, the shop would be ready on time. The room looked finished except for furniture and painting, which wouldn't take long to complete. The power tools were silent and piled in a corner ready to be picked up. "Hey, kid. Got a minute?"

He followed her into the living room. "Are the men leaving soon?"

"Yes. They work fast, don't they?" She hugged her nephew. She never wanted to make him feel unwanted or that he was an inconvenience. "Listen, I know we've been busy getting the inn ready, and I want to check with you. Are you okay with all this going on? You don't feel I'm ignoring you, do you?"

He hugged her back. "Nope. I like it here. There's a lot to do."

"Well, there will be even more to do once school starts." She winked and glanced over at her grandmother asleep in the chair. "I have a favor to ask. You know Luke, right?"

"Uh-huh."

"I would like to meet him for dinner tonight. Are you okay with that? It would mean you would be home with Nana."

He nodded. "I like Luke. Sure."

"You can even order whatever movie you want."

"*The Hulk?*"

"A kid after my own heart. I won't even have to pay for it. Haven't you worn out your DVD yet?" She scrunched her nose and rubbed it against his.

"Nope, it's still good."

"Ooooooooooooooooo." Nana yawned and stretched. "That felt good. I always made fun of old people who napped during the day, and now I'm one of them."

Danny crawled up on his grandmother's lap.

"You're not old. Just tired. Aunt Kristen has a date tonight, and me and you are watching *The Hulk*! Can we make popcorn?"

Nana smiled. "Luke?"

"Maybe." Kristen smiled and turned away.

"Well, it's about time if it is. He's cute." Nana shooed Danny from her lap, then stood and smoothed her apron, neatly folded the blanket, and laid it over the back of her chair.

"We'll discuss the final stage of the salon. They're nearly finished. Luke's not even picking me up. I have to drive myself." Kristen rolled her eyes.

"And that bothers you?"

Kristen thought about it for a moment. "Yes, it does. Why would he do that?"

Nana turned on the Christmas tree lights. "Maybe he's as cautious as you are."

Hmm. Kristen hadn't considered the possibility. She knew nothing about him but surely would learn something soon. *Time to solve the mystery of Luke Baldwin.*

Chapter Ten

The traffic lessened once he passed the Delaware Water Gap so he made up time and got home an hour earlier than he anticipated. He emptied his car of boxes he would need to go through. Most likely half the stuff was garbage, but he didn't have the time to stay in Jersey to sort through things.

His mind was focused on Kristen. He planned on sticking to his policy of not dating clients, but she wouldn't always be one. Having never gotten his hot dog, his stomach roiled with hunger.

No messages from the assisted living place or his aunt so his mother must be doing okay. He would make it a point to see her tomorrow.

All he wanted to do was meet Kristen for dinner. He could taste the salty fried dumplings doused with teriyaki sauce and green onion.

He got the boxes settled into his office. No need bringing them upstairs to the apartment. If he tossed most of the stuff, why bother with unnecessary junk? Any pictures stored in the boxes he planned to scan and trash, or maybe bring them to his mother and see if doing so helped her to remember moments of her past.

At times he wanted to hide from the world. He never thought he carried so much emotional weight. Only now did he realize how much his mother had done for him. No help from her family, and he never met his father. He wasn't sure how he was related to Aunt Gladys. The connection was never explained, and he called her aunt as he was instructed.

Enough with the pity party.

He needed to lie down for a few, so he could be refreshed and sharp minded for his non-date. As soon as he stretched out and closed his eyes, his phone rang.

Deborah.

He didn't have the time for her now—she would have to wait. He was happy with his choice to put a couch in his office. Sometimes he didn't want to trudge upstairs to stretch out for a few. He noticed the midday nap was becoming a regular part of his routine. Of course, the three-hour drive didn't help either. Especially because he left so early in the morning.

Sleep evaded him so he focused on the ceiling fan. Too cold to put it on but he could count the holes in the aged fake-bamboo on the blades.

Hard as he tried, all he could do was think about how ugly the fan was and needed to be replaced. Cosmetic repairs were low on his list, and hardly a priority. He needed to build a client base first. Once money started flowing into his business, he would splurge on replacing last century fans.

He closed his eyes, squeezing out the bright glare from the snow. He always remembered snow being on the ground for Christmas. Brookside Falls reminded him of old, black-and-white holiday movies. Live boughs of holly decorated the center of town, and evergreens displayed ornaments made by local children.

Though he didn't go to school in town, he took every chance he got to visit. Even moving back, he chose to establish his office in the Haineswood section just on the outskirts of Brookside Falls.

The towns often got confused until the holidays. Residents of Brookside Falls tended to drape real boughs of garland along railings of the larger homes and place candles in the front windows. The people of Haineswood focused on window lights and lighted snowflakes on streetlights.

The memories lulled him into limbo and brought him closer to sleep. If he focused hard enough, he could imagine the horse-drawn sleigh gliding through the center of town.

Zzzzzzz

Drifting.

Drifting.

"Luke!" A shrill female voice vaulted him out of his much-needed slumber. "Luke." He rubbed his eyes willing his aunt Gladys to go away so he could sleep. But she was determined and wouldn't leave until she had her say.

The wrinkles fell out of his pants as soon as he stood. "Uh. I'm coming." He saw her face scrunched against the glass window in the front door and felt bad. For a fleeting moment, he wanted her to leave so he could relish his quiet time.

He realized he was lucky to have her, and she was a huge help with the relocation. If he didn't have plans with Kristen, he would have asked Gladys. He wasn't one to cook for himself. It seemed like a lot of mess for one person.

"Good afternoon." Gladys walked inside with the song in her voice and a free-standing walnut coatrack with antique brass hooks.

"How are you always so cheerful?" He took her

coat and hung it on the new addition to his office.

"From Deborah's store. You can thank me later. Have you seen her?" Gladys walked over to the empty coffee maker and shook the burned pot. "This should never be allowed."

"I know. I got wrapped up in things and forgot the warmer plate was on."

"So, don't use it or keep some liquid in it. The carafe will end up busting on you at the worst time. Don't worry, I think I have another hanging around my staging warehouse."

"Thanks, but I don't need it. The deli is next door."

"Oh." Her chin dropped and she rolled her eyes. "You have money to throw around? At a buck fifty, you'll be in hock because of your caffeine addiction."

He was rethinking feeling guilty earlier about her visit. He forgot how much energy she sucked out of the room when she was wound up. "Thanks for stopping by, but I can assure you everything is fine plus I have a date for tonight so I have to get ready."

"A date?" Her brows arched. "So soon? You barely settled into town."

"It's really a business meeting."

"Who with?" Gladys smiled.

He hesitated, and she stared at him like she could read his mind.

"It's someone I know, isn't it?"

He nodded. "Kristen."

Gladys slapped her hand upside her cheek. "Oh, how adorable. She's adorable. You two are perfect for each other."

"Please, it's a business meeting to discuss the salon and inn renovations. She asked me." He didn't let on he heard her when he dropped the phone in the car.

"Hmm. A modern girl. That could work. You okay with that approach?" She folded her arms across her chest. "You're not intimidated by an independent, take-control woman, are you? Because that's what she is."

He looked at his aunt and did everything he could to stop from busting out laughing. "Ah, no, I'm not intimidated, so yes, I'm okay with it. I'm sure she's even planning to pay for her half of the dinner bill."

"Well, go on and get ready."

He helped her on with her coat, and then gently pushed her toward the exit.

"You keep me posted. And don't let her pay for her dinner. I don't care how modern it is. Even if it's *only* a business meeting, you pay. Simply write it off as a business expense."

He smiled and closed the door as she left, most likely to go visit someone else unannounced. Sure, because that's what a grown man would do.

****

Kristen's eyes took a few seconds to adjust to the dim light of the restaurant. The scent of ginger and soy sauce filled the air. She hadn't eaten a stir-fry meal since leaving New Jersey, and she was craving one.

She stopped at the host station and looked around. There he was at a table for two by the back wall. The candlelight enhanced his chiseled profile even more. She took a minute to take in the moment she joined him at their table. This could be the only moment he didn't annoy her. She slid off her jacket, shaking her head slightly to give her hair that-tossed-for-your-pleasure look, and walked up. "Good evening." She stood for a moment, giving him an opportunity to do something

129

gentleman-like.

Nothing.

She put her jacket on the back of her chair and took her seat. "This is a nice place, isn't it?"

"Yes. The food's good." He read his menu.

Does he wear contacts? His eyes couldn't be that shade of green on their own, or could they? She struggled with her vanity and refused to take out her glasses. Normally, she didn't care, but tonight she wanted to play it sexy—well, as sexy as she could. She flipped her hair over her shoulder and leaned toward the candle to see the menu better. The words swam on the page, no matter how she steadied her gaze and embraced the little bit of light. Not ready to let him see her in glasses, she chose something she was sure was on the menu.

"Good evening. What can I get for you?" the server asked as he set a pot of jasmine tea on the table.

"I'll have pork lo mein with dumplings and spareribs." She closed the menu and sat back with ease.

"Sorry, miss. We do not have pork in any of our meals, and our dumplings are filled with vegetable or chicken. Steamed or fried." The server smiled and waited for her to choose something else.

What Asian place doesn't serve spare ribs or pork lo mein? She reached under the table for her purse and slyly pulled out her reading glasses. "Um, you may take his order first."

As he watched her adjust her glasses and read the menu this time, Luke smothered a laugh with his hand. "I'll have fried chicken dumplings and garlic chicken with brown rice. Thank you." He handed his menu to the server. "Are you ready?"

"Yes, chicken dumplings as well, steamed, and honey-glazed walnut shrimp with white rice, please." She handed her menu to the server, then turned her attention to Luke. "So, you've been here before." *Stupid question.* She knew he had been with his date. She made a feeble attempt to make conversation.

"With my sister. She was the second person who told me about this place so I figured it must be good. She's extremely picky."

Kristen removed her glasses. "Your sister? I didn't know you have a sister. I didn't think you were from here." She tightened her smile, not wanting to show her excitement.

"She owns an artist co-op in Jackson Corners."

Kristen poured him a cup of tea and nearly spilled it on the table.

"She does a wonderful thing for the art community by giving them a venue to display their work." He picked up the handle-free cup and stopped it short of his lips as he looked at her in the candlelight.

"Like gnomes?" She sipped her tea, unsure if she should reveal her secret.

"I imagine so. She gets a lot of strange items. I'm sure she has a few standing around." He placed the cup on the table and leaned toward her.

"Or?" She smirked.

"Okay. Maybe." He leaned back in the chair and folded his arms across his chest.

Oh, hell. She wasn't good at being mysterious and felt awkward and silly. "I met your sister. Her name is Deborah?"

"Yes."

The server placed two plates of appetizers on the

table.

"I met her on one of my outings. I bought a family of gnomes, now living at the foot of the inn porch. You helped me get them into the car. I also bought candy dishes I won't fill until Christmas Eve."

"Too tempting?" He shoved a fried chicken dumpling into his mouth.

"Serious chocoholic. I can't keep it in the house." She set chopsticks in her hand and picked up a dumpling. "I love these." She took little bites, because she was nervous and didn't want a mouth full of food while talking, though he didn't seem like he was interested in much conversation. Maybe he was tired from the drive, but he was the one who'd asked her to dinner. She didn't know what to make of him.

Her rumbling stomach overtook her desire for conversation, and so the dumplings won. At least she still had a chance with him, and he hadn't been to the Asian fusion restaurant with a date.

"I'll be right back. I want to check on Danny." She slid out from the table and caught the corner of the tablecloth with her bracelet. As she stood, a plate of dumplings crashed to the floor. "Ooooohhh." She leaned down to gather the mess and prayed the floor would open and swallow her.

The candle fell over, and flames ignited the tablecloth.

"Watch out!" Luke used his napkin to dampen the flames lapping at his chin.

The server ran over and dumped a pitcher of water on their dinner.

Their food was ruined and possibly their first date.

Luke leaned down to help her. "Are you okay?"

She wanted to run or hide—to be anywhere but there.

Diners stared as their quiet dining was disrupted.

She stood straight and smoothed the front of her turtleneck. "And that concludes tonight's floor show. Thank you for coming." She bowed and took her seat at the table.

The customers' applause did little to squash her embarrassment. She buried her head in her hands, then leaned closer to the wall. "I'm so sorry."

The server quickly cleaned the table.

Luke smiled and reached across the table with both hands, taking her hand in his.

She immediately connected with him.

He laughed and rubbed her hand between his. "I think it's funny. I can definitely say this will be a memorable first date."

Date! He said date! She giggled inside like a school girl. Kristen Anderson, who rarely dated, was actually enjoying herself—despite nearly burning down the restaurant.

The server placed two more orders of dumplings on the table and walked away, without mention of the incident.

The meal proceeded without any more drama, and for the first time, she was at ease with Luke. Though he didn't talk much during dinner, the night's events gave her an opportunity to get past the business relationship.

When the bill arrived, she peeked at the total. How much someone tipped was one method she used to weigh a person's generosity. She noticed the bill didn't include the second round of dumplings, but Luke covered the cost as if charged, including the tip. Nice.

She liked a considerate man. Being a hairstylist and former server, she knew how important leaving a healthy tip was, especially for good service.

"Do you have thirty-one cents?" He straightened out the dollar bills.

"Ah, okay." She fumbled for her wallet and handed him the change. "Here you go."

"Thanks."

The server picked up the dinner check and cash.

Luke waved his hand. "No change. Thank you."

Kristen took her cue from him and stood, careful not to upset the table setup for an encore. He held her jacket as she slipped her arms into the sleeves. When he placed his hand at the small of her back as she left the restaurant, she smiled. "Well, that was embarrassing." She clutched the top of her jacket closed. "I can never go in there again."

"Why? No one got hurt. If anything, it livened up the evening. The music in that place was like being in an elevator."

"And the food?" She stayed close as they walked down the street, his hand lingered at the small of her back. The air smelled like snow, and she thought she saw a flake pass a streetlight. The walk cleared her thoughts of Nana and Danny. She had no clue what Luke had planned, and she reveled in the temporary reprieve of not being the one to do the thinking.

"Not counting the food you tossed on the floor, dinner was excellent. Do you need to get home soon?"

She smiled. A quick glance at the bank clock read seven-thirty. "I have some time."

"Good. I enjoy walking looking at the storefronts when they're decorated for the holidays."

"So do I. Do you find this time of year gives you hope?"

Luke slipped his hand into hers. "I do."

Her heart raced as she embraced the warmth of his hand. What else did he have planned?

****

Luke did his best to relax and strolled along Main Street. What he thought was a non-date was quickly turning into one. He hadn't meant to take her hand, but it happened without thought. "So, Danny must keep you busy."

"He does, but he's a great kid. My grandmother has been a godsend, not only asking us to move in with her, but she provides a steady, secure, if somewhat sweet nutty existence."

He didn't want to pry, but his curiosity grew. He wanted to know more about her. What made her happy? What was she looking for in life? He had been so caught up in taking care of his mother and working to support them, he never took time for a social life. The few dates he did go on didn't mesh with his no-nonsense approach to life.

His mother used to tell him he took life too seriously. *Lighten up. Enjoy yourself.* He never thought he was unhappy, so he didn't think he was missing out on anything. He looked at Kristen. The top of her head stopped at his shoulder. She was shorter than the few women he dated so he wasn't used to towering over someone. "Your grandmother seems like a nice lady. My aunt talks about her a lot. Then again my aunt talks a lot." He laughed.

Kristen shrugged. "I guess when you're as involved with the community like your aunt is, that's to be expected. So, what about you? What brings you here? I mean, I know what it's like to live in a city, as quaint as this town is, it's not hopping with entertainment. Well, except for the hayrides around Halloween."

He hesitated to open up about himself. What's the use in doing so? To kill time and make small talk? He wasn't a fan of chit-chat as his mother called it. "Family stuff brought me here."

"Ah, same with me. Once I left here, I never expected to come back, except to visit for holidays. Funny how things change."

"Yep, I never thought I would be back here either." He tucked her hand into his jacket pocket as he slowed his pace, taking in the ambiance of the decorated storefronts.

"It was difficult when Carly and I were taken from our home and brought to my grandparents' house."

He stopped and faced her, releasing her hand. "You didn't grow up here?"

Kristen looked into his eyes and shook her head. "Nope. Our parents were killed in a car crash. I'm originally from New Jersey. My grandparents took us to live with them. So, I'm a little bit country, but a lot of city.

Her smile made him smile. She was like him in a way. *You do what you have to for your family.* There's time for yourself. But maybe not when you want it to be. "Do you mind if we continue walking?"

"Not at all."

"I've been cooped up in my car and office most of the day so it's nice to stretch my legs." He thought about taking her hand again, but when he caught her plunge both of her hands into her jacket pockets, he took it as a sign not to—yet. "I can smell snow in the air, can you?" He stopped and took in a deep breath. *Invigorating.* "I love snow—except when I have to shovel my car out of a plowed-in spot."

"I do like the snow but mostly when it's falling at night and doesn't result in messy mounds of black slush."

Kristen walked closer, her elbow knocking into his ever so slightly. "You were happy with the dinner?"

She nodded. "I was. The food was much better than I expected it to be."

"That's what I thought when you set the place on fire." He stopped and held his stomach as he laughed, barely catching his breath.

"You will not let me forget, will you?"

"Not in our lifetime. I can't wait to see the story in the local paper."

She stopped short, and her eyes grew wide. "No. That wouldn't happen. Do you think?"

"Are you kidding? In a heartbeat. What else is there to write about in this town? No crime. How many recipes can they print? You will make the front-page. *Kristen Anderson Nearly Burns Down the Best Restaurant in Town.*"

She hung her head.

"Don't worry. It's not like you'll be newsworthy for long. I'm sure something else will happen in the next decade." He wanted to hug her but squelched the thought. The business-maybe-date situation was very awkward to balance. He was enjoying her company, and for the first time in his life, he wanted to sit down and spend the night talking to someone. She was interesting and fun. So far, she appeared to be easy going, which was a huge plus for him. A drama free relationship suited him.

He didn't have the capacity to tolerate what he considered to be trivial rants and complaints. Kristen carried herself with confidence and preferred direct conversation. She was someone he wouldn't mind hanging around and get to know her better.

But business first.

He needed a distraction. The movie already started, and he would probably fall asleep anyway. Also, he couldn't assume she would want to sit through a six-month-old movie. With Danny at home, she was surely thinking about him. "I think I know what would be perfect right now." He slipped his arm through hers, turned her around, and headed in the opposite direction. Enough sightseeing, the stores were closed and not much of anything else to do for the evening. He planned to put her through the ultimate test.

Chapter Eleven

The chilly air was no competition for the exhilaration rushing through Kristen's body. The nip in the air barely registered with her, so dessert at Casey's Ice Cream Shoppe was an acceptable choice.

Luke held open the door.

She walked into the store, eager to savor the sugary sweetness from the ice cream case. Glass jars with silver tops housed orange, yellow, green, and red candies ready to be mixed into a milkshake or ice cream sundae. A slight twinge ran through her teeth from potential sugar overload. As she thought how she'd literally have to light a fire under his behind to spark a reaction, she laughed. Whatever it took, she was glad it worked and he'd come around.

"I thought this place would have a better dessert selection than the restaurant. I hope you like ice cream." He stopped at the case to browse the selection.

"Of course, I do. Who doesn't like ice cream?" She threw up her arms. "No one I know. Chocolate cone please."

His eyebrow rose. "You haven't even looked at all the flavors."

"I know what I like. Chocolate." Yes, she was definitely feeling more comfortable around him. The way he'd laughed when she'd nearly burned down the restaurant put her at ease. Yeah, he was a guy she wanted to know. But how would he feel about a woman with a seven-year-old child? "Thank you." She took the cone from the clerk and watched Luke order his ice cream.

"Pistachio, black cherry, and rum raisin on a sugar cone, please." He took out a twenty.

She was eating ice cream on a winter night as Nat King Cole sang about roasted chestnuts and Jack Frost biting someone's nose. She stood next to Luke, licking her ice cream, waiting, watching to see how he handled himself. She was a firm believer she could tell a lot about someone by how a person treated another.

He handed the clerk a twenty and waved his hand for the kid to keep the change. *Hmm, is he showing off?* So far, he paid for food they weren't charged for and let the kid keep a fourteen-dollar tip—yet he'd asked her for thirty-one cents at dinner.

She sat at a table in the corner and waited for him to join her.

He tossed his jacket over the back of the chair.

For the first time, she noticed the subtle blond strands woven within the darker brown hair. She loved his hair—not too long, enough to let everyone know he was carefree, which his tipping habit proved. She leaned closer while licking her ice cream. "Question. It's nothing major but I have to ask. You are a very generous tipper and gracious for covering my show props."

He sat back and stretched his legs practically on top of her foot. "So?"

"Why did you ask me for thirty-one cents for the dinner bill?"

"I thought we were going Dutch." He switched his

legs and finished the scoop of rum raisin.

"For thirty-one cents?" She bit into her cone, which was nearly gone, and wanted more. She should have at least gotten a double dip.

"I don't like carrying change, and I don't like passing the change from the broken bill onto the server. Simple. No change, so I don't have to worry what to do with it."

"What about the eighty percent tip for the ice cream guy?"

He leaned in close. "Come here."

Would he kiss her? Her stomach tightened. He was going to, her instinct told her so. She finished the last of her cone and inched toward him.

"Come here." He said it again, softer, "You see that girl at the end of the counter?"

Kristen moved closer. "Yeah."

"I bet she's the ice cream kid's girlfriend, or he wants her to be. So, I throw the kid a few extra dollars and help him make enough to take her to a movie."

Kristen leaned back in her seat. It didn't matter he hadn't kissed her, she could easily fall in love with this guy. Never had she met a man so generous to others. And it confused her because of how standoffish he had been. How their relationship began didn't matter, they had taken the first step and would surely be another, even if she had to schedule it herself. She stood and walked over to the counter. "Can I have another scoop of chocolate? In a cup please." She gave the kid a five-dollar bill for a two-dollar scoop and let him keep the change.

Luke finished his cone.

She motioned for him to follow her outside, ice

cream cup in hand. "It's a beautiful night."

"Yes, it is. Christmas was always a magical time here—the time I spent here." Luke stared at the red and green lights in the ice cream store window.

"I thought you grew up here." She cocked her head.

"For the most part. I lived with my mother on the outskirts of Brookside Falls, but I also lived in New Jersey."

"What part?"

"South Jersey. Exit 105."

"North Jersey, here. Sussex County."

"My mother and I moved around a bit." He shrugged his shoulders. "I also spent time in Jackson Corners where my brother and sister lived. My sister still does."

"Deborah, the one I met at the antique store." She clutched the front of her jacket, as the night grew colder.

"Yes, she's a good person. I like her and try to see her as much as I can when I'm up here. It's hard for her to venture out because of the store. She doesn't make enough to hire a manager so running the business has become her life."

She attempted to dissect his expression but couldn't tell if it was sadness, hurt, or missing his family. She wanted to ask more questions. This was the most vulnerable she had seen him. Not that he had any reason to be before, but their prior meetings were focused on the salon and the business side of him was quite different from what she was seeing now.

"I didn't come up here as much because there wasn't much demand for my line of work. But technology changed. I can pretty much live where I want as long as I have a strong Internet connection."

This was her opportunity to be nosy without being out of line. "Yeah, ah, why did you take on the inn?" She pressed her key fob.

He opened her car door.

Was the date over already? She wanted to kick herself for being so forward. He held open the door. She silently resisted.

He gently took the empty ice cream cup from her hand. "Will you get in the car? It's freezing. My leather jacket isn't cutting it in this wind."

"I like the cold." She slid into the driver's seat.

"Apparently, because your jacket isn't good for anything except looking pretty." He closed the door.

She tried too hard? She sucked at first dates, not that she had many, but enough for her to remember she sucked at them. She turned the ignition key and rolled down the window. "The cold makes me feel alive."

He stood back from the car.

Her heart sank a bit as she sensed this was the end of their date, if it even qualified as one. "Well, thank you for dinner and dessert. Again sometime?" She was frustrated he never answered her question.

"Absolutely. I'm tired from the drive. I'll stop by your place tomorrow to check on the progress. We can make plans then." He slapped a hand on the roof of her car. "Careful driving home."

No kiss. As she watched him eat his ice cream, all she thought about were his lips. She looked at the clock on her dashboard and thought of Danny. She wanted to get home to kiss him good night before he went to bed. She rolled up the window and as she pulled away, Luke faded into the distance. At least she'd have another chance.

****

Luke pulled into the empty parking spot in front of his building. He was exhausted but exhilarated at the same time. Kristen wormed her way into his heart when he wasn't looking. She passed the ice cream in winter test with flying colors. Not really a test but it did show him she was game and liked to have fun. He needed that in his life.

The red message light on his desk phone blinked in the darkness of his office. Up until a few hours ago, he would have answered voicemail upon seeing the signal—not tonight. All he wanted was his bed. First, he checked the water reservoir of the Christmas tree. It could use a little to top it off.

He walked into the bathroom, each step louder and a reminder he was alone. Funny, he never paid attention to things like that before. He was usually preoccupied with work and ignored most distractions.

Gladys must have been by because a liquid soap dispenser and stack of paper hand towels nested in a woven basket on the sink counter. He appreciated his aunt helping out, but he needed to enforce boundaries. He forgot she had keys. Apparently, she didn't think her realtor duties ceased upon closing the deal. That they were family didn't matter.

He watered the tree then sat in his chair, leaning back and relaxing. The flashing red light challenged him to check his messages. He stood firm and refused. Unable to stand the reminder of an unanswered phone call, he locked up his office to head upstairs to his apartment.

Deborah.

He forgot to call her back. The town clock perched on the corner of the bank read eight-thirty-two. Too late to call her. She didn't use a cell phone so he couldn't even text her. He would catch up with her in the morning. So unlike him to forget something, but he was sure she would understand. His sister was good that way. As set in her ways as she was, she always had a soft-spot for him, and he could sweet talk her.

He stepped outside on the steps of his office. *Quiet.* The center of town had little life after sunset. All alone, like he was the only person on the block. He drifted his gaze above the stores. Yep, only his building had an apartment. The other buildings looked like the upper stories were used for storage. Chances are his place was originally a catch-all. Apparently, the owner maximized financial gain by updating and converting the space into an apartment.

The shore in winter wouldn't be much different, except for the sea. Most of the shore towns were boarded up in the off-season. He kind of missed driving through the deserted towns to stand at the ocean's edge.

A gray-striped cat sauntered up to the steps and stopped.

"Hey, buddy. Is it always this quiet around here?"

The cat cocked its head.

"You're not much for talking either, huh?" He stepped down to the sidewalk, where the cat sat waiting. "Not skittish. Cool. Are you hungry?"

The deli was closed, and he thought about what was in his food cabinets. Not much. He did have some milk in the refrigerator in his office. "You wait here." He went back inside and rummaged through the small, dorm-size refrigerator. Yep, enough milk in the container. He found a tin foil carry-out container that would work for a dish. He rinsed it out and brought the meal to his furry neighbor.

The cat stood on the landing and waited.

"Here you go, buddy." He watched the feline lap a little milk. *Hmm, not overly hungry.* No tags or collar. Must be a house cat on the town. It was too cold to let his new buddy stay outside for the night, but he wasn't equipped to board a cat. Dogs he could deal with. He had zero experience taking care of cats. His knowledge was limited to a cat needed a litter box, and that couldn't happen.

He checked his phone. Eight-fifty-seven. No store was open to buy cat supplies. With caution thrown to the wind, he texted Kristen.

—*Call me if you're awake.*—

Within seconds, his phone rang.

"Hi. Did you forget something?"

Her voice sounded sweet as could be. "No, but you are the only person I know in town. I have a predicament."

"This time of night?"

Oh no, he hoped she didn't think he wanted to—his timing couldn't be worse. "I have a cat staring at me, and I don't have any food. I gave him what milk I had."

"That should get him through the night. He's probably eaten a few mice for dinner anyway."

He was royally screwing up this call. "Okay but what about bringing him in the house? I don't have anything. A cat needs litter, right? I've never owned a cat."

"No indication of ownership? Collar, tags?"

"Nope."

"He's probably a stray hanging around the deli. If he is, he might not want to stay inside. If it makes you feel better, throw some old towels or T-shirts in a box and out of the wind. He probably lives by the dumpster behind the deli anyway."

"I didn't think of that. He was hanging out on the stairs, and I figured he needed food and shelter."

"That's sweet, but it's not going to go below freezing tonight. He'll be fine."

He felt like an idiot, calling her for nothing. "As long as I'm bothering you, I'd like to tell you how much I enjoyed dinner."

"I had a lovely time. I promise not all my meals are as exciting as tonight's so I might not be as entertaining the next time."

Next time? A smile replaced the subtle humiliation he felt. His heart was light and fear of getting involved in a relationship fell aside. The move promised a bright future, at least personally. "Thanks for the cat advice, and have a good night. See you tomorrow."

****

"Aunt Kristen, there's a big truck outside." Danny climbed onto the window seat, engrossed in the activity in the driveway. "Wow."

"They're here early. Did you eat breakfast?" Kristen grabbed him from behind and scooped him up in her arms. "You're having fun?"

"Waffles. Yeah, and it's snowing."

"Goodness, you're growing fast." His feet tapped her just below her knees. Which reminded Kristen, she needed to buy him more winter gear. He was wearing out his snow pants, and winter wasn't at its worst yet.

His daily trips through the woods tore at his clothing, and she was happy watch him explore.

Still excited from her date with Luke, she paid special attention applying her makeup. A lot of effort was required to obtain her natural glow. She took care choosing a soft, off-white turtleneck and her favorite black jeans accompanied by black ankle boots.

From the dining room, she could hear Tom instructing the deliverymen where to put the chairs and hair dryers. Luke told her the shop would be finished before the inn opened, and he'd kept his word. She was glad the project would be done any day. She thought dinner would have been enough to raise their relationship to another level, but it proved not to be as romantic as she hoped.

"The dishes are done. I'm taking Danny to the market with me. Gloria is joining us with her grandson." Nana put on her coat and adjusted her furry black hat.

Kristen remembered the hat from when she was a kid. She and her sister Carly made fun of it, because it looked like a cat sleeping on top of Nana's head. Once, they'd examined it to make sure it wasn't a cat, given their grandmother's penchant for stuffing her pets. "Wonderful. I worry he's spending too much time in the house." She grabbed his coat. "Have a good time. See you later. Love ya." She hugged her nephew, who seemed to be growing an inch taller each day.

"Bye." He waved with his bundled-up hand.

"Bye, sweetie. Have fun." Her stomach ached as the car pulled away from the house. She waved as Danny looked back through the back window. He brought so much joy to her life she couldn't imagine being without him.

Luke never said what time he was stopping by, but she wanted to be ready. With Danny gone most of the day, she would have time to weave her way into Luke's past.

First, she had to focus on finalizing the shop setup. She looked forward to getting back to work and was glad she'd never let her Pennsylvania cosmetology license lapse. She peeked into the shop from the hallway—the neutral colors worked well. The medium cocoa walls gave the shop a country, yet modern, feel. The white accents made the room pop. She was glad she'd gone with the black fixtures.

A knock on the front door caught her attention. A warm sensation flooded her body—she sensed Luke. A quick stop at the hall mirror confirmed her hair and makeup were understated. Sometimes she tended to go a little big with her hair. She tugged her sweater down on her hips and opened the front door.

Luke stood on the porch, the morning sun framing him, sunglasses hiding his eyes and coffee in hand. "Morning. I see the last of the equipment arrived."

She stepped aside to let him in. He was dressed casually, jeans and a turtleneck. She liked his look. He usually wore khakis and an oxford shirt. Even his shoes were different. Work boots instead of boat shoes. Nice. "Good morning. Yes, they arrived early. I have to say you run a smooth operation. Everything has been on time or earlier. You've made this an easy process."

He took a sip of coffee. "I enjoyed this job. Different. I've never done a job like this."

Did she dare approach him again? Hell, yeah! "I'm glad you brought that up. You never did answer my question. Why did you take on this job? I knew right away this was more of a favor than a matter of money."

He walked with her to the salon. "True. Gladys was looking for a streamlined way of financing this project for your grandmother since they're good friends." He shifted his weight as he leaned against the wall, sunglasses perched on top of his wavy hair.

She yearned to run her hands through each silky strand, even if only on a professional basis. "I told you I'd lived with my mother and didn't spend much time in this town." Something haunted showed in his eyes. Every time she looked into the deep green windows of his soul, her heart sank a bit. A twinge of sorrow filled her chest. Something was buried within him that he wasn't sharing and she didn't want to pry. He needed more time, and she understood.

The salon had been a convenient distraction to keep her from being immersed in grief over losing her sister. She sensed Luke carried the same type of hurt. His pain seemed to have been with him much longer. Maybe not the best time to start a relationship. Danny was still settling into his new phase of his young life. She would be busy helping out with the inn and running the salon.

She reached out her hand and took his empty cup, leaving it on the lobby counter. She led him into the salon. "Well, I think it's a wonderful thing you've done. I'm sure my grandmother appreciates it. I thought she was crazy when she told me she was reopening the inn, but I think she's bringing something back to this town that's necessary. What do you think?"

Luke walked around the perimeter as he checked each corner and piece of woodwork and made sure the floor tile was laid to perfection. He ran his finger along the inside of the window. "It looks good."

"All we have to do is sweep up, and we're out of here. Good luck with your new business, Kristen." Tom shook her hand.

"Thank you. You do wonderful work. I'd recommend you anytime." She waited for Tom to leave and then turned to Luke. "I'm hungry. You?"

She had him to herself, and no one was home. The time provided the perfect opportunity to delve into the secret of Luke Baldwin.

If only she was willing to open up about herself.

Chapter Twelve

"I am but I need something. Be right back." Luke ran out of the house. *How stupid!* He was losing his usually cool manner around Kristen. Was it because he had more time to notice he actually had feelings for another person? His self-imposed solitary life was slipping away. He jumped into his car and took off.

He planned to present Kristen with a small, tasteful, flower arrangement for her new salon. It completely slipped his mind to stop at the florist. Fortunately, he called in the order so all he had to do was stop and get the flowers.

A ten-minute drive got him to where he needed to be. He rushed out of the car and into the empty store. "Sorry I'm late. Luke Baldwin. Pick-up," he announced to a middle-aged woman.

"Flowers in a vase?" She peered over her glasses as she cleaned rose stems.

"Yes. Roses with stuff."

"Yeah, you got that right. I'm sure she'll love the stuff." The clerk laughed and went into the back room, returning with a clear, round, glass vase filled with white and lavender roses. "The stuff is baby's breath."

"It's very nice. How much?"

"One-fifty."

"What?" His chest tightened.

She raised an eyebrow and placed the vase of

flowers on the counter. "One hundred and fifty dollars. Let me guess...you didn't mention price, but you wanted a dozen of the most difficult to find roses in December. With stuff."

He nodded.

"I see you don't buy flowers very often."

"Apparently not. I hope you take credit cards."

"In this business? Of course, who carries cash?" She took his charge card and zipped it through for approval. "Hmm, good thing your bank approved the purchase. I can give you your flowers now."

"Are you always this funny with your customers?" He took back his card and slid it into his wallet.

"Only with the ones who think flowers are as cheap as what they find in a grocery store. You'll never find lavender roses amongst produce." She smiled and handed him the vase.

"You are a funny girl. I'll make sure I ask for you the next time. What's your name?"

"Joan."

"Thank you, Joan. I'm sure I'll see you again." He turned to leave.

"Wait a minute. Let me secure that." She put the flower arrangement in a box and taped it to the vase. "Put this on the floor of your car and drive slowly. The box will remain steady while you're driving. I guarantee my work, not the handiwork of an impatient driver. Nice to meet you, Luke."

"Um, how did you know my name?"

"Credit card." Joan peered over her glasses. "Unless you're using someone else's."

He smiled and laughed. "No, it's mine. Good detective work. I'm a little flustered today."

"Well, she must be special. Enjoy your day. I hope to see you here again."

"Your shop is my first recommendation for floral arrangements." He took the flowers and headed toward the door.

"Good. I need to make a payment on my cruise."

Joan. He would remember her name. She made him feel welcome to town. He wasn't used to people taking the time to talk. The conversations he got involved with were no more than what did he want in his coffee.

He considered bringing something else but didn't know Kristen well enough to understand what she liked. Even the flowers were a stretch. Completely uninformed, he relied on something his former assistant once said. She mentioned how she loved white and lavender roses.

Securing the flowers in a box was a smart idea. He hadn't thought how to travel with a water-filled container and delicate flowers. He placed it on the floor and was off.

His stomach started to growl. Breakfast was a half-stale donut and black coffee because he used all his milk for the cat, who sure enough was living behind the deli dumpster. He would make it a point to buy a few cans of food and litter to have on hand for cold nights.

It broke his heart to know his fur buddy was sleeping alone in the night, though the cat didn't seem bothered at all.

He carefully drove back to Kristen's house, glancing every so often to make sure the flowers hadn't tipped over. All this new-found care for his mother, Kristen, and the cat was exhausting. Not that he minded but it was an adjustment of responsibility. Even being closer to Deborah and Gladys made him feel he needed to be more involved and spend more time with them.

And he didn't mind at all. He had to get better juggling his schedule instead of his world being only about him. *I guess that's being an adult.* He turned onto Kristen's street and leaned over to hold the flowers in place as he took the turn too hard.

Made it.

If he ever ordered flowers again, he would have them delivered. The nerve-racking experience tested him, and the last thing he needed was to take on errands that stressed him. He thought small-town life was supposed to be calm and easygoing. It had been nothing but, on the go, and worrying about things he never gave notice to before. Then again things were bound to settle down.

Putting off Deborah was the one thing he needed to come to terms with. He wasn't fair to his sister and did care. At times he resented having to be the one to make the trip so they could see each other. She was always reclusive, and her seclusion got worse as she got older. His sister did promise to work on her fear of driving—at least locally.

He killed the engine and gingerly carried the over-priced but pretty flower arrangement up the front steps of the inn and hit the doorbell with his elbow.

The door flew open. "I thought you—"

"These are for you. Congratulations on opening your new shop."

Kristen's smile was one of pure surprise and appreciation. He loved when she smiled with excitement. Her exuberance was infectious. What would it take to work his way into her heart?

****

The day before Christmas Eve provided way too many calories with peanut butter, chocolate chip, sugar, and shortbread cookies lining the kitchen countertop. Nana always had something ready to nosh on and did her best to keep family traditions intact.

Kristen stood at the kitchen table and remembered Carly rolling out shortbread dough on the butcher block the first Christmas after their parents were killed. The accident happened the prior year when a deer ran across the icy road. The car veered off the road and down a ravine. Her parents were killed on impact.

The girls returned briefly to New Jersey with their aunt Josie but she couldn't keep them. Kristen remembered the night her grandparents arrived in New Jersey, because it was the last time she had been there until she was old enough to move back on her own. Her memory could never delve into all the details of her parents' deaths. She focused on the happy moments instead.

"Hey, you okay?" Luke rested a hand under her hair on the back of her neck.

The warm touch surged through her body. Her neck relaxed, inviting him to linger. "Yeah," she whispered, "I'm thinking." She looked into his eyes, searching for the hurt. A tear escaped her eye.

He wiped it away.

For the first time she allowed herself to be vulnerable. The silence of the empty house pummeled her. She aged within minutes. Her parents, grandfather, sister, Danny—even the birds, turtle, snake, and hamster—all were who she was, where she was going, and what she wanted.

The palms of his hands rested against her face and pulled her to his chest, and then wrapped an arm around her body. His breathing deepened with each second, his lips lingered on hers. He gently combed her hair with his fingers.

No more business got in the way. Her body melted into him. His lips were even softer than she imagined. Tragic memories were pushed aside by his embrace. She thought she would pass out from the intoxication of his kiss. She didn't want to but she gently pulled back her head to catch her breath.

"I've wanted to do that since the day I met you." He loosened his grip but didn't let go completely. "It's taken too long to…"

She placed a finger against his lips.

He lightly kissed the tip of her finger and pulled her closer. His arms tightened around her waist, and he buried his face deep in her neck.

As she welcomed his warm breath against her, she closed her eyes. She was getting too close. Each breath weakened her will. She stepped back and placed a hand against his face. "Then why have you been such a jerk?"

"Not only are you an arsonist but you sure know how to kill the moment." He laughed and took a chocolate chip cookie.

She wanted to reach into the air and grab the words that escaped her lips. *I ruined it.* The words were out there, and the choice was his to make. He could choose to leave. *Please, please don't.* He could ignore it. Maybe. Or he could use it against her every chance he could. Yes. That was the most likely option.

"Lunch." She ripped open the refrigerator door and plucked a few slices of lunchmeat from a tray. Surely, the platter was for the grand-opening tomorrow night so she rearranged the food to cover the empty spots on the platter. That's what garnish was for—to cover missing food. "Ham and cheese good?"

He nodded and smiled. "With mustard."

She didn't want to dwell on her abrupt question but nervousness replaced the passion. Anxiety crept in, and, well, she was capable of saying inappropriate things. She brought the sandwiches to the table. "I tend to say random stuff. Sometimes I have no filter."

He took a bite of his sandwich and nodded. "Maybe you need food."

What an unintentional fool she could be. All those weeks, how could she ruin it now? She picked up her sandwich and looked down at the table while she ate, sipping a seltzer with lime between bites.

Luke wiped his hands with a napkin and finished his ginger ale. "So, how have I been a jerk?"

She looked at him mid-bite. "Seriously?"

"Yes. No pretense. I mean, I kissed you, and you kissed me back. I say we are at a different stage in our relationship." He sat back and stretched out his legs in front of him, crossing them at his ankle.

She put down her food and threw out an index finger. "You are distant. I would spend time with you and then lie in bed confused."

"In the girlie room?"

"Yes, in the girlie room."

"I hate that room. The room itself is nice but the wallpaper has to go."

"Can I finish?" She narrowed her eyes.

He swept out his hand.

"At times you are so aloof...like I shouldn't be around you. I never know how to take you." There she said it. The feeling gnawing inside for weeks was out in the open.

"And that"—he threw out his hand—"is the exact reason why you might think I'm being distant. I don't want to be. But it's simple. I do not mix business with pleasure. It's not a smart or professional thing to do."

She put her elbows on the table. "And the kiss?"

"The way I see it, the job is over so business is over. Well, the final check has to clear, but I'm sure your grandmother is good for it."

She stood and laughed, then cleaned off the kitchen table. Luke washed the dishes. She moved behind him, eager to have him embrace her again.

He turned and slid his hand down her back. "I..."

"Aunt Kristen! I got another hamster!"

Kristen pushed away Luke and frantically ran her fingers through her hair to smooth it, so she didn't look like she went through a wind tunnel. She hitched her sweater down around her hips. She didn't know how to act around Danny when her personal life was involved, and she didn't want to make any mistakes.

****

As the young voice pierced the calm of the house, Luke startled. He hadn't expected Kristen to back away as abruptly as she did, either. He steadied himself.

"Aunt Kristen, look!" Danny ran into the kitchen, waving the boxed hamster in the air. "Look. Nana said I can have another one."

She looked past her nephew and stared at her grandmother. "That's nice. Go put it in the cage."

Lita Harris

"Well, you can't have one. It'll be lonely." Nana shrugged and smiled. She dropped the grocery bag on the table. "I see someone's been eating the cookies."

Caught, Luke held up his hands. "What can I say? These are the best cookies I've ever eaten."

"Thank you, dear, but I bet you say that to all the old ladies." Nana patted his shoulder.

"No, seriously, they are." His mother's idea of a homemade cookie was a freshly opened package of store-bought cookies. He loved his mother dearly, but life was rough with Mom being the sole provider. Close family was one of the things he liked about country life. Even he and Deborah were working on strengthening their family ties. Brian's death five years earlier made him realize the only family he had left from Jackson Corners was his half-sister and Aunt Gladys.

"Well, I'm glad you like them. Will you be staying for dinner?"

He looked at Kristen for approval. Her smile told him to stay. "As long as I can have more cookies for dessert."

Nana winked at Kristen. "Good."

"One minute." He dashed to the front door.

"Pork chops and applesauce for dinner with string beans. Good?" Nana slapped a butcher-wrapped package on the countertop.

"That's fine. Though I'm..." She spun as Luke walked up behind her. "Thought you'd left."

"I wanted to give this to you tonight. It's the finishing touch for your salon." He took her hand and walked her to the door between the inn and the salon. "Are you coming?" He waved to Nana to follow them. "Danny!" Luke gathered them in front of the salon door

160

as he waited for Danny to get downstairs.

The banister provided a quick entrance for Danny as he slid down and jumped to his feet at the landing.

"I want to thank you for letting me work on this project. I have to admit, when my aunt asked me to do this, I turned her down. Normally, I don't take on small, residential jobs, but she convinced me to do it. The short of it is, I'm glad I did." He stood tall. "Now that everything is finished, one more item needs to be hung. I wish you luck with your business venture." Luke ripped the brown paper from the package, turned it, then held it above the doorway, and looked back over his shoulder. "Well? What do you think?"

Kristen's eyes filled with tears.

Nana's plump cheeks grew rosier.

The smile on Danny's young face showed his appreciation for what Luke had done.

Carly's Place was officially in business, with the hand-carved sign that looked great hanging over the salon door.

Kristen knelt beside her nephew, and he hugged her tight.

"Thank you. I know we never firmly decided on a name but…" Kristen wiped a tear from her cheek.

"I took a chance this was the name you would settle on. Glad you like it."

Nana slapped her face. "Oh my, that's tomorrow. I have to check my lists. Is everything ready? Are the beds made? Are the towels done?" She buzzed about the lobby counter, checking room keys and the guest book.

"Nana, everything is fine. The pantry's stocked. Everything has been cleaned. The sheets and towels were done yesterday. It's only six rooms." As she stated each item, Kristen ticked off her fingers.

"The hostess setup." Nana spun. "There always has to be tea and coffee."

"Right there, Nana." Danny pointed to a small buffet table readily supplied with tea, sweeteners, and pots ready for percolating.

"Good." Nana took off toward the kitchen.

Luke squeezed Kristen's arm. "I know where we can pick up good ice cream for dessert. Do we have at least an hour before dinner?" he called out to Nana.

"Yes," she yelled from the kitchen. "And Kristen, don't think I haven't noticed my keets are missing—twenty-five to be exact. I expect they'll be back for the New Year?"

Kristen rolled her eyes. "Yes, Nana, they'll be back."

"Hey, buddy." Luke knelt down. "Grab your coat. We're going for a ride."

The thunder of his little feet echoed throughout the hallway.

Luke ushered them into his car, putting Danny's booster seat in the back. "Seatbelt on?" Luke refused to start the car until Danny was buckled up in the back seat.

He slipped into the driver's seat and caught a glimpse of Danny through the rearview mirror. His heart raced with excitement of how comfortable he was around a child, and the direction his life was taking.

Chapter Thirteen

Kristen watched as he looked in each mirror before turning the car around. She fought to conceal the glee swirling within her stomach as Luke interacted with Danny. Any guy coming into her life had to pass her "nephew test" and care for Danny as much as she did.

Luke turned onto Main Street and kept driving.

"You're not stopping at the market?"

"Nope. You can only buy boxed ice cream there. This occasion calls for homemade. Has Danny ever been to the one we, um, the one in Haineswood?" He caught himself.

She was pleased he didn't want to be the one who told Danny about their budding relationship. Her nephew was her responsibility.

Luke parked in front of the ice cream parlor where he brought her for dessert on their first date. "Okay, champ. Here we are."

As he walked into the ice cream parlor, Danny's eyes lit up. He rushed over to the wall-long case of ice cream three containers deep. "Wow! Can I get whatever I want?"

"Sure." Kristen placed a hand on his shoulder.

Danny stood on his toes with his nose pressed against the glass and pointed to the container. "Vanilla walnut, please. A lot."

Kristen laughed. "A quart will be fine."

"Chocolate for you, right, Aunt Kristen?" Danny said.

"Does she ever order a different flavor?" Luke asked Danny.

He shook his head, not taking his gaze off the selection of ice cream in the freezer. "No, it's always chocolate. I try to make her get the same as me—but she never does. Chocolate—always chocolate. She says, why try a different flavor? She knows what she likes."

"What does your grandmother like?" Luke asked.

"Cherry vanilla. It's her chocolate," she interjected.

"Choice of ice cream is a telltale sign. A woman who isn't easily swayed on her flavor is not easily swayed at all. Also, a quart each of cherry vanilla, chocolate, blueberry pie, and vanilla walnut." Luke pointed to the ice cream case. "They have a hundred different flavors. You have to try at least one."

Kristen also had a theory about men and ice cream. A man who gets a different flavor of ice cream every time he orders is someone who cannot commit. She hoped she was wrong and his desire to try something new each time was limited to his choice of ice cream.

Danny paced in front of the display case.

Her immediate response was to grab a hold because she didn't want him wandering too far, even though only a few feet. Losing track of Danny was more her fear than his.

"Here you go. All packed for the ride home. Enjoy." The clerk handed the ice cream sack to Kristen.

Luke threw a fifty-dollar bill on the counter. "Merry Christmas."

This kid can retire soon if Luke keeps coming in

here for ice cream. She shook her head.

Luke held the door for Kristen and Danny. "Deborah! I'm shocked to see you out. Did you drive?"

"I'm a little shaken but I managed."

As he reached over to hug her, he held the door with his foot. "I'm so happy you're confronting your fear. Kristen, this is my sister, Deborah. Deborah—Kristen and her nephew, Danny."

Deborah slowly extended a hand to Kristen. "We've met. Good to see you again."

Kristen shook Deborah's hand. "It's good to see you, too." She noticed how Deborah kept an eye on her, as though she was concerned for her brother. She could sense Luke's sister was probably somewhat controlling and distant. The way she kept her gaze averted downward seemed that she was not eager to connect. Was she taken back by running into Luke, accompanied by a woman with a child?

She thought back to how Carly could be over-protective, cautious, and ready to pounce on anyone who would do wrong to her baby sister. She was just as fierce protecting her nephew, so maybe she ought to give Deborah a break and extend a welcome gesture instead. "We're having a pre-celebration of the inn's opening day and Luke is staying for dinner. You're more than welcome to join us." Kristen pulled back her hand.

"Thank you, but I don't want to intrude on a family dinner." Deborah stepped aside.

"No imposition at all. You're Luke's sister, so, of course, you're welcome to come."

Deborah looked at Luke.

He nodded for her to join them.

Kristen thought, it would give them more time together to catch up while he spent time with her. After all, the dinner wasn't a date but a very efficient gathering by her standards. It would also be the perfect opportunity to get to know Deborah and learn more about Luke. People usually behave differently in the company of family.

"Thank you, but I'll pass for tonight." Deborah brushed past them. "Nice to see you again. It truly was. Stop by the store anytime."

Somehow, Deborah's response wasn't unexpected. Deborah was distant and removed when they met in the store. Like she sensed something about Kristen and wasn't comfortable with whatever issue she imagined to worry about.

She and Luke were still getting to know each other. Not the right time to throw family drama into the mix. In time she would see how the situation would shake out and if they needed to learn how to co-exist. "Please know you're welcome to come over anytime." Kristen took hold of Deborah's thin hand. A chill ran up her arm.

****

Luke waited outside and made sure Deborah was in the ice cream shop and out of earshot. "My sister can be somewhat, um—"

"Unfriendly?"

"Abrupt is more like it. She does talk to people but not many. I'm shocked she's in town. She's become agoraphobic, and it's difficult to get her outdoors. She even set up a living area in the back of her store so she wouldn't have to go home." He walked toward his car.

"Why do you think that is?" Kristen grabbed his

hand and slid it into her pocket. "Danny, not too far. Make sure you know we're behind you."

"I think the loss of our brother and parents became too much grief for her to consume and process. She's quite empathic and gets easily drained in large crowds. I don't even think she makes money off her business, but the building is paid for so it's more like a hobby and keeps her busy."

"There is some nice stuff at the shop. A lot of stuff."

"To the point of being a hoarder." He thought back to what Deborah was like before the family tragedies piled up. His sister was an obsessive neat freak. Everything in her life was in order and accounted for. Deborah made sure Brian's clothes were cleaned and pressed. She had given up her life for her family, and now no one appreciates the sacrifices she made.

He sensed he was on the edge of caring because he didn't grow up with his siblings. A complicated relationship at best, and he was trying his hardest to connect to Deborah. "Thank you for asking her to come to dinner, that was nice." He squeezed her hand.

"I thought it would be a good opportunity to get to know her better. And I know my grandmother, you will not have to cook for weeks."

"Me not cook?" He stopped walking and held her back.

"Yep, you. Single guy. You inherit all the leftovers." Her smile revealed every perfect tooth in her mouth.

"Wonderful. Do we need to pick up something for the table?"

"No. She will have everything."

"Especially cookies. She's always baking cookies," Danny yelled.

"Ah, wait. Follow me." He grabbed Kristen's and Danny's hands and waited for the streetlight to turn green. "I know just the thing." Across the street, he pulled them into the florist shop.

"Hey, Mr. Moneybucks. I didn't expect to see you so soon." Joan placed an arrangement of yellow and orange chrysanthemums in the see-through refrigerator. "What can I do for you today?"

"What did she call you?" Kristen whispered.

He shook his head. He wouldn't let on he complained about the cost of the flowers he gave her. "What kind of flowers does your grandmother like?"

Kristen looked in the cooler and scanned the counter and walls for other options. "She's not much of a flower person. She kills anything she touches. Family trait."

He pictured the over-priced roses, withering in her care. But that's not what it's about, right? You give a gift and that's the end. Once it has exchanged hands, you have no more investment. He would have liked to pay off his credit card first before the flowers died.

"Get her a poinsettia plant. That's something with half a chance of surviving." Kristen giggled.

"Joan, how would a plant like that stand up to a black-thumb?"

"As good as anything. You never know what will affect a plant. You know, it's like a person. You water it and that might be all you need to do. Sometimes, you have to put in a little extra TLC."

He looked around the shop, discreetly searching for price tags but none were evident. "I'll take two of those things she said."

"Poinsettias," Danny corrected.

"Thank you. Two of those." He opened his wallet and went right for the credit card, expecting the plants to cost more than he carried in cash.

"I think Nana will like those. She has plastic ones around the house." Danny hung on the edge of the counter, his nose resting on the ledge.

"Good. As long as she likes them." Luke handed the credit card to Joan.

"That will be twenty-five dollars." Joan took the card from his fingers.

Not bad. The next time he would ask before he bought flowers. He wasn't cheap, but he weighed the cost and value of everything he did. Spending hundreds of dollars on flowers to die in two days seemed wasteful. However, two plants with the possibility of surviving at least a season was a much smarter financial move. He waited as Joan added a green velvet bow to the plants and wrapped the containers in red glitter foil paper. He thought it looked pretty, and he never paid attention to things like that.

Joan handed back his card. "Nice doing business with you again. I hope Nana enjoys her present. The care instructions are buried at the base of the plant. You can always call if you need guidance."

"Thank you, again. Have a nice evening."

"Can I carry one?" Danny jumped up and down.

He handed a plant to Danny and then the other to Kristen.

"Why do I have to carry one?" She held the poinsettia.

"I have to drive. Can't drive balancing it on my

knee." He waved his car keys.

"How did you get mine to my house?"

"You don't want to know, but I made a promise to myself, I would never do it again. I was right." He laughed as he opened the car doors for Kristen and Danny. Off to the family dinner, he hoped for an enjoyable evening. His heart was warm and the company inviting. But would Deborah show?

****

Luke pulled into the inn parking lot. Traffic was light, and the plants made the trip without incident.

"Dan—" Kristen slammed the car door.

Danny ran up the front stairs and into the house before either of them could get the plants out of the car.

"I guess he didn't want to help." Luke laughed.

"Sometimes he's very helpful, and other times, not so much." Kristen took two plants. "I think we'll manage." She walked up the stairs.

Danny had left the front door open. "At least he's considerate." Luke smiled.

"I think it's more forgetfulness than concern."

Before walking through the door, Luke hesitated. "Is that fresh bread?"

"My grandmother makes bread, biscuits, or rolls with just about every meal. She's been using starter that she received from her mother."

He took a deep breath.

Kristen walked ahead and placed the plants on the side table in the foyer. "You can dole out these later."

He placed his plant next to the other, and then placed his jacket on the coat hook. "Dinner smells good."

"Nana said sit down to eat." Danny laid out

silverware on top of neatly folded, linen napkins on the dining room table.

Kristen joined her nephew and poured ginger ale into the glasses from a pitcher that sat in the middle of the table.

Luke stood aside, staying out of the way and not interrupting the family dynamic. Everyone sat except Luke. "I want to make a toast."

Danny was the first to raise his glass of ginger ale.

Kristen and Nana joined him.

"I want to thank you for letting me be a part of this business venture." He gestured to Kristen with his glass. "I think what you're doing is wonderful for this town, and I wish you a prosperous business and one you will enjoy. Cheers!"

Everyone raised their glasses in unison. "Cheers!"

The doorbell rang as Luke pulled out his chair to sit at the table. "Do you want me to manage the door?"

"Sure." She rested a hand on her grandmother's wrist. "Are you excited about tomorrow?"

"Yes, dear. And you?"

"I'm very excited. Nervous about the ghost of Christmas past thing, though." She speared a pork chop from the platter.

"Oh, don't worry. Gladys will be here, and she'll take care of the drama. Most people who come to these inns expect the place to be haunted, even if it's not. Eat your dinner." Nana scooped string beans with slivered almonds.

Luke smiled and stood in the dining room archway. "Look who decided to take you up on your offer."

Deborah extended a hand toward Nana. "I don't mean to intrude. Kristen was nice enough to ask me to dinner tonight. We ran into each other at the ice cream shop."

Nana sprung from her seat and pulled the empty chair next to Luke from the table, and then waved her hand toward the seat. "Sit down. No problem at all. I was wondering what I would do with all this food. Glad you could join us."

Deborah sat in the chair as Luke pushed it in. She took her napkin and spread it across her lap. "This is a lovely home you have. I remember it as a little girl, and I always wanted to come inside to snoop around. I'd walk past it when the county fair was in full swing."

"I hope the county fair starts up again or the town does something else, at least. All this beauty shouldn't be wasted. There's so much to offer here—cross-country skiing, pumpkin picking, apple season, pancake breakfasts, snowmobiling." Nana stopped talking long enough to fill her plate and take a bite.

"Aunt Gladys says that all the time." Deborah took a pork chop and applesauce.

"As a business owner, you should appreciate the opportunity," Luke chimed in.

"You have a lovely shop. Deborah's shop is where I got the gnomes." Kristen smiled.

"And the holly candy dishes, I believe," Luke added.

"They're on the lobby counter and scattered about the living room. I won't fill them until the guests arrive because I'll eat all the candy myself." Kristen laughed.

Danny rose from the table and left the kitchen.

"He's a cute kid." Deborah rested her fork on the edge of her plate.

"Thank you. My sister passed away a few months

ago. She lived in Florida, and Danny never experienced snow or had to wear a heavy coat, so he's enjoying himself here."

The tune *Silver Bells* wafted into the kitchen.

"Yep, that would be him. He's beginning to like Christmas music. I'm sure he turned on the tree, as well. He'd never seen a real Christmas tree, either, until he moved here."

"Did they celebrate Christmas?" Deborah took a roll from the basket.

Kristen wasn't sure what to make of the question but didn't want to be rude. She cleared her throat. "Yes, but not with a real tree. A fake one. Not very festive but it gave her what she needed, I guess." She noticed Deborah kept an eye on Danny at all times. Even when he was still, Deborah paid a little too much attention.

"Danny, are you excited about Christmas this year?" Deborah picked up her fork and stabbed her pork chop.

Danny sat at the table. "I miss my mom." He squirmed in his chair and stuffed a spoonful of applesauce into his mouth.

Kristen wrung her hands under the table. She didn't understand why Deborah had an interest in Danny. "As I said earlier, this is his first Christmas without his mother. We're all going through an adjustment." She shot a glance at Luke aimed at getting his sister under control.

"Of course. I'm sorry. I didn't mean to upset anyone." Deborah's shoulders slumped slightly.

Luke cleared his throat. "So, Deb, how has business been at the store?"

She set down her glass. "Fine. As good as can be

expected, under the economic circumstances. I was thinking about closing the store after this holiday season."

"No, you can't." Kristen blurted. "This town, well, area, needs something like your store. There's nothing else like it for miles."

Deborah smiled. "Thank you. Maybe Jackson Corners isn't the right place." She relaxed.

Kristen witnessed a sense of peace settle into Deborah's eyes.

"Oh, enough with talk of closing a business and fake trees. It's Christmas after all, and we need to be merry." Nana stood with her hands on her hips.

Kristen understood that her grandmother never liked confrontation or sad stories, and this past year supplied enough sadness for the next decade.

"Ice cream and cake in the dining room in five minutes. All of you out. Scoot." Nana waved the backs of her hands to shoo them out of her kitchen.

Kristen escorted everyone, except Nana, into the living room. Nana usually let her guests sit around the table picking from their plates, but not tonight. She had to get things in order for the morning.

Deborah stopped in front of the tree. "It's beautiful."

"Yep." Danny propped himself on the window seat and stared at the snow. "Santa comes tomorrow night."

As she watched Danny search for his mom's star, Kristen fought back sadness. He hardly mentioned it anymore, and she was hoping he wasn't forgetting his mother. She was counting on the full house of guests to keep him busy and distracted. Gladys had done a great job selling the vacancies, and tomorrow the guests would arrive.

"I must go. Please tell Beth I can't stay for dessert. I have some things to tend to at the store."

As a result of Deborah's abrupt nature, Kristen stiffened her shoulders. She wondered why she'd been so friendly in the store, but uncomfortable with Luke's sister in her own home. "Oh, I'm sorry to see you leave. I'll let my grandmother know you had to rush off." Kristen forced a smile. "See you over the holidays?" Not that she wanted to but she was raised to be polite, no matter how hard she had to bite the inside of her cheek.

After all, it was the Christmas season and she made a promise to bring tidings and joy to everyone.

Chapter Fourteen

Luke followed his sister to the front door. "Is something wrong?"

"No. I want to get home before it's too late. This has been stressful enough."

"What? Dinner?" His sister confused him at times. He did his best to be patient with her quirks, but he usually had time to prepare himself. Twice in one day, she caught him off-guard.

"Dinner was lovely. You know my paranoia. My body is telling me it's time to go. Thank you again."

He watched her get into her twenty-year-old sedan. The car likely had five thousand miles on it, if that. Deborah pulled away so slowly he figured it would take her thirty or forty minutes to make the fifteen-minute drive.

Ahhhhh. Cinnamon filled the air, and he headed back to the dining room. "Deborah apologized for leaving so soon but she gets anxious with driving in the dark."

"Oh, I can understand." Nana nodded then grabbed a pie server from the sideboard. "I never liked driving in the dark and rarely drive in the daytime now. Too many irate people on the roads. Everyone is in a hurry going nowhere fast. Everyone wants to be first at the same red light as me. Good thing the senior center has a shuttle. And since Kristen moved in, well she's a huge help. This girl's not afraid of anything."

He glanced at Kristen, happy to be next to her. He could understand why her grandmother would be generous describing her.

"Cake?" Nana handed him a plate. "You can scoop your own ice cream. It's hard on my hands."

The dessert was loaded with caramel sauce poured over a banana layer cake topped with homemade whipped cream. "Yes, thank you." He took the offering before it slid off the plate into his lap.

"Enjoy. It's one of her best recipes. She only used to make it for Easter, but I talked her into making it for Christmas as well." Kristen dipped her fork into his dessert and swiped a bite. She slowly slid the fork from her mouth, licking her top lip.

"It smells—" *Ring.* He glanced down at his phone. "Sorry. I need to answer this call."

"Of course." Kristen took a mouthful of cake.

He stepped away from the table into the foyer. "Hello?"

"Mr. Baldwin? It's Jocelyn from West Haven. I'm calling about your mother. Don't get alarmed. She had a fall. She seems okay, but she is asking for you."

His stomach dropped. "What happened?"

"The incident happened after dinner. She stepped away from her group at the table and fell. I'm not sure if she lost her footing, fainted, or miscalculated her movement. She's with the nurse right now."

"I'll be right there. Thank you for calling." Luke slid his phone into his jean pocket and ran his fingers through his hair. His first instinct was to call Gladys, but she had done so much that he didn't want to upset her if his mother was okay. He went back to the dinner table and stood alongside Danny.

"And then this giant turtle—"

"Um, I have to run. I'm sorry to leave so abruptly. But I have to go."

Kristen started to stand. "Is it Deborah?"

He laid a hand on her shoulder and eased her back into her chair. "My mother. She's in West Haven, and something has happened. They've assured me she's okay but I won't sleep unless I know for myself."

"Nana, can Danny stay with you? He won't be any trouble, right?" Kristen squeezed her nephew's shoulder.

Danny sighed and rolled his eyes. "I'm fine. I know the drill, after dessert, help Nana clean up, take my shower, brush my teeth, and a half an hour of TV, then bed."

"Perfect. We'll be right back." Kristen tossed her napkin on her plate.

"You don't need to go." He meant it. His mother wasn't Kristen's concern, and he wasn't comfortable with her getting involved. He had a difficult time dealing with his mother's illness, and the last thing he wanted to do was drag someone else into the mix. He would consider her tagging along if they were further along in their relationship.

She rested a hand on his. "Listen. I'll stay in the car. I'd like to go for the ride in case you need to talk. I don't want you to feel alone. Plus, if I stay here, I'm guaranteed to eat another piece of cake and, well, it's never a good thing."

He was grateful for her concern. *Damn her smile.* It got him every time. "The company would be nice."

"I can be as vocal or quiet as you want. I promise

not to change the radio station."

He smiled. Her penchant for levity might be welcome. Who knew what he would walk into? "Okay. And no eating in my car."

She put back a chocolate chip cookie she wrapped in a paper napkin. "Killjoy."

He took her jacket from the coatrack in the foyer and held it out as she slipped into it. "I don't like cleaning my car."

"Understood. But what about if we broke down and weren't found for days? Then you would be looking for a cookie."

"I think we'll survive. I know people. We'll be rescued without incident."

Kristen turned and looked into his eyes.

He leaned into her. "This might be uncomfortable."

"Only if you make it to be. With the stuff I have to deal with in my life, I'll be fine. I'm a strong woman."

Yes, you are. He leaned closer, her cake breath smelled sweet. He held her shoulders and kissed her on the forehead. "Okay, if you insist on going, come, but I am not responsible for anything you might encounter."

"Not a problem. I'll play with your radio and eat a cookie while you're inside." Her cheeks blushed.

"Ugh. Is this what I have to put up with? Stubbornness and—"

She waved her finger. "Ah, don't worry you'll get used to it."

If she only knew how right she was. Kristen was a woman who could easily be a part of his life. But how would he convince her?

****

"It's here! It's here!" Nana yelled up the staircase.

"Get down here. Our guests arrive today."

Kristen made her way downstairs, barely awake. The shower hadn't even helped—she shuffled to the stove and poured a cup of tea. "Muffins?" Kristen took in the aroma of freshly baked goods.

"Yes, cranberry and don't you touch any. And I noticed ten more budgies gone." Nana waved a fist.

"Don't worry. That'll be my Christmas present. A little late but all stuffed, glass-eyed budgies accounted for." She took a swig of tea. "I mean you don't want any of your guests to steal them, do you?"

Nana clutched the skirt of her apron. "Do you think they would? I hadn't thought of that. Good thinking."

Kristen realized the devastation her grandmother experienced when she lost a beloved keet. Nana kept every bird that ever lived with her. She set a pitcher of orange juice on the table next to a bottle of pure Pennsylvania maple syrup.

The best thing about being back in Brookside Falls was not having to cook for herself—not that she ever really did. Nana made sure a home-cooked meal was on the table every day—at least breakfast and dinner. She finished setting the table. "Waffles today?"

Nana nodded then placed a platter on the kitchen table. "I couldn't let that syrup go to waste. Homemade sausage links also, courtesy of John the Farmer."

Danny took his time coming down for breakfast, so she had some free moments to discuss something that bothered her.

"How is Luke's mother?" Nana wiped her hands on her ever-present apron.

"She's fine. I didn't go into the building. By the time we got there, his mother was asleep, because she was given a sedative to calm her. The aide assured him she was okay. He'll go back and see her today."

"Oh, that's wonderful. Eat."

"Nana, I need to talk to you." She waited for her grandmother to take a seat. "What do you think about Deborah?"

Nana sat back, poured a cup of coffee, and topped it with cinnamon. "She's a bit odd. I thought her questions regarding Danny were out of line."

"My thoughts exactly. Why would she be so concerned about him? I mean, her own brother was here, and they barely spoke." Kristen was slightly annoyed at how little Luke contributed to the conversation at dinner. All he did was stuff cake down his throat after his sister left.

Kristen broke off a small piece of waffle and swirled it in fresh maple syrup. "I thought she was rude. The whole time she was here was weird. I asked her to come because I was being polite since Luke was with us. She turned down the offer and then she showed up. Okay, no biggie. But then her interest in Danny was downright uncomfortable. I was glad she left early."

"Who knows why people do the things they do. Don't let that get in the way of your relationship with Luke. You'll never win. Family is family, no matter how estranged they might be."

"They're estranged?" Now Kristen was curious, and she put down her fork on the plate and leaned forward. She sensed an onslaught of the juicy information she sought.

"I don't know Deborah but I know about her from Gladys. Like you, Deborah's parents died in a tragic, damn barn fire. The husband left a pile of oily rags too close to a kerosene heater. It doesn't take much to set an old building up in flames."

"Nana, the story."

"Well, they died putting out the fire and Deborah took care of her brother Brian."

"There's another sibling?" She placed her elbow on the table and chin in her hand.

"He was a free spirit and did what he wanted to do. Traveled the world while Deborah stayed home and took care of the family farm. Little by little, she sold it off. Do you know how difficult it is for a woman to take care of a six-hundred-acre farm?" Nana shook her head.

"That's interesting." She wanted Nana to hurry before Danny got to the breakfast table.

"So, Deborah took care of things and then her brother died…right in town in Jackson Corners. The snow was heavy and roads were slick. Brian plowed into a mailbox and tree in front of the post office. How the kid couldn't have seen that is beyond me. Alcohol's my guess. These young kids drink and drive like maniacs. Watch Danny."

"So, Luke had a brother?" Kristen sat back, arms crossed and legs stretched out before her, ankle over ankle.

"Yep, but he never spent much time with him. Different mother. The father was a hound dog. Luke and his mother lived in…"

"Haineswood." The word escaped her like it took every bit of effort to form. "But you didn't know Deborah?" How could her grandmother not know her? She knew everyone in town. But then again, Luke did say they were from Jackson Corners, and he and his mother lived near Brookside Falls. Different school systems so it was possible. Maybe that's why he didn't talk much about it. "What about Gladys. Did she tell you much? How is she related to Luke and Deborah and Brian? When did he die?"

Nana poured another cup of coffee. "It's funny. As much as Gladys talks, she doesn't talk much about her family. What I know is she was the sister-in-law of Luke's mother. I liked Luke the minute I met him. Quiet, but he seems like a nice guy. I see a sparkle in your eye when he's around. Don't let the sister thing get in the way."

Kristen sighed and rubbed her temples. "I'll be right back." She climbed the stairs and stopped outside Danny's door. Silence. The little time she lived with him was enough to teach her that a quiet seven-year-old wasn't good. She flung open the door and walked inside.

"Noooooooooo." Danny jumped up and slammed the door closed. "Leave it closed."

Her heart skipped a beat. She knelt, grabbed his shoulders, and looked him square in the eyes. "What's wrong? Why are you still up here?"

He broke away, shaking.

Carly's death must finally have hit him. She wasn't prepared for this. *Oh, God, how do you help a seven-year-old grieve the death of his mother?* His only parent. "Please tell me what it is."

"You'll get mad." He covered his face.

"Of course, I won't get mad." She softened her voice to reassure him.

"Yes, you will." He backed away.

"Danny. Please. Tell me."

He took a deep breath. "My snake got loose."

"What!" She jumped on the bed, pulling at her shirt with the feeling the snake was slithering up her sweater. "Do not kid me."

Danny crawled under the bed. "I'm not. I have to find him before the guests arrive. I don't want them to hurt him."

All she could think about was grabbing the nearest rock and smashing the snake. She shouldn't have allowed him to keep it. Grieving compromised her rational thinking. Once the snake was found, if alive, it would be the last one he would ever own. "How did it happen?" She stood on the bed and hugged her chest with her arms so tightly, not even a slip of paper could slide in between.

"I was playing with it, and it wiggled out of my hands. I'm sorry, Aunt Kristen. I didn't mean to do it." He flipped up the bed skirt then poked his head out from under the bed. "I swear."

"I know you didn't, sweetie, but you have to be careful. We can't have animals running amok through the house, especially with strangers staying here." She wanted to hug him but no way was she getting off the bed.

Danny slithered over to the closet.

A black tail poked out from under the door.

"I found it!"

Kristen sighed but was not getting down until the snake was secure in its tank and a boulder placed over the cover. "Good. Put it away. Your breakfast is cold, and that's even if Nana still has it out."

Danny walked across the room clutching the snake with both hands. "Waffles?"

As the reptile's tail swung beneath her nephew's grip, she trembled. "Yes."

"Ice cream?" He dropped his pet into the tank and covered it.

"No ice cream. It's too early." She slowly extended one leg to the floor as Danny secured the snake.

"Nana lets me have ice cream with waffles." He placed the rock on top of the metal screen and stretched a bungee cord around and clipped the ends together.

"Not while I'm home."

"Luke's here!" Nana yelled up the stairway.

Kristen's heart pounded, and she jumped off the bed and ran down the stairs with Danny in tow.

"Hi there." Luke stood at the foot of the stairs. She wanted to kiss him but was uncomfortable in front of Danny. Too soon. The poor kid had to deal with so much change. The last thing she wanted to do was make Danny feel Luke was taking her away.

Danny jumped from the third step and nearly stomped Luke. "Hi." Without a break in momentum, Danny ran into the kitchen.

"He's excited about something, huh?" Luke leaned toward Kristen. His breath swept her neck.

As she caught a whiff of his woodsy scent, she sighed. "It's been an eventful morning. He hasn't eaten breakfast yet because we were snake wrangling."

"We?" Luke lifted one brow.

"Fine. He searched for the loose snake, and I was the lookout standing on the bed."

"I thought that might be closer to the truth." He rested the palm of his hand at the small of her back. "I want to whisk you away, but I know you're busy today. I want to apologize for my sister last night. She can be off-putting."

All the words she'd spent rehearsing since Deborah's visit were for nothing. Not only did his good looks and casual manner make her smile but he was perceptive and aware. A rare combination not found in any of the other men she had been involved with. However, Deborah focused on Danny, and she had to find out why. But Christmas Eve was no time for an unpleasant, serious discussion. She missed Carly terribly and chose to spend this day celebrating the opening of the inn and be grateful for Nana and Danny. "We'll talk about that later, okay?" She pressed a fingertip to his lip. "Right now, I want to enjoy the holiday. Don't you?"

Luke took her hand, smiled, and then kissed her fingertips. "I was never big on Christmas."

"Why not?" She peeked into the kitchen to check on Danny, who was finishing his breakfast. No evidence of ice cream. She took Luke's hand and walked into the living room. The tree ablaze with colored lights, and the tinsel swayed in the light breeze from the heat of the fire burning in the fireplace. Chocolate drops filled the holly candy dishes from Deborah's store.

The inn looked like Christmas, but no matter how hard she tried, the holiday cheer she desperately sought eluded her. She thought about her parents, her grandfather, and now her sister. She turned to Luke and stared deeply into his eyes. "Tell me your story."

She took a risk, ballsy as she was, her spontaneous question might change the course of their relationship. But that was her. She didn't care what someone owned or how much money a person made. She wanted to know the individual—the soul of who they were. With her hand still in his, she pulled him down onto the couch to sit beside her. She waited for his reply.

He shifted in his seat. "I don't have much of a story. I was raised on the outskirts of Brookside Falls. My parents weren't married because my father was married to someone else."

"That someone else being Deborah's mother?" She gently squeezed his hand.

"Yeah, something like that." He smirked.

"Something like that or exactly like that?" She sat back, crossing her legs.

He shifted in his seat. "I really don't like to talk about my family life. It's not interesting anyway." He patted her knee and walked over to the tree. "Nice ornaments." He gently cupped a foam snowman with red eyes. "Someone make this?"

"My sister, Carly. She was the crafty one."

"You're the stylist." He released the snowman and slid his hands into his pant pockets.

"Hair is different. I'm not much in the way of imagination and crafts." His cool demeanor settled in. Many times, she refused to discuss her family's tragedies, yet she broke her promise of enjoying the day without sadness.

A bang on the front door jolted her and swung open before she could answer. A big paper bag of fresh rolls was first through the door.

"Yeesh, it's cold. Snow's on the way. Happens every year. Time to head south." Gladys dropped the bag of rolls on the floor and switched her boots for high heels.

Nana hurried to the door. "It's about time. I

thought the rolls would never show up. I have guests arriving soon."

"Quit your complaining. The rolls arrived in time. Your first guest wants a sandwich." Gladys hugged Nana.

"Huh? What do you mean?" Nana stepped out onto the porch. She stepped back inside the house. "What are you talking about?"

Gladys stood with her arms outstretched. "It's me!"

"I don't have room for you." Nana picked up the overflowing bag of rolls and headed back to the kitchen.

"You do if I'm paying for it, Beth. Check your register, Anna Franklin room two." She stepped deeper into the foyer. "Luke! What a surprise!"

He got up and walked over to his aunt. "Nice to see you. Do you need help with anything?"

"My bags are in the car." She straightened her skirt and ran her hands over her temples.

Over the past year Gladys and Nana became even closer friends. Gladys was the first person to see Beth when Carly died. Gladys lost a sister to ovarian cancer too, so she was compassionate to the grief Nana experienced. She was bothered Beth was all alone in the large house. Too much room to think about what was missing. Beth always complained how nearly every family member died before her, and that's not the way it should be as far as she was concerned.

Kristen stayed out of the way as Gladys scuttled across the room to behind the lobby counter. She grabbed a feather duster and swiped at the wood, catching whatever little bit of dust there might be.

Nana was still in the kitchen with Danny.

With Gladys in charge, Kristen thought the moment was opportune for Luke to catch up with his aunt, and her to slip away for some alone time.

She grabbed her jacket from the coatrack and stepped onto the front porch. Green, red, blue, and yellow miniature lights glowed in the boxwood bushes along the front of the house. A quick glance into the house showed her everyone was busy. A memory of Carly at the kitchen table making cookies made her smile, so she headed for their favorite place.

A few moments of solitude would calm her spirit and help clear her head. Had she taken on too much?

Chapter Fifteen

Fine, dry snowflakes landed on the tip of her nose as she made her way through the abandoned trails behind her grandmother's house. The sixty acres didn't seem as big now that she was grown but was still a lot of land. She would have to hire someone to care for the grounds. And Nana was definitely in no position for such heavy work.

She stopped beside the path, seeking mistletoe. Every year her grandfather tried to grow at least a sprig so he could hang it in the doorway of his house. No one could convince him he lived in the wrong part of the country for growing mistletoe. He believed if you tried hard enough it would happen.

The wind swirled around her feet. She pushed her hands deep into her pockets and tipped back her head as the sun warmed her cheeks. For a moment, she experienced peace. She hadn't spent much time in the outdoors since moving back to Brookside Falls. When she was a kid, the trails were her solace. Birds were her friends as they sat on the tree branches and sang as she strolled by.

She stopped at a log bench her grandfather handcrafted, weathered but still solid. Her mind must be overworked, she thought she saw Carly sitting on the bench. It had to be her imagination and the past playing tricks on her. She sat on the bench and picked up a holly branch that must have come off in a storm. She crossed her legs and twirled the sprig in her hand, hesitated, then brushed the holly across her cheek. "I miss you, Carly," she whispered. "You'll never know how much. I can't believe how much time we missed together, and for that I'm sorry." Tears rolled down her face. She was alone with her thoughts with no grandmother, nephew, or errant animal running circles around her, for the first time since she came back to Brookside Falls.

Silence.

She stopped breathing to take in the calm. Not a bird or squirrel stirred. She released her breath, closed her eyes, and focused on the quiet of the forest. Stillness. What felt like hours in the woods was only a few minutes.

A breeze swept by, not too cold but enough to make her stir. An owl flew overhead—she recognized the beat of its wings. She and Carly would close their eyes and guess the sounds of the woods, even identify the trees by sound.

Carly insisted each tree had a distinct sound because of the size of the trunk, shape of the leaves, and flexibility of the branches.

She heard a noise—something moving—coming up behind her. Her body tensed, and she opened her eyes but was blinded by the sun.

"There you are. Your grandmother's been looking for you. It's pretty back here. I can understand why you went for a walk. It's a gorgeous day."

She shielded her eyes so they could adjust to the sun's glare and Luke came into view. "I do love it out here. I've been away so long I forgot how important this was."

"What a wonderful place for Danny to run around. Think of all the snakes and frogs he'll find. The spring peepers are really cool." Luke laughed.

Kristen stood. "They're my favorite. March is prime peeper season. I would stay awake until the last peeper peeped. Have you ever seen one?"

"No, I hear they're really tiny." He draped an arm around her shoulders.

She moved closer, her hip touching his. His difficult sister escaped her mind. He was what mattered and right then he was doing everything right. She held his left thumb. "You see this? The size of your thumbnail?"

"Uh-huh." He focused on her gesture.

"That's how big a peeper is—as big as my thumbnail."

He rubbed her thumb and hugged her.

She was enthralled by him, something she'd never experienced before. "I caught one once, and that's not easy to do."

"I imagine it isn't." He turned. "I have something to tell you, and I'm not sure how you're going to take it."

He squeezed her as if guarding her from the sadness sweeping through her heart. Her stomach tensed. Was he leaving? She couldn't bear any bad news. Not today. She gazed into his eyes as he spoke. Windows to the soul, they were, and no matter the words—the eyes always told the truth.

His chest heaved as he took in a breath. "We've met before." His shoulders softened as the words escaped his lips. "I wanted to tell you when we had our first business meeting, but I couldn't. I thought I recognized you at the church parking lot, but I wasn't sure. That's why I asked for your name."

She stood back, hands in her pockets, shoulders practically up to her ears. "When did we meet? I'm sure I would have remembered you."

"Years ago, at the county fair. I was fifteen, and you were standing next to the ice cream stand eating a chocolate ice cream cone."

"Did you speak to me?" She struggled to remember.

"Not in the traditional sense. You stood there and I knew you were special. I walked up and said, 'excuse me' as I threw away a napkin, so I could get next to you."

She tilted back her head. She remembered going to fairs, but she had been to a few so not one stood out. "I'm sorry I don't remember."

He sucked his teeth. "You might remember what happened next. I dropped my blue snow cone…"

"On my new sheer, white blouse!" She laughed. "Oh, my God, that was you?"

"Guilty. I was mortified and took off." He kicked a stone into the brush.

"I thought you were being rude. You ruined my blouse." She chuckled. She had been at the fair with Melissa and Judy, who she hadn't seen since they graduated high school.

"I'm sorry. I was a stupid teenager and apparently not as cool as I thought." He held out his arms.

"I have a confession also." She wrapped her arms around his waist. "The first time I looked into your eyes I knew, but I couldn't figure out the connection. I didn't know why, but the feeling wouldn't leave me." She pulled him in closer.

He wrapped his arms around her and gently tucked her head in his neck. He slid his fingers in at the base of her neck and tipped her head back ever so slightly.

The chill in the air gave way to the heat from their bodies. The two stood with snow at their feet, bare branches softly swaying around them.

He leaned in to kiss her impatient lips. She wanted him to hold her forever. She hoped he wanted the same. Not even the wind could slip in between them. Was this happening too fast? She slowly moved away from his lips and looked into his eyes—she could see he was hers.

"You know what I want?" he whispered.

"What?" She smiled and tilted her head to the side.

"I want time alone with you. We're always surrounded by people."

She gently slipped from his embrace and her hands ran down his arms and she squeezed his hands, broke away, and shoved her hands into her pockets. "Alone, huh?"

He swung an arm around her shoulders and turned them toward the inn. "Not what you think."

He softly squeezed the top of her arm.

"I want to spend time with you and without burning down a restaurant."

"I'll try my best." She kissed him on the cheek, then strolled back to the house. Time alone. Would Luke accept Danny as part of the package? She would have to make her expectation clear. Nana could not keep Danny entertained. She decided to leave the conversation with Luke until later.

Christmas music grew louder as she neared the inn. The melodies played through the speakers her grandfather installed on the back deck and front porch.

"Are these the gnomes?" Luke pointed as he walked up the front stairs.

"Cute, aren't they?" She stopped and rested her hand on top of the largest gnome's hat.

"Cute for gnomes, I guess. I never gave lawn ornaments much thought." He held her hand as she walked up the stairs and opened the door.

Could he love Danny as much as I do?

****

Luke held open the door for Kristen and walked into the foyer welcomed by Christmas bells and carols.

"I see you have guests already." He took Kristen's jacket and hung it on the coatrack.

A man and woman stood at the lobby desk. Gladys checked them in as Danny struggled with the luggage. Nana was busy placing small dishes of chocolate chip, peanut butter, and shortbread cookies throughout the lobby and living area.

Luke walked up to Danny and took the largest suitcase.

"I can do it," Danny insisted.

"I know you can, but I want to help and get away from the cookies. Otherwise I'll eat them all." Luke let Danny lead the way.

"Nana wouldn't like that." Danny spoke looking back.

"No, I guess she wouldn't." He followed.

Danny walked up the stairs then hesitated in front of a door on the third floor, and tilted his head.

"You okay there?" He paused, waiting for Danny

to continue.

"That was my mother's room. No one can stay in there." He continued to the guest room.

His heart sank as he stood with the little boy, who had been through so much and being brave and strong so everyone would think he was okay. At least that's how he figured it to be. He remembered when his mother didn't feel well, and he would stay home from school to take care of her.

Most of his life, his mother struggled to maneuver through the world with ease while keeping her sanity intact. He looked back at his childhood with the eyes of an adult and was in awe of how they survived tight financial times. As a child, he knew nothing of what was needed to keep a home. Other than being a responsible latchkey kid, he thought life was wonderful. He realized his mother's loving generosity made his world feel that way.

His heart broke for Danny who had no idea how fast he was growing up, whether he wanted to or not. At least the little guy had his aunt and great-grandmother to give him a solid home foundation.

The luggage was settled in guest room six on the third floor.

"You put me to shame carrying those suitcases like they weighed no more than a bag of feathers." He stretched his hands to loosen the tension from the weight of the handles digging into his palms.

"I run a lot. Aunt Kristen said it makes me strong and helps me focus."

"She's a good aunt, isn't she?"

"Yep, the best." Danny's smile stretched from ear to ear.

He watched Danny run his hand down the comforter and smooth out a small wrinkle, thinking it odd for such a young kid to be concerned with something so tedious. He was lucky if he made his own bed, never mind care about a bump in the linens.

"No wrinkles allowed?" He smiled.

"Nana always says a job worth doing is a job worth doing right. She must have missed one."

"She's a smart woman." Luke smiled.

"Yeah, I like her a lot. She lets me bring home animals Aunt Kristen won't let me have."

He finished and headed to the stairs.

Danny slowed down in front of Carly's old room, again.

Luke knelt down beside Danny. "You miss your mom, don't you?"

"Every day."

The seven-year-old with an old soul looked deep into his eyes. Luke could tell Danny fought back tears by the glistening tears pooling in his eyes. He wrapped his arms around him. "I miss my dad every day too, buddy." The little body shuddered within his arms. Luke held him tighter as Danny wept. He gently rocked back and forth until the sobbing ceased. He bowed his head close to Danny. "I'll tell you a secret."

Danny wiped his nose with his shirt sleeve. "What?"

"I still cry for my father, and I know I always will. You know it's okay to do that, don't you?"

"I don't let my aunt or Nana see me cry." Danny sniffled.

"It'll be our secret, okay?" Luke held up his pinky.

Danny hooked his pinky into Luke's. "Okay."

"From this day, anytime you need to let it out, letting tears free, or you need someone other than your aunt or grandmother to talk to, you call me. Got that?"

Danny swiped away tears trickling down his cheeks. "Anytime?"

Luke nodded.

"I'll need your phone number." Danny held out his hand.

He smiled at the contradiction and honest emotions of a seven-year-old. He reached into his back pocket and pulled out his wallet. "Tell you what. Here is my business card. You can call this number whenever you want."

Danny smiled. "Thanks."

"Anytime, Bud."

He hugged Danny, then continued downstairs. His heart grew three times during his conversation with Danny. What was this family doing to him? He never allowed himself to get emotionally involved. Overcome with joy as if a well was unplugged and gushed water and his heart been held prisoner for an entire lifetime.

When he first considered his relocation to Haineswood, he had one goal—to put his mother in an environment that would make her remaining years comfortable and hopefully jar some recollection of what was the happiest time in her life.

Little did he know he walked into a world that gave him a new present every day. He stepped off the bottom stair, excited to join the family.

Danny wiggled his fingers, motioning Luke to bend down. "I know where the extra cookies are hidden."

Luke smiled and took Danny's hand into his. "I bet

you do buddy. I bet you do."

****

She instantly fell in love with him when she overheard Luke soothing Danny. He couldn't have known she was within earshot while checking one of the rooms. She stacked the towels in the linen closet then made her way down to her own bedroom. With Gladys at the helm, and Luke a willing helper, Nana and Danny could manage the rest.

The warm air comforted her as she sat on her bed and fought to stay awake. Tired from worry whether all things were falling into place, exhausted from not sleeping enough hours, and the comfort of her mattress beneath her, she propped herself up so she wouldn't doze off. Carly's diary lay on the nightstand. She picked up the book and held it against her heart.

"I miss you." A tear ran down her cheek. The memories she enjoyed at the house were still there, but her parents, grandfather, and sister weren't. Danny and Nana were the ones who would be with her to make new memories. And maybe Luke, if he was willing.

A rapid tap on the door startled her. "Aunt Kristen?"

That kid has the damndest timing. "Come in sweetie."

The door flung open as Danny raced into the room.

"No snakes?" She straightened herself preparing for reptile battle.

"No snakes. He's locked away."

"Good. Come here." She spread her arms ready to catch him. "What's up?"

"I like Luke." His tiny body curled beside her. The warmth of his small protected image let her know she

199

was taking good care of him.

She smiled at the admission of his acceptance. Her only option to allow someone into her life was someone who would be kind and patient.

"I like him too." She brushed aside his hair. "You're going to be my first customer in my new shop. Why do you like Luke?"

"I just do. He's very cool."

She laughed. "Where did you hear that expression?"

"From you. You say it all the time."

She thought for a moment. "You're right, I do." She chuckled. "So, how's it going downstairs?"

"Good. Nana said 'it's a good thing Kristen moved my budgies.' There are too many people in the house, and she doesn't want her birds hurt." He stretched his arms.

She kissed the top of his head, something he didn't like it but too bad, she enjoyed smothering him with kisses and would do so as long as she could. "We should be downstairs. We can't have Nana doing everything."

"Oh, she's not. That Gladys lady is while Nana talks to the people. That's all she's been doing. Talk, talk, talk."

"Well, I'm sure we can help." She placed the diary in her night table drawer. One day she would let Danny read the journal. For now, it would be her stories she would tell.

She made her way downstairs. "O Come All Ye Faithful" played through the piped stereo system and the aroma of hot cider permeated the air. Popcorn balls were neatly piled in a bowl on the counter. Gladys must have brought the sticky treat. Nana wouldn't have made them. She'd tried it once and cleaned up corn syrup for weeks. She swore she would never permit popcorn-ball-making in her kitchen again. Plus, she rarely allowed anyone in her kitchen when she was cooking.

Darkness settled in, and the weatherman promised a white Christmas. A fire burned in the hearth, a turkey roasted in the oven, and family gathered together—a perfect evening. The only meal planned at the inn was breakfast, but her grandmother couldn't have a house full of people on Christmas Eve and not feed them a holiday meal. So, she decided a small turkey would be practical. After all, the guests would be hungry after traveling all day. She might lose money on the inn but at least she would be happy while doing so.

Kristen found Luke in the kitchen filling plates with cookies. "Hey!" she snapped. "Knock it off."

"I'm replacing what's been eaten. I swear. I'm not taking anymore." His eyes grew wide, and he licked his fingers.

"Gladys is amazing." She took a cookie from the plate.

"Yes, she is. She's the one who made sure Deborah and I got to know each other better after Brian died."

She cocked her head to the side. "Brian?"

"My half-brother. Deborah's full-blooded sibling. I didn't know him well."

Should she tell him she knew? No, she wanted him to tell her about his family connection.

"He was killed in a car accident in front of the post office in Jackson Corners." He set the plate of cookies on the counter.

"How sad. When?" She folded her arms across her

chest.

"Five years ago, on New Year's Eve." He reached to the back of the kitchen counter and poured himself a rum and coke.

She ran her hand up and down his arm gently. "I'm so sorry. Holidays suck when things like that happen."

"Yeah." He chugged the drink. "What really bothered me is we started to get to know each other and then he was gone. As kids, we were kept apart by our parents, but when he went to college in Oregon, we got in touch. He had problems. I guess all teenagers do."

She sat at the kitchen table wondering what he was like as a young boy. How did he fill up his day being an only child? "Did you?"

Luke turned to the counter and then poured another rum and coke. "Not really. I stayed in the house most of the time. My mother worked a lot, and I didn't have a sitter, so I wasn't allowed to go outside if she wasn't home. I guess that's why I became an architect. I used to study the walls a lot." He laughed.

She walked over and hugged him from behind. "Do you drink much when you're sad?" The last thing she wanted to do was bring an alcoholic into her family. She remembered ruined holidays when her uncle Ted drank so much that he was asked to not come back to her grandmother's house.

He put down the glass, turned around, and then kissed her forehead. "No, I rarely drink. But this is an evening to celebrate. This drink will be the last one tonight."

She hugged his waist. "We can hide in here all night. The two of us. Alone." No sooner had she spoken those words than Danny barged into the room.

"Luke, we need the cookies."

"Oops, sorry buddy. Can you take these out to the dining room?" Luke handed the plate to Danny. "Thanks. Be in there in a few."

She waited for Danny to leave the room. "Was Brian younger or older?"

He sipped his drink "Seven years older. Deborah is the oldest. She has another fifteen years on me. Like I said earlier, I'm sorry for her being intrusive, but that's her way. She took on the mother role after Brian was killed."

"An accident in front of the post office?" She recognized the street.

"Brian had a serious drinking problem, passed out, and plowed into a mailbox and a tree. I didn't take a drink for years. This will be my third this year." He lifted the glass.

She took the glass from his hand, then walked to the sink, and placed the drink on the counter. "Three this year? That would be three times with me. Don't make me the reason you find it easy to pour yourself a drink."

"No, no. I didn't mean it like that." He ran his fingers through his hair. "I didn't mean to sound like you made me drink."

"I didn't think you did, but if you never drank another drink again, I would be there right beside you. I was never fond of liquor anyway. My family rarely had beer in the house, except for holidays." She washed her hands, and then dried them on a towel hanging from the handle on the refrigerator door.

He leaned over, grabbed the glass, poured the liquor down the drain, rinsed the glass, and filled it with ginger ale.

She raised her glass to his. "Now you're hitting the hard stuff. Merry Christmas."

"Not being connected to my brother and sister was easy." He scratched his head.

His lips moved to form words, but nothing came out. She should be with the guests at least attempting to help, but she couldn't walk away.

"Our last names were different, so not many people connected that we were related, and we didn't live in the same town."

"His name wasn't Baldwin?" She squinted her eyes.

"Nope. Reeves."

Her stomach dropped, and her breath caught. *Brian Reeves!* She clamped a hand over her mouth to smother a gasp. The glass in her other hand rattled. The letter in Carly's diary. He couldn't be the same Brian. Could it?

She finally had confirmation of Danny's father. How would Luke fit into her life?

Chapter Sixteen

Unsure what Kristen's next move would be, she focused on the evening and saved the uncertain relationship questions for another day.

Luke put his empty glass in the sink. "I think we should make an appearance and help out. My aunt will be singing every song written since 1824."

"Why start there?" Kristen pondered.

"She likes that era. Once she starts singing *It Had to Be You,* there will be no stopping her. Especially if she hits the hard cider."

"Ah, it's not that hard. Nana doesn't spike it much."

"No, but my aunt does. I can guarantee she has poured a fifth of vodka into the cider bowl. Make sure Danny doesn't drink any."

Kristen's eyes flew wide open. The thought of her nephew accidentally drinking the wrong batch of beverage frightened her. She ran out of the kitchen with Luke fast on her heels. Kristen searched for the bowl of hard cider on the lobby counter next to the appetizers, but the bowl wasn't there.

"Danny?" Kristen called.

No response.

"Danny?" She threw open the kitchen door, no sign of him. Nana, Gladys, and the couple who checked in earlier were chatting around the table.

"I'm sure he's fine." He grabbed her shoulder.

She melted at the touch of his fingers gently rubbing away the tension as to assure her everything was okay.

"I'm being a parent." Kristen pushed away his hands and flung open the back door.

He backed off.

She agonized over her missing nephew like a mama bear who lost her cub. "Danny?" She called out the back porch.

Luke walked close to keep a safe distance from an unexpected swat. "I'm sure he's fine. It's not unusual for boys to have secret hiding places. At times I wish I still had mine. Many nights I would hide under the— come with me." He grabbed Kristen's hand and made his way to the basement. He turned and held an index finger to his lips and then hers. He pointed to a light that peeked out from under the door and nodded.

Slowly, Kristen opened the door. "Danny?"

"Yes?" A quiet voice escaped from underneath the stairs.

Luke led Kristen down the flight of stairs.

Sure enough, Danny was huddled underneath the staircase. She walked to the bottom, and then squatted on the floor next to Danny. "Honey, why are you hiding here?" She wrapped an arm around her nephew who seemed perfectly content to make the basement his apartment.

"Boris likes it here." Danny held out a two-foot garter snake.

"Agh!" Kristen's heart raced, and her palms were clammy. "Is that the same one?"

Danny shook his head. "No, I found this one in the

woods about an hour ago. I thought it might be too cold for him so I brought him inside."

Kristen shivered and flicked her hands, attempting to rid herself of fear. "Danny, you cannot house every lone reptile. Understand?" She watched Danny stare, questioning her sincerity.

He nodded, curled up the snake, and placed it in his jacket pocket.

"Hey, Bud. Do you want to find a nice warm home? I'm sure he'll be much more comfortable in a gigantic pile of leaves or a hole in the ground. Come on. Whatcha say?"

Danny stared at Luke.

As if his trustworthiness was suspect. "Sounds like a great plan. You two take care of that thing. I'm resting a bit." Kristen shooed them out of the basement.

****

Luke put a hand on Danny's shoulder as he accompanied him up the stairs. "Snakes are cool, aren't they?"

"Yep."

He didn't agree, but who was he to challenge the interests of a seven-year-old? He wove his way through people gathered between the dining room and foyer, and then picked his jacket from the coatrack.

As he stepped onto the front porch, the cold air hit his lungs like a punch to the chest. The weatherman was wrong again. What was supposed to be an unusually warm December day for northeast Pennsylvania turned out to be cold, gray, and damp.

Fresh snow would be welcome, because at least the air would be drier. He thought about the one fun day he spent with his brother.

Brian had made a bunch of snowballs and threw them at Luke when he came to visit. What began as a contest of territory turned into a fun snowball fight. His cheeks hurt from smiling about the memory.

He wished he would have asked more questions about his father. As a child, life seemed forever and was taken for granted. By the time he was brave enough to voice his curiosity, his mother started fading into the darkness. At first depression took hold, and then dementia. He would never dare ask his father questions about the scandal. He was content with what he had and didn't see a reason to upset the status quo.

Danny turned to the right, forged ahead, and broke trail into the woods behind the inn.

Luke's loafers weren't designed to traipse through terrain suitable for critter cover. But the experience of watching Danny determined to find an adequate home for his newest pet was worth the adventure.

"Find a place yet?" he called out to Danny.

"Over here. Straight ahead."

He followed the young, backwoods trail expert and stopped at the top of a rock as big as a small car. It seemed to be the highest point on the property. "Are you sure we can be out here?"

Danny nodded. "Of course, Nana brings me out here all the time. Wild blueberries and strawberries grow over there."

Luke followed the direction where Danny pointed. *Nice bear eating grounds.* Wild animals scared him, but he wouldn't let on. He didn't want to upset the kid. If Nana was brave enough to spend time in the woods, then the area must not be too dangerous.

But bears love blueberries.

"I guess most of the animals are asleep for the winter, and it's past blueberry season." He dug his hands deep into his jean pockets.

"Yep. That's why it's weird I found this snake. He should have been in hibernation under rocks or under a log out of the cold. A woodchuck or a fox must have scared him out of his home. He'll be safe up here under the rock."

Warmth radiated through his chest as he witnessed Danny dig a hole under the base of the boulder and lay the coiled snake in the ground. "You seem to know quite a bit about the animals out here." He was impressed with Danny's outdoor skills.

"You have to understand it's their home. They want to live without being bothered."

Luke smiled wide. He never thought he would have children. Work was his life. However, if he did decide to have a child, he hoped the kid would be like Danny.

"Come on, Bud. Time to go." He wanted to get back to the house to join the party and spend time with the woman who brought happiness to his life.

****

The front door slammed open.

"Aunt Kristen. We're back!" Danny ran into the house, dropped his coat on the foyer floor, and then waved his dirty hands.

"Wonderful. Wash. And use soap. And hang up your coat." She shooed him away.

"I could stand to freshen up also." Luke leaned in and kissed her.

She smiled as Luke wandered into the kitchen with his wildlife mentor. Her heart melted with joy as she witnessed the bond growing between them. She grabbed a tray and gathered empty glasses from the lobby counter and living room coffee table. Uncomfortable with letting down her guard, she paused for a moment, and then walked to the window.

Snow fell slowly. The animals were quiet and hiding in their homes. For the first time in months, all seemed well in her life.

Danny was in the dining room with Luke. She didn't like to drink, but she needed something to steady her nerves. She brought the tray of dirty dishes into the kitchen and settled on a ginger ale. Not the most effective mood stabilizer but soda would have to do.

Her world spun out of control while the party continued on the other side of the door. So many questions. Was this the reason Luke had been brought into her life? Had he known all along Danny was his nephew? She stepped out of the kitchen and rushed past Luke. "I'll be right back."

Taking two steps at a time, she sprinted up the stairs. She threw open the bedroom door, ripped open the nightstand drawer, and pulled out the letter. She sat on the bed with a thud. The room spun as she laid a hand over her eyes to block glare from the overhead light. "Carly, could it be?" she whispered.

She held the diary to her heart. If true, and Luke and Deborah were Danny's aunt and uncle, how did it all fit together? How would she and Luke fit together? *Could they?* She rolled over on her stomach and pulled the pillow over her head, holding the sides tightly against her ears. She'd promised her sister she would do her best for Danny and protect her nephew at all costs.

Luke! He must have known Danny was Brian's son. Deborah's questions made sense now. Her interest in Danny was more than a casual interrogation. A rap on the door echoed through the pillow.

"Kristen, are you okay?"

"Go away, Luke." She screamed into the mattress, and then rolled onto her back, loosely laying the pillow on top of her head.

"Did I do something wrong?" He turned the doorknob and poked his head into the room. He walked in quietly and rested his hand on her knee.

She shot up, tense and aggravated. "Please leave."

"What?" His face twisted. "I don't think I said or did anything to offend you."

Her breathing deepened. She had to know the truth. "Do you know anything about this?" She held out the letter.

"What is it?" he asked calmly.

She handed him the letter and sat back on the bed, her arms wrapped around her knees as they dug into her chest.

As he read the letter, his mouth dropped open.

She waited for evidence, anything to prove he knew. Perhaps, a knowing eye as he read the words or a lack of surprise with each pass of a sentence.

He held out the piece of paper.

"I have one question. Did you know?" Her gaze locked with his.

He ran his hands through his hair. "Not at all. I didn't know Brian had any kids."

"How could you not know?" She wanted to believe him.

A bead of sweat surfaced on his forehead. "I told you, Brian and I weren't close. He did his own thing." Luke walked to the window seat, sat, and rubbed his temples.

"I want to believe you, but now I understand why your sister was asking so many questions. She has to know. And if she does, why didn't she say anything?"

"I-I don't know. Honestly. I don't." His brows knitted together.

He seemed to not know what to make of Brian's connection to Danny. She wanted to believe him, but the stakes were too high.

He stood, then walked to the bed, and sat beside her. His mouth hung open, but he didn't speak.

For a moment, she wanted to hug him and tell him she knew he was telling the truth, but she couldn't. She picked up the diary and held it between her hands like she was praying. What could she do? Her mind was empty. As much as she tried to make sense of the situation, she was at a loss. "I can't talk now. I'm going downstairs to enjoy the evening. I don't want to discuss this at all." She stood and walked to the door. "Neither of you will take him from me. I never want to see you again. I don't want you around him." She stood in the doorway and stared as he lingered.

Still on the bed in her room, he slumped, his fingers hovering over the red leather cover for a few seconds and then retreated.

She expected him to open the book but figured he wouldn't do it with her standing there. How many other secrets was he keeping from her?

He left the diary and its contents alone then walked past her.

She closed the door and followed him to the living room. She sat on the floor, arms folded and legs crossed next to the fireplace.

Nana was telling a few of the guests about the history of the house.

Gladys listened while she stood behind the counter with her elbows propped and resting her chin in her hands.

Luke stood in the archway of the living room.

He waited, as if seeking Kristen to acknowledge him. She didn't. Did she really think he knew and would take Danny from her? His eyes pleaded with her.

He grabbed his jacket from the hall closet and left through the back door.

She sat on the living room floor, stared into the dancing flames, and breathed slowly. Attempts at meditation usually failed but she did her best to focus her anger into calm.

Carly, I'm doing my best.

She fought to shut out the noise of guests milling about the inn. A slight hum vibrated from her throat. Christmas music faded into the background as her focus and intention grew stronger with each breath.

Of course, the person who came into her life with half a chance of being her partner would present complications. *Wasn't that the way?* No matter how she did her best—

"Love you!"

Little arms hugged her neck from behind and jolted her from her meditative state. "I love you, too. My little snake wrangler." She slid her hands into Danny's, and she held his, pulling him onto her lap. A text popped up on her cell phone screen.

—We need to talk but I had to take care of something first. Luke.—

Her heart twinged as she placed her phone on the

coffee table, uncertain she would ever see him again.

****

The automatic doors slid open as Luke walked into the West Haven Assisted Living Home. The night air warmed a bit, and he needed to clear his head. He walked to the reception desk and waited until he had the attention of the aide talking on the phone.

Each time he walked into West Haven, he was more relaxed. The facility did its best to look like a home. Heavy mahogany woodwork trimmed the doorways and matched the crown molding on the ceilings. Planning the move over the phone had been difficult, but his aunt Gladys assured him West Haven would be a perfect place for his mother to live. Gladys was right. He was pleased with his decision.

If it weren't for the emergency door buttons, he would never know West Haven was a care facility. In the lobby stood a nine-foot tree, adorned with miniature, multi-colored lights and handmade ornaments, likely made by the residents.

"Can I help you?"

The woman at the desk broke his concentration of admiring the holiday decorations.

"I'm here to take Amanda Baldwin for a ride around town."

"Oh, you must be her son, Luke." The woman stood, reached over the counter, and shook his hand.

He returned the gesture. "Yes, I am. Can I get her?"

"I'll buzz the aide. Your mother has been talking about you all day, while waiting for your arrival. You're as good-looking as she said you were. I'm Chrissy."

"Um, thanks." He stood, taken back by the admiration, but at the same time happy his mother was having a good day. He hoped it stayed that way—at least for his visit.

"Eva? Would you escort Amanda Baldwin to reception please?"

"Thank you, Chrissy. I'll wait over here." He pointed to the leather couch a few feet away from the desk area. As he thought about the last time he had a conversation with his mother before her memory started to fade, he smiled. She asked him if he would marry or stay focused on his career. He wondered if his mother realized she had moved to a new facility.

Kristen was constantly on his mind. When he woke in the morning, she was the first vision he saw and the last when he went to bed for the night. He had to find a way to convince her he didn't know anything about Danny.

"Luke, here she is. Enjoy your night, Mandy."

He stood and hugged his mom like he hadn't seen her in years. The fact she didn't rely on her wheelchair pleased him. She didn't physically need it but using it made her feel more secure when she was having a period of forgetfulness. "You're having a good day I see." He took his mom by the elbow and escorted her to his car.

"I like this place. Most times I forget I'm here, but when I do remember, I know I like it. Gladys was here today."

"We're lucky to have her here." He helped his mother to the parking lot, then opened the door, and got her settled into the front passenger seat.

"Is this a new car?"

"No, Mom. It's the same one I've had for eight years."

"It looks so new."

"I take good care of it. Are you in the mood for ice cream? I hope so, because I am." He pulled out of the parking lot not expecting an answer. Years passed since he could have a consistent dialogue with his mother, but he enjoyed spending time with her.

He drove carefully as not to upset her. She wasn't a fan of fast cars—not that his mid-size sedan was capable of competing in a stock car race. But he noticed over the years, fast movement could throw her into an antsy episode, so he did his best to control what he could. He glanced at his mom. She looked healthy and wore a smidge of makeup.

"Peppermint," Amanda blurted.

"I'm sure they have peppermint this time of year." The ice cream store wasn't too far, and the parking was easy. Even though most stores were open later than usual for the holiday, not much traffic clogged the streets. Maybe he was the only one who waited until the last minute to buy presents.

The lack of gifts he needed to buy made him a little sad. He no longer had an assistant. His mother had everything she needed. The only other person in his family he would buy a present for was Gladys, if even as a thank you for her help over the past summer and fall.

He thought about Kristen. Was it too early in the relationship to buy her a present? Did they still have the beginning of one? He had another day to think about getting a gift. Maybe he should hold off on buying a present and see if she calmed down enough for them to talk.

Deborah never wanted any gifts. She always said seeing him was enough, and she had a store full of stuff, and she didn't need a thing. Just customers.

At least he wouldn't have to travel from New Jersey anymore to see everyone. He missed the ocean, and this Christmas would be the first year without his morning holiday stroll. No matter how chilly the wind off the Atlantic Ocean, he would take off his shoes and socks and walk along the edge, as water rolled to and from through his toes. Maybe he would visit New Year's Eve and spend the next morning at one of his favorite Jersey haunts. "Mom, do you mind if we stop in a store before we get ice cream?"

Amanda shook her head.

Good she was still with him. He parked the car in front of Enchanted Muse. Unsure what he would find in the store, it intrigued him enough to see what they sold. Maybe he could find a peace offering for Kristen. If he did, would it matter?

Chapter Seventeen

Kristen didn't want to be mad, which she considered a wasted emotion that took up precious time. But she couldn't help but think Luke and Deborah had some kind of plan in mind for Danny.

She puttered around the living room, and then stood at the bay window and pushed aside the lace curtain. A male cardinal landed on the holly bush against the porch railing. At times, she expected a bird to be a sign of someone she lost.

Kristen thought back to the moment she accused Luke of having an ulterior motive. He seemed genuinely surprised when she told him Brian had a son. She could see his pleading eyes boring through her, while he did his best to convince her to believe him. She suppressed her gut reaction to say she believed him and carry on like nothing happened, she couldn't. Not until she had information she believed to be the truth.

Doubt crept in as she realized how secretive her sister had been. If Carly hadn't told her own family who her son's father was, then it wasn't much of a stretch to believe Luke didn't know. Her heart softened at the possibility of Luke's role in the family saga might be innocent.

But she didn't trust his sister. Kristen's instincts gnawed at her gut the minute she ran into Deborah at the ice cream store. At the time, she didn't know what made her uneasy—after the dinner interrogation and reveal in the letter—but the uncertain feelings in her soul made sense. She had to pay more attention to her intuition.

Noise from the hallway grew louder. She fixed the curtain and walked to the foyer. "Danny?" No answer. *He's probably playing with his animals.* She couldn't wait until summer when he could release his collection into the wild. Next year she would be ahead of the game and build some type of winter home—outside—away from the main building. "Danny?"

She walked out into the hallway. Gladys could be heard two floors up. Her theatrical voice carried with ease. "Danny?" She spoke softer as to not frighten the guests. His floppy brown hair made him stick out in the crowd gathered in the lobby. "Come here."

Her nephew looked at her and pointed to Gladys. "Story time. Scary story."

She stood at the foot of the stairs, half-listening to what Gladys said.

"And then sleigh bells rang through the night, but no one was there. Legend has it every year on Christmas Eve, old man Stewart still waits on the front porch to greet Santa Claus."

Geez. She's turning this into a sideshow. She walked up behind Danny and tugged at the collar of his flannel shirt. She leaned into his ear. "You know it's a story? It's not true. Some marketing gimmick she created to keep the rooms rented through the holidays."

"There's no old man Stewart?" Danny pouted.

"Oh, I'm sure at one time he lived here, but not in the way Gladys remembers him." She looked down at his sad face. "What's the matter? You like ghosts?"

He shook his head. "I think they're cool."

She hesitated to feed his interest. Carly would tell her ghost stories, and she enjoyed being entertained, but not scared. Come to think of it, she was about Danny's age. "Come on. Grab your coat. We're going for a short walk."

"Hat, too?"

"Always a hat, even if it's warm, tuck it in your pocket, because you never know when you'll need it."

Danny threw on his coat without closing the zipper and squished his hat on his head.

As she watched him rush to get ready, she sighed. Technically, he had done everything she told him. She wouldn't squash his creative spirit. As long as he was warm, it didn't matter his gloves didn't match.

He opened the front door and grabbed two cookies off the serving tray on the side table. "Nana has these everywhere."

"She's going through separation anxiety over losing so many budgies."

Danny laughed. "Where are we going?"

She slipped on her jacket, and matching hat and scarf. "A short walk. You said you like ghost stories, so I want to show you a place I thought was haunted when I was a kid. Will you be scared?"

"Nah. The only thing that scares me is when Nana says she's making turnips." Danny shivered.

She patted his head and leaned down to hug him. "You can thank me for saving you from that ghastly fate. I don't like them either, and I've been successful by keeping her distracted. You know one day you have to give in, and suck it up. At least try one turnip."

Danny held her hand and squeezed it. "Well, if you

try one, I will too."

Her heart jumped every time he moved closer. She was scared and unsure how he would adapt to her as his guardian. They saw very little of each other before Carly died. The thought of her walking into his life and picking up where his mother left off was paralyzing—but things seemed to be going well.

Deborah's sneaky way about wanting to know about Danny brought out the mama bear in Kristen. She squeezed her nephew's hand as hard as she could without causing him pain. She would always be there for him.

No one would take him from her.

No one.

The ten-block walk was longer than she remembered, but Danny didn't complain, and she needed some way to burn off cookie calories. She stood at the intersection light waiting for it to turn green. "We're almost there."

"What is this place you're taking me to?"

"You'll see." The light turned green. "Come on. It's right over there." She walked to a small, white clapboard house. The roof sagged, and the windows appeared to be painted shut. She held his hand tight as they walked to the chipped red brick back steps and a rotted wood railing. "Be careful. Are you sure you're not scared? There's still time to go home."

"Nah, I'm fine."

She walked up the stairs and wiped away dust from the window in the back door. "Can you see?"

He nodded, and then stared into the vacant house.

The building had been abandoned for as long as she could remember. One of her wishes in life was to go inside and explore the old Stephens house.

"What's spooky about this place?" Danny stepped back and wrinkled his nose.

"I guess maybe my childhood imagination made it seem scary. The place doesn't appear very spooky. It's an old abandoned house, with no one maintaining the grounds or building."

"Can we go home now? Nana promised to make hot chocolate."

"Yeah, I could use some myself." She walked away from the house, thinking things didn't always turn out to be how they seemed—no matter how perfect.

Was she wrong about Luke?

****

"Good evening. Last-minute shopping for the holiday?"

A young girl greeted Luke as he closed the door behind him.

Peppermint and chocolate wafted through the store. At first, he thought he walked into a candy store but on further examination he viewed a mixture of books, CDs, jewelry, Christmas ornaments, and a cat.

He gently nudged the feline with his foot. "Stuffed?"

"No, very much alive. She sleeps a lot. I think the chimes in the music keep her calm." The salesperson smiled.

"You have quite a collection here. My sister has a shop similar to this around the corner."

"Oh, Deborah's store?"

"Hi." He nodded. "My name is Luke. Yours?"

"Julie. My mother, Marina owns this place. She asked Deborah a few times to go into business together.

Better to be friends than competitors, you know?"

"Interesting." He narrowed his gaze. He vaguely remembered his sister mentioning someone wanted her business but she didn't trust the deal.

"My sister can be—"

"Strange?" Julie laughed.

"I call her eccentric." He smiled. "Well, nice to meet you." He guided his mom through the maze of shelves and tables. The store was a little bit neater than Deborah's but not as organized, which made him nervous walking through the tight aisles.

"Oooo, this is nice." Amanda picked up a pottery, tie-dyed elephant.

"Really? I don't think you have much use for that." He took it from her and returned it to its spot on the table. He didn't have a problem with spending money on her, just not on something he considered wasteful, and was nothing more than a dust collector.

"Luke? Why are we here? Who is that woman?" Mom scanned the store, her eyes wide.

"Mom? Look at me." He waved a hand in front of her face. "Ice cream. Remember? We are going for ice cream."

Amanda stared.

Her eyes looked bewildered and teary. He was grateful for the time she was able to focus, but there would be no dessert.

"Can I help with anything?" Julie came from behind the counter.

"Thank you, but no. I need to take her home." He walked his mother toward the front door.

She stopped short. "Oh my. This looks like home." Mom reached out to pick up a snow globe.

"Let me help you." Julie held the snow scene for Amanda to admire. "This is made by a local artist. It's a scene of the Brookside Falls town center. Alan makes them for the different seasons. This is winter. I'm sure you don't need me to tell you."

"It's my home." Amanda ran a finger along the curve of the glass.

Luke shook his head to signal to Julie his mother's memory failed her.

"It's a lovely scene. And the snow—well it's fitting this time of year. I guess it could be anyone's home." Julie cupped the snow globe.

"Come on, Mom. It's getting late." He nudged her to move.

Julie held the delicate piece against her stomach, protecting it with both hands. "Thank you for visiting. I hope to see you soon. And I hope you get your ice cream."

"She will. She'll have some at home. Thank you for your time." He ushered his mother out of the store. He wanted to get her home before she became too agitated.

He thought he was doing a good thing. Apparently, he was overly optimistic. At least she spent some time out of the home. He didn't like the fact his mother was cooped up in a strange building all day. West Haven did have a lovely setting and he was happy with his choice but—maybe the short days and long nights of winter made him feel isolated.

"Luke?"

He looked behind him, keeping hold on his mom as they approached his car.

Julie rushed up to him.

"Here. Merry Christmas." She handed a gift-wrapped package in a small bag to his mother.

Amanda slid her fingers in the handles and held the bag against her body.

"You shouldn't…" His heart warmed at Julie's generosity.

Mom smiled.

She was pleasant and content. He opened the door.

Amanda slid into the passenger seat.

"Hey, it's Christmas." Julie folded her arms across her chest, fending off cold.

"What do I owe you?" He reached for his wallet.

"Nothing. It's a gift. The globe seemed to make her happy. Isn't that what this time of year is about? Hope, peace, and happiness?" Julie shivered, her teeth chattered.

"Yes, it is. Thank you. Have you been told you're an angel?" He closed the car door and smiled as his mother clung to the snow globe.

"Not recently. But I am trying to earn my wings." Julie beamed a smile.

"Thank you again. If you keep giving away your inventory, your mother won't have a store to run. Merry Christmas." He watched Julie disappear into the shop. *Nice kid, but couldn't be more than nineteen.* He wasn't used to people being so friendly. Maybe he needed to interact more. He'd spent so much time working and huddled at his desk as the world passed him by, that he forgot how to make small talk.

He slid into the driver's seat, and then turned the key. He hung his hands over the steering wheel as he leaned forward and watched the store light go off. He glanced at his watch. The ice cream store was probably closed. He would try another time, during the daytime when his mom seemed to be better.

As he drove back to West Haven, he analyzed how his entire life had been influenced by women. He couldn't think of any dominant male figure in his life. That thought brought him to Danny and Kristen. He adored the kid, and he would be in the same position as when Luke was a child. Not a bad thing, but he lived the emptiness of not having a father in his life.

He had one more stop to make after he dropped off his mother. Could his day get better?

****

"Are you ready for some hot chocolate? It's getting late." Kristen removed her scarf and hung it on the hook in the hallway.

"I've been ready ever since you dragged me to that not-haunted house." Danny stuffed his hat and gloves into his jacket sleeve and handed it to her to hang.

"You know, maybe we shouldn't be hanging our stuff out here in the open where it looks messy. We have guests now." She gathered their belongings and put them in the cedar chest beneath the coatrack. She scooped her nephew in a bear hug. "Do you know how much I love you?"

"To the moon and back." He rolled his eyes.

"Does that embarrass you?"

He nodded.

"Too bad. Your annoyance will make me do it even more. Like in front of your school friends."

"Aunt Kristen. Don't."

"I will. Nothing can stop me. Except a mug of hot chocolate. Beat you to the kitchen." She pushed open the door and found Nana putting a platter of chocolate chip cookies away in the pantry.

"No, Nana. Don't hide the cookies. Aunt Kristen, save those. They're for us." Danny jumped on a stool next to the island.

"I'll take a few for us." She took a dinner plate from the shelf to the left of the stove, and then placed six chocolate chip cookies for a snack.

Danny's maturity surfaced. She wasn't sure if it was age, life changes, or she never paid attention before. His mannerisms were those of his mother. The straight way he held his back when he helped himself onto the stool. How he flipped the forever-in-his-eyes-hank-of-hair away from his face.

She glanced around the room. The three of them would take on what life put in their way. Nana with her experience, Danny with his youthful exuberance and fearlessness, and Kristen with her ability to stand firm in the wake of heartache.

"Is Luke coming back tonight?" Danny clipped a cookie and shoved it in his mouth.

She glanced at the clock. "I don't think so, kid. It's late, and he said he had something to do." Maybe he was never coming back. After she calmed down, it hit her about how unfair she might have been. She didn't give Luke an opportunity to talk. She was so shaken by what she found that she wasn't thinking straight.

Luke texted *her* so that must mean he would be in touch. Had she ruined their relationship that was barely off the ground? She couldn't have sabotaged things so soon. Her average time for relationship implosion was three months. Usually, when the *nice* period was over and everyone involved relaxed and their true colors surfaced. She didn't have the patience for games, and she hadn't found any guy who was above playing games. Hopefully, Luke was different. She poured milk into the old stainless pot always used for making hot chocolate. "Nana, would you like some?"

"No thank you, dear. The caffeine will keep me awake, and I have to sleep and be up early."

"If the hot chocolate keeps you awake, wouldn't that be better? You wouldn't have to waste time sleeping." She stirred chocolate into the simmering milk.

"You're a funny girl, Kristen." Nana pushed open the kitchen door to leave. "Oh, and don't think I don't know about two missing budgies. I would appreciate it if you left my birds alone. Goodnight."

She placed her hand over her mouth, stifling a laugh. "Did you take the birds?"

Danny took another cookie. "Nope. Maybe the guests think the budgies are souvenirs."

The kid has a great sense of humor. All in all, he seemed to be doing well. "Here you go. Piping hot. Be careful."

He pulled his sleeves over his hands and hugged his mug of hot chocolate. "Whipped cream, please."

"One minute." She scoured the refrigerator for a yellow bowl with a red poinsettia. A family heirloom and the only bowl her grandmother used for whipped cream. Ready-made and waiting to be used. "It has to be in here somewhere, hiding in this ridiculous maze of food."

"Try the top right shelf."

"Huh. Yep, that's where it is. How did you know?" She carried the bowl to the island and slapped a dollop of homemade whipped cream in Danny's drink.

"I'm a good detective. Plus, she always keeps it there. None for you?"

She nodded. The truth was her mind was preoccupied. The image of Luke explaining himself kept rolling through her head. She hoped she didn't do too much damage. She refrained from calling him and seeming needy. He told her he had to take care of something. She would leave him alone and wait to hear from him.

She hoped. The last drop of warm chocolate hit her tongue, and she swore no more sweets after the holiday season was over.

"Finished with your hot chocolate?" The sweet aroma lingering in the air made her nose itch.

"Almost. I know. Bedtime."

She nodded.

"And brush my teeth."

"Yes, after every meal."

"I don't do it after lunch in school." He smiled.

"Don't tell me that. I believe you do."

"Nope."

"Do you need me to tuck you in tonight, or are we officially beyond that ritual?" She leaned against the counter, facing him, and watching his reaction.

He wrinkled his nose. "We're past it."

"I thought so." No more kisses made her a little sad. The tedious routines were coming to an end. In a few short months, she watched him change from a frightened child to a young boy who was taking on the world, and everyone better watch out.

She would always be ready to run into his room to comfort him, but she was taking her cues from her nephew now. When she would drop him off at school the few times in Florida and kiss him goodbye, he would reluctantly let her, and then ran away like she had the plague. She remembered being like that but when she was older. Distance behavior must start earlier with boys.

"Done." Danny jumped down from the stool and put his empty mug in the sink.

"Thank you, sir. Good night and remember to brush every tooth not just your two front teeth." She hugged him, knowing she could get away with it when no one was looking, and she treasured those moments.

"Night."

She walked him out of the kitchen and watched him run up the stairs two at a time. As soon as he disappeared around the bend, she stepped out onto the front porch. Flurries fell, and she folded her arms against her chest. She leaned against the post. "You've got a good kid there, Carly. We miss you terribly. Send me a sign every once in a while, to let me know I'm doing okay. Goodnight, sis. Love you."

If only the rest of her life fell into place.

Chapter Eighteen

After dropping his mother at West Haven, Luke stopped at home. He needed time to mull over what happened earlier with Kristen. He wasn't one to leave things unsettled.

He dumped his coffee into the sink and put his coat back on. He ran down the stairs, jumped into his car, and peeled out of his parking spot. He punched off the radio—holiday music was the last thing he wanted to hear. His apartment retreated in the rear-view mirror.

Lighted wreaths adorned the town square of Brookside Falls. Carolers strolled beneath the fifty-foot Norway tree donated to the community. Luke ignored the festivities of the townspeople and made his way onto the highway—the fastest way back to Jackson Corners. He wasn't going to let Deborah ruin his relationship with Kristen.

Fifteen minutes later, he pulled up to the front of the store. The lights were off in the back apartment, but she had to be there, because her car was in her parking spot.

He knocked. "Deborah! Open the door!"

The etched sidelight allowed him to peer into the store. He placed his hand above his right eye and leaned close to the glass. Nothing. But he knew she was there, mourning like she did every Christmas for the past five years. The self-appointed mother, martyr, counselor—

an all-around busybody. Instead of living her own life, she imposed upon others.

Once again, he banged on the door again, and a light went on in the back room of the shop.

She appeared with a shawl draped around her shoulders and carried a white votive candle as she approached the front door. Deborah opened the door.

He pushed his way through, nearly crashing into the wall.

"What's wrong?" She stepped back. "Why are you so upset?"

"I can't believe…" He paced in a circle, holding his chin.

"Why are you so excited? Is everything okay?" Deborah clutched her shawl at her throat.

Drawing a deep breath, he leaned against the wall. "Did you know Brian had a child?"

Deborah stepped farther away.

He didn't intend to scare her, but he was furious. Never had he become upset with her to the point of anger. Annoyed, yes, but never so mad he wanted to scream.

"I…" She placed the pine-scented candle on a table and gathered her shawl around her arms. "I never told you because he didn't want people to know."

Luke glared. "You knew?"

She lowered her head. "Yes."

"Did you know that child is Kristen's nephew, Danny?" He crossed his arms as he stared into her eyes, searching her face for clues as he waited for the truth.

"Yes, I did." She sat on a bench along the wall.

"So, you knew the night at the ice cream store. You knew when Kristen invited you to dinner. You declined, changed your mind, and came anyway." He shook his head. "I can't believe you didn't tell me about this. You knew I was getting involved with her. You didn't think I should know?"

She got up from the bench. "I'm tired. Can we discuss this another day?"

"Absolutely not!" He put out his arm to hold her back. "I've been the illegitimate child in this family long enough. I've tried my best to forge some sort of relationship with you and Brian. I'm tired of feeling like I don't belong. What happened is not my fault!" He breathed deeply and rested his hands on her shoulders. She seemed much older and shorter. The darkness that hung over the room intensified the heaviness he carried. They'd worked hard to be a family, but most times their relationship only worked on her terms, especially since Brian died.

"Listen, I don't want this to come between us, but I want to know why you never told me about Brian having a son. Especially now I am getting involved with the woman who is raising him."

Again, she sat on the bench and pulled her shawl tight across her chest. "Brian never had much to do with his son. He didn't acknowledge him when he was born. He never even gave him his name." Deborah blinked back tears so eager to dampen her cheeks. "His dismissal of his child was the one thing I despised about him," she lowered her voice.

Luke relaxed his shoulders and rubbed his temples with his thumb and middle finger. "What?" He spoke softer. He didn't want to be the one to send her spiraling deeper into the grief she had been clawing her way out of for years.

"I forgave a lot of the stupid things he did, but not owning up to being the father of his own child—I couldn't accept that. It reminded me…" She looked up with a weak smile. "…of Daddy and you. The difference was Brian wasn't married. He had no excuse for making a kid illegitimate and ignoring him." Her head dropped, and her shoulders heaved up and down.

He sat next to her. The two of them—all alone to deal with the poor choices made by their family—in the darkness, illuminated only by the flicker of a lone candle.

Deborah lifted her head and wiped her nose with the edge of her shawl. She got up, walked over to the counter, and came back a picture. "Look at this." She held it out to Luke.

"It's Brian's picture when he was in college. So?" He held it like it meant nothing.

"No, back here." She reached across Luke and flipped around the picture. She pulled off the back and handed him the letter.

Luke opened the letter and instantly recognized it. "Kristen showed this to me tonight. Carly kept a copy in her diary. That's how Kristen found out who Danny's father was. Carly never told anyone."

"Neither did Brian. Small town gossip, in my opinion. I imagine it was worse for Carly." Deborah took the picture.

"You think that's why they didn't tell anyone?" A lump formed in his throat. The day had been an emotional rollercoaster.

"Could be. Makes the most sense to me, especially with Brian being away. And face it, he was irresponsible with most everything he did. Look at how he died. Alcohol. He couldn't hold his liquor." She walked back to the counter, and then returned with a letter. "There's something I haven't been able to do."

He took the envelope and leaned against the storefront window to catch light from the street lamp. "It's addressed to Carly."

"I know. I could never bring myself to open it. I found it in his car the night he died. My guess is that is why he went to the post office. I took it so the police wouldn't." She rested her head against the wall.

He stood and tapped the letter in the palm of his hand. He wanted to tear it open, but the contents were private. But whatever was in the letter belonged to Danny like the letters Deborah and Kristen possessed. Those two letters proved Brian was Danny's father. "I know it's been hard on you. All your life you took care of the family. I know your mother was detached from you and Brian after your father strayed. And I always believed you blamed me somehow, whenever you looked at me. But you know I'm not responsible for his behavior. I'm the result." Luke was relieved to finally tell her. For years, he'd held his true feelings in and finally his heart was lighter.

"I know. It was easier to blame you, somehow. I realized a long time ago it wasn't the right way to look at the situation. But every time I looked at you, I was reminded of what destroyed our family, the Reeves family." She wiped a tear.

He looked dead into her eyes. "How did you think I was affected? An illegitimate child, not given my father's name. Not even allowed to live in the same town or go to school with my own siblings. Birthdays spent alone." He paced back and forth, breathing deeply to quell his anger.

"I know. I truly do know, but not at that time. And I'm sorry." She stood and hugged him. "We have to bring this letter to Kristen. It's only right she be there when we open it."

Luke let out a sarcastic chuckle. "She doesn't want to see me. She told me so. Her actual quote was, 'I never want to see you again.' So maybe I should let her be for a while."

"Not if you love her. It's been too long now, so don't wait any longer." She picked up the candle.

"What do you mean it's been too long?" He reached out and held her arm.

"Oh, Luke, I've known since you were a kid you were in love with Kristen. The gossip ricocheted all around school how you made a fool of yourself at the fair, not on purpose, but I knew from the moment you laid your eyes on her."

She left him standing in the light shining through the window as she walked back to her apartment behind the store.

She returned a few minutes later with her purse and coat then she blew out the candle. "Let's go.

For the first time, he agreed with his sister. But would Kristen be willing to talk to him?

****

Kristen stopped and pressed her ear against Danny's bedroom door on the way to her own room. Blankets rustled, and she was sure he had the covers over his head with a flashlight nuzzled in the crook of his neck. As long as he was reading, she didn't mind. He surprised her with his book collection. At seven, he owned more titles than she read in her thirty-three years. She kissed her palm and pressed it against her nephew's door. "Sleep tight, buddy."

Her whisper was too low for him to hear, but she did it every night since he came to live with her. From his first scared night in Florida to the comfort of the family inn, he was settling in, and she loved taking care of him. Though he was pretty self-sufficient for a young boy, she was determined to impress upon him the importance of family.

With the thought foremost in her mind, she stole away to her bedroom for much-needed alone time. The threat of snow made her long for her patchwork quilt, handmade by her grandmother, and fuzzy socks decorated with holly.

Settled onto the bed, she slid deep into the middle and stacked three pillows behind her head. No matter how big the bed, she always slept in the middle. She reached for an old mystery paperback she found on the shelf of books in the downstairs gathering room, as her grandmother called it. She thumbed through the brittle pages and tossed the book to the side. She wasn't much of a mystery fan anyway.

She took Carly's diary from the night table drawer and rested the book on her chest as she lay back, lost in the softness and comfort of her bed. She must have reread her sister's entries a dozen times and memorized every word. The passage where Carly wrote of Brian's sister, but never mentioned a brother, confused her. Maybe Carly never met Luke. But she knew Brian since they were teenagers, so how could she not know anything about his brother?

Their history was so confusing. She put aside the journal, maybe she was misinterpreting the passages in the book. Without her sister to fill in the blanks—any further thought was an assumption. She envisioned Carly sitting in the window seat of her room—knees curled up to her chest, staring out the window, looking for words to fill the pages.

A few more hours to Christmas. Songs filtered in through the windows from the carolers walking the streets of Brookside Falls. Joy weaved its way into her world, and for a moment, she wanted to run outside and join them. But sleep was sneaking up, and she was fighting to stay awake.

Her gut told her Luke would be back, and she didn't want to miss him. The minutes ticked by, and her upset lessened. Maybe the hopefulness of the season, or she simply believed everything would be okay made the night better.

Even though she would have preferred to stay at the shore in New Jersey, life for Danny would be much better in Brookside Falls where he could explore the woods and run around without the restrictions of living in the city. The shore could be their vacation spot.

Ring.

She bolted upright. Luke? A quick glance at the caller ID let her know it wasn't him but her friend Gina. "Hello, stranger. I was thinking about my old home."

"Hey, Kristen. How are things going?" Gina shoved a potato chip in her mouth. The crunch with each word gave it away.

She sat upright and hugged her knees against her chest. The quilt swirled around her fuzzy-covered feet. "It's going well. Danny is adjusting. My grandmother seems happy to have us here."

"She still has all those stuffed birds you told me

about?" Gina laughed.

Kristen smiled. "Not as many. Me and the kid have been attempting to thin out the brood, or flock, whatever a lot of parakeets are called."

"Not to be mean, but I think it's called crazy."

Gina was never one for subtlety. They met when Kristen got her first job as a hairstylist down at the shore. At first, they didn't get along. Competition for clients was fierce, but once Gina realized Kristen wasn't after her clientele, things cooled down and they became fast friends.

"What are you doing for the holidays? My mom's having over the family, you know, same stuff every year."

She would miss Christmas dinner at the Rozella house. The food went on for rooms of tables covered in whatever fish, fowl, beef, or pork Gina's mother cooked. Each main dish had at least five different sides, usually pasta salad, shrimp cocktail, chicken soup, tortellini soup, broccoli rabe, green beans, and mashed potatoes—food madness. She was guaranteed to gain at least five pounds at dinner. She did her best to stay away from the appetizers and antipasto, which were calorie enemies for sure. "I'll miss the care packages. I never had to cook for the next week."

"Oh, honey, who are you kidding? You never cook."

Gina was right. As much as Kristen tried her best, if somewhat sporadic culinary attempts, she promised she would learn how to cook even to take some of the pressure off her grandmother. "I'm trying." Kristen laughed. "And stop munching those chips in my ear."

"Stopped. Anything new up there? Meet someone?

How's the shop coming?"

"Well, I did meet someone, but I'm not sure what the deal is. Nothing serious yet, and it's complicated."

"Tell me."

"Nothing to tell yet. I'm focusing on Danny, making sure he's finding his footing with school work. He'll be starting regular school after the holidays. My grandmother has been a huge help. And the shop is finished. I have to check the punch list and order supplies, which shouldn't take too long. Will you come up to see it? I think you'll be impressed."

"You kidding? I was impressed when you told me what you were doing. All those years, us working for someone else. It's nice to see one of us moving ahead."

"Hmm, and it's funny." She sat upright, flipped her hair behind her shoulder, and then tucked a pillow against her belly. "I didn't have any plan to open my own shop. The arrangement fell into place through no suggestion of my own."

"Well, I'm glad things worked out, sweetie. I'll see you soon. Please keep me up to date."

"Will do. I have to go too. Love you." She ended the call and smiled with joy, realizing for the first time how much she had accomplished in a few short months.

She glanced at the time. Way too early for her to go to sleep. She climbed off the bed and walked to Danny's room and tapped on the door. "Hey. You still up?" She opened the door quietly and poked her head into his room. "It's the night before Christmas Eve. I say we're entitled to another round of hot chocolate. Meet you downstairs." She headed down to the kitchen, excited for the next chapter of her life. Talking to Gina gave her the emotional lift she needed. What would the holiday bring?

****

The Brookside Falls Inn was alive with Christmas lights strung through the trees in the front yard. Scotch Pine wreaths, each adorned with a red velvet bow, and pinecones were complete with a battery-operated candle and hung on the front windows and door. Snow fell as he pulled up to the house. Luke loved Kristen, and he had to make her believe him. He had to convince her he was not a player in the web of deceit. "You have the letters, right?" He pulled into an available parking spot.

Deborah checked her purse. "Yes."

The history of Danny's parents whittled down to words on two pieces of paper. Unsure if sharing them would be the smart thing to do but sure to be the right thing. Danny had a right to know the truth surrounding his birth, even if it would be years from now. "Ready?" Luke took a deep breath and turned off the car.

Deborah nodded and patted the purse held tightly on her lap.

Luke got out of the car and opened the door for his sister. Anger was futile, he knew better. Even if Brian had a troubled past, his son should have the right to know one day. Luke directed his sister to walk around the side to the back of the house. He figured fewer people would be hanging around in the kitchen, and he could have a private conversation. His assumption was correct; no one was in the room. He quietly opened the kitchen door and slipped into the room.

Kristen sat on the living room window seat with Danny.

Luke checked his watch. Nine o'clock—he couldn't wait much longer. He had to convince her he had never known Brian was Danny's father. He put his finger to his lips. "Sssshh. Stay here."

Deborah stood by the sink.

He pushed open the swinging door and walked over to Kristen. The crackling fire and music muffled his steps. He reached for her as he approached.

"Luke!" Danny spun around on the window seat. "I thought you left for good." He jumped up and hugged him.

"I had to take care of something." He patted Danny's head while looking straight at Kristen.

She continued to watch the heavy snow as it fell.

"Do you want a cookie?" Danny stood next to Luke, holding his hand.

"No, buddy, not now. I need to talk to your aunt."

She ignored him.

"I need to talk to you, Kristen. I have something to show you now," he said in a calm but firm tone.

"Sweetie, get ready for bed. I'll be up in a few minutes to check on you." She kissed her nephew on the cheek.

"Do I have to brush my teeth again?"

"Of course, you do. You drank hot chocolate. Scoot."

Danny started to leave and hesitated. "You're not mad at Luke, are you?"

"Bed." She shooed him away and watched him leave the room. Taking in a deep breath, she steadied herself. "I told you I didn't want to talk to you." She stood and shoved her hands in her back pockets.

"We have to talk. I have to make you believe I didn't know"—he looked around and lowered his voice—"about Brian and Danny." He ran his hand through his hair, frustration consumed him. He took her hand and pulled her into the kitchen.

"What's she doing here?" Kristen's eyes narrowed.

"Both of you, sit. Please." He pulled out two chairs.

Deborah sat.

Yet Kristen hesitated.

Luke planted his hands on the kitchen table. "You must listen. I didn't know until you showed me the letter that Brian was Danny's father. I swear to you. I didn't know."

Kristen slid into the chair, and then sat with her arms across her chest.

He was at a loss for any other way to convince her he was innocent, but he would do whatever means it took to convince her. Could he make her believe him?

"How do I know you and Deborah aren't conspiring to take away Danny?"

He shook his head and threw up his hands. "I don't know how to convince you. I don't know what more I can say."

Deborah cleared her throat. "I have something we should read together." She removed the unopened letter from her purse. "I don't know how much you know about our brother, but he had a lot of problems. Brian was an immature, free spirit—sorry, I digress. I knew about Danny, but Luke didn't. Brian didn't tell anyone but me. After the scandal with my father and Luke's mother, well, Brian hadn't wanted his child to go through the same hell Luke did. Anyway, this letter was found in Brian's car the night he died." She handed it to Kristen.

"It's not opened." She handed it back to Deborah.

"I haven't been able to read it. I figured the day would come, and it has. I think it's only right we do it together, since I'm sure it must be tied to both families because it's addressed to Carly." Deborah handed back the letter to Kristen. "I think you should be the person to open it."

Luke pulled up a chair.

Kristen carefully opened the envelope. "From the writing, I assume Brian was left-handed, like Danny."

"Silent Night" streamed through the speakers.

She unfolded the letter and read it aloud.

Dear Carly,

I hope you and Danny are doing well. I'm finally getting my act together. I've moved back to Jackson Corners to get away from the bad influences feeding my addiction. I haven't drunk any alcohol for a week. It's hard, but I agree. If I'm to be in Danny's life, I have to be sober.

I have a confession. I know we made a pact not to tell anyone I was Danny's father because of my father's history and my inability to be a good parent. I did tell Deborah. I didn't mean to, but it came out one night as I was confessing my sins. No one else in my family knows—no one. I know Deborah will keep the secret; she's good that way.

I want to take another month of sobriety before I head down to Florida. Thanks for sending pictures when you can. I know it's hard to keep track of me moving around so much. It's a good thing Danny has at least one stable parent.

Always know I do love you and understand your reasons for making me stay away until I could get sober. It sucks it took so long. See you soon.

Love,
Brian

Kristen stared at her hands while her lips trembled. "So, Carly never knew."

"We don't know that." Luke chimed in. "We don't know if they ever spoke on the phone before he wrote the letter. It sounds to me like they had some discussion."

She waved the letter in the air. "Why would he write it?"

"Brian actually started writing down pretty much everything. That was his way of being accountable. That way if he drank and couldn't remember, he had something to get him back on track." Deborah stood. "You keep the letter. I just ask you give me a copy when you can."

Kristen gently folded the paper. "Of course."

Luke wanted to give her time to process the news. Brian's letter was the only evidence he had that proved he didn't know about Danny until Kristen showed him her letter. "We'll go now."

She stood and motioned to Luke. "Follow me."

He was willing to take cues from Kristen. Whatever it took to make the situation better. Leaving Deborah behind, he followed Kristen up the stairs to Danny's room.

"He's been asking for you all night. Do you know how difficult it is to be mad at someone who is adored by a seven-year-old?" Kristen leaned her ear against Danny's bedroom door, and then cracked it open. "Good, you're still awake. I wanted to give you a goodnight kiss before you went to bed. And I figured you wanted to see Luke before he left." She sat on the edge of his bed.

Danny snuggled close. "It's difficult to see Mommy's star tonight. The snow got in the way."

"Oh, it's there. Give me a hug and off to bed. I'm sure you'll get a big surprise tomorrow." She kissed him on the forehead and hugged him tight as a tear slid down her nose.

"Luke, I think Santa gave me my present early."

"How so, buddy?"

Danny reached up and hugged Luke. "He brought you to me and Aunt Kristen."

Luke's breath caught as he fought back tears and wished for the best.

Chapter Nineteen

Kristen was pleased the day promised to be sunny and warmer. Nana was busy booking sleigh rides and setting out a never-ending rotation of cookies from the oven to the gathering room.

"Who's next on the list?" Nana wiped her hands on her apron printed with strands of Christmas lights. She wore her poinsettia silk flower with a yellow and red light in the center that simulated the seeds of the flower. Later that night, she was sure to adorn her neck with a necklace made out of plastic colored light bulbs that lit up whenever she laughed.

Kristen set aside Christmas Eve morning to be available and help where needed. They turned down reservations. People called to see if they could at least make a reservation for dinner. Nope, sorry, was her answer because meals were for guests only.

Whatever Gladys did to advertise the reopening of a previously-closed-for-decades inn was a success. Kristen definitely needed Gladys to work her magic for the salon since that income was needed to carry them through the year after the inn's winter business died down.

Of course, they would try to find ways to expand guest interest and urge them to come back in spring and summer. They could focus on the county fairs in the fall, and maybe set up tours with the local pick-your-own fruit farms in the area. Another option was to advertise surrounding businesses. Jackson Corners, sprinkled with hands-on artisan stores, could be an easy enticement to bring tourists to the Brookside Falls area.

"Kristen, dear." Nana waddled.

Her concentration broken, she returned to the organized chaos of her grandmother. "What do you need?"

"Here. I forgot to go to the bank. Would you please run this deposit down there? Marty already picked up my outgoing mail, and I wrote checks."

Sigh. She lost count of how many times she told her grandmother to stop sending the checks until the money is in the bank. "Sure, no problem. Danny!" Her nephew was likely bored and could use an hour or so outside the inn. It wouldn't be so bad if the guests had kids with them, but none did. Danny wouldn't start school until after the New Year, and he hadn't made any friends in the neighborhood, mainly because the homes were so far apart from each other.

If only she could figure a way to encourage him to be more social and not depend on her so much for companionship. He needed friends his own age. So did she.

Of course, Gina was only a phone call away, but she missed having someone to go see a movie with or spend some time wandering through the mall. Having someone to catch up over a cup of coffee would be nice.

"What's up, Aunt Kristen?" Danny huffed and puffed and nearly ran her over before stopping short of plowing down Nana.

"We're taking a walk. Grab your jacket."

"But I…"

"Whatever you're doing, you can continue when we get back." She slipped on her jacket and flung her scarf around her neck.

"Okay, whatever you say." Danny removed his jacket from the cedar chest and pushed his arm through the sleeve, knocking his hat and gloves out the opening and onto the floor.

"How many times do I have to tell you to take them out first?" She shook her head.

"It's more fun this way."

"Hmm, I'm sure." She wondered when she became a stickler for good behavior. Not that she didn't have some stories of her own but a different realm of expectations swooped down on her the minute she realized caring for her nephew would be her life. She patted him on the head. "Come on. Let's go."

"Brrrr, it's freezing." Danny pulled down his hat over his ears.

"We won't be out long. The fresh country air will do you some good." Geez, she sounded like her grandfather. Maybe her grandmother was right and he was still lurking around the halls of the inn. Her first thought was to walk to the bank, but the wind kicked up and bit her on the nose. The ring of sleigh bells caught her ear, and she turned to see where they were coming from.

The postman was at the reins. He slowed down as the horse trotted closer.

"Got the day off, Mr. Parsons?" She shielded her eyes from the sun glare bouncing off the snowbanks.

"Yep, I do this every year since Pete retired. He started this tradition, and I didn't want to see it retire with him. So, I bought the getup. Hat and all." Paul Parsons tipped his top hat with a black satin band adorned with a sprig of holly.

"It's a nice tradition. Thank you for keeping it alive."

"Ever ride in a sleigh, Danny?" Mr. Parsons leaned down and smiled.

"No, sir." Danny shook his head.

"Well, you will today. Hop in."

"Is it okay?"

Danny's eyes begged. "I think so. It's rude to turn down an invitation." She hoisted Danny into the seat. She climbed in behind him and spread the red-plaid, flannel blanket across their laps and pulled it up to their chins.

"Wow! This is cool!" Danny jumped around in his seat. "Look at his butt."

Mr. Parsons turned around and looked down at Danny.

"I'm sure he means the horse. He's a seven-year-old boy." She shook her head. "Stop being silly."

"I've never been behind a horse. It looks different from behind."

"I'm sure it does." She pulled his head into the crook of her neck. "Just be gracious. Mr. Parsons, will you be driving by the bank?"

"I can if you like. Bring you back also. I have some folks to pick up at your grandma's inn. It will be a perfect exercise for Trixie here."

"Thank you very much." She leaned back and snuggled with Danny to keep him warm. Only his eyes peeked out from the blanket. She closed her eyes and thought how nice it would be to have Luke sitting beside her. Time had a way of pushing aside her anger.

****

A quick check at the office revealed no calls. Business slowed during the holiday week, and Luke expected the lull to continue through the New Year. No sense in making daily stops until after the holidays. He didn't know how to relax and dismiss the obligatory need to go to work every day. This Christmas Eve would be different. No business calls. No sitting at the desk shuffling through papers. He spent many holidays holed up in his office, mainly as a way to ignore the festivities. He believed the road to success was paved with work and no interference. Frivolous moments didn't contribute to building a successful business.

Since moving to Haineswood, he was seeing life differently. Meeting Kristen and Danny showed him what true happiness was in spite of heartbreak.

He ran his fingers down a branch of his Christmas tree. The needles sprung back like the evergreen that had been recently cut. *Still healthy*. He would leave it up until the New Year and take the tree down on January first. Why not reap as much enjoyment as he could?

A topping off of water in the base and he was done with the office for the day. His heart was light in spite of what happened with Kristen, and he wanted to visit her, whether she was willing to see him or not. But first, he had some errands to run. He locked the door behind him, and then stopped into the deli. "Good morning, Leo. How are you today?"

The deli clerk turned and smiled. "You're in an unusually good mood."

"Must be the season." He mixed his coffee with

cream and sugar, grabbed his usual buttered roll, and then placed a fifty-dollar bill on the counter. "Thank you, and have a nice Christmas."

"Luke, you—"

He waved a hand above his head as he walked out of the deli. Christmas brought out his generosity. He learned not to weigh his happiness against how much money he had in his wallet or the balance of his bank account. Even if things didn't work out with Kristen, he wasn't going down without giving his all. He watched his mother grow older, as her life slipped away, and no one by her side. He didn't want that for him.

Traffic was light, and he pulled up to the florist shop. He wasn't sure if Joan would be open but gave it a shot. He smiled as he entered the door. His favorite shopkeeper stood behind the counter tying a red velvet bow onto a wreath decorated with silver balls, snow-tipped pinecones, white birch branches, pink angels, and gold-glitter bells. "Hello. Are there enough decorations?" He laughed.

"This one is a special order for a resident at the assisted living in Jackson Corners. Every year she asks for the same thing. Each item means something. Personally, it's not my favorite arrangement, but it's what she wants."

"West Haven?" He raised his brow.

"Yes."

"I'm going there today. That's why I stopped in, to get something for my mother. I could also bring your delivery."

"I knew you were sent to me for a reason. My angel from New Jersey."

Blood rushed to his cheeks. Not much made him

blush, but Joan had a way of making it happen. "No problem at all. Do you have small, potted, decorated Christmas trees?" He looked around but didn't notice any.

"On Christmas Eve?" Joan peered over her glasses and laughed. "Of course, not many. But I do order extra because someone is bound to need a last-minute gift. How many do you need?"

He counted off on his fingers. *Deborah, Mom, Danny, Kristen, Nana.* "Five."

Joan closed one eye and tilted back her head. "Take what I have left and they're yours. I should have eight but only pay me for the five you want. Consider the extra three payment for delivery and time saved."

"Deal." Unsure what he would do with extra trees, he reached across the counter and shook Joan's hand. The warmth of her personality ran up his arm. He was liking his new town better each day.

"Be right back."

He glanced at his watch. Hours flew by, and it was later than he thought so he mentally juggled his schedule around for the day.

Ring.

The bell over the door interrupted his thoughts.

"Luke, dear. I never expected to run into you here."

He turned and was accidentally smacked in the cheek by his aunt Gladys as she reached up to hug him. "Funny seeing you here also."

"Oh, I come here often. Joan is the best florist in the county. I have some last-minute gifts to pick up, I guess as does everyone today." Gladys shoved her black square purse up her elbow with her white-gloved hand.

Her outfit reminded him of actresses from television shows from the 60s.

"Here you go." Joan pulled a kid's steel red wagon behind her hauling the trees. "Decorated and all. I even threw on some tinsel I had lying around. You might think it's old-fashioned but I like the stuff. Hey, Gladys. Your nephew is becoming my best customer." Joan laid the wreath in the wagon. "The recipient's info is in the card attached to the bow."

"They're perfect. The size I was looking for." Luke took the wagon handle. "Can I use this to take them out to the car?"

"Of course, leave it next to the bench out front, and I'll send the bill to your office. I have the information. Register is closed for the day."

"Thanks." He caught a look of concern between the women. Must be a female thing.

"Does he know yet?"

He overheard Joan ask Gladys.

"No. I figure it's best Deborah tells him."

Still within earshot, he heard his aunt's failed attempt at a whisper. He loaded the trees into the back of his car and placed one in his aunt's car with a note.

Thank you for all you have done. Merry Christmas.
Love,
Luke

But what was his sister hiding from him?

****

Mr. Parsons pulled back on the reins, bringing Trixie to a halt. "And here we are. Back at the inn. I hope you enjoyed the ride."

"That was so much fun! Can we do it again?" Danny jumped out of the horse-drawn sleigh and patted the animal's rump.

"Thank you so much, Mr. Parsons, it was a wonderful ride. You see the town from a different perspective." Kristen stepped down from her seat.

"Yes, and that's why it's so important for me to keep the tradition going. Progress and corporations can ramp up the speed of living as much as they want, but every person needs to sit back from time to time and relax. Take in life from a different angle." Mr. Parsons tipped his hat.

She reached into her pocket.

"Oh, no. No charge, especially for you, dear. You helped bring the inn back in business. That is enough payment for this old man's heart. Consider this trip my trial run for the season."

"How long will you be operating?" She shielded her eyes from the late morning sun.

"Starting at dusk. It's a prettier trip around town. Do you mind if I use the trails behind the inn? I wouldn't be too late. Probably no later than eight."

"That would be fine. I'm sure you'll get more business if the guests see you coming through the woods. I like how the lights outline the sled."

"These battery-powered lights are amazing. This will be the first year I'm doing it. You don't think it's not too much?"

"I think it's perfect. Thank you again. Oh, how long into the season?"

"I plan to be available for tours until New Year's Day."

"Wonderful. I'll spread the word."

With a gentle tap of the reins, he convinced Trixie to proceed ahead.

"Did you ever see a horse drawn sleigh in Florida?" She rested a hand on her nephew's shoulder and smiled she'd made him happy.

"Nope. One, there's no snow in Florida. And I don't know if they have horses."

"Oh, I'm sure they do, but not on the beach pulling a sled. Hot chocolate?"

Without a response, Danny ran up the front steps.

She knew the mention of hot chocolate had him heading for the kitchen. She didn't bother to run in after him, Nana surely had a pot ready to be poured. She fiddled about the front of the inn, straightening the gnomes. The biggest one tended to tip over at the slightest gust of wind.

A car pulled into the gravel parking spot.

Bent over, she peeked through her hair without lifting her head.

Luke.

She hid her smile, unhappy they didn't have their talk and she had questions, but her gut fluttered with happiness to see him. She had done a lot of thinking since he came over with Deborah. And something told her his sister was still hiding something. She composed herself, then stood to greet him and three Christmas trees. Her folded arms gave no indication she would help—at least not without an explanation.

"I come bearing gifts that keep on giving. Plant them in the woods, and they will grow to be big Christmas trees one day."

"That's if they have roots. Usually a potted tree like this is the top that has been cut off, stuck in dirt, and made to look like a viable tree."

"You mean I got hustled?" His jaw dropped.

She grabbed her stomach and held it to keep from hurting while she laughed. "Hustled? By whom?"

"Joan my personal florist."

"Well, yeah, if it's Joan then most likely you got taken."

Luke hung his head and sighed. "One is yours for the taking, so choose."

"Hmm." She walked close and tapped her lips with her index finger as she mulled over the selection. "This one has a red package, I like red. But this one has a shiny silver bow—"

"Will you please take one?"

"Silver bow wins." She took the red ornament from one and placed it on her new tree. "There, best of both choices."

"I only offered you a tree because it was heavy to carry."

"Figures." She smiled, took the tree, and held open the door.

He walked into the inn. "It's beautiful. You must have a warehouse of Christmas decorations."

"Not quite but close. It's been so many years since they have been put out, but if Nana finds a box and if it's red, green, silver, or gold, it must be hung. Organized hoarding, I think it's called."

Luke maneuvered through the hallway to the lobby, clinging to the trees, careful to not disturb some precariously placed antique decorations.

"What are those for?"

"Not what, who. Nana and Danny."

She smiled. The fact he gave Danny his own tree was—well—her heart melted. How many men would do something like that? "Wait. Is this a ploy to get close to Danny? So you have leverage?" She narrowed her eyes and crossed her arms, blocking his entrance to the kitchen.

"No. I thought it would be nice if everyone had their own tree. Don't you think they'll make interesting night lights? Did you notice?"

She looked at the tree. "No, I didn't." She wavered between upset and happy. "That will be a very cool night light." At night in her room with only the light of the Christmas tree was a pleasant image. Luke did good. She placed her tree on a side table and held open the kitchen door. "They're in there. Danny's surely stuffing his face with enough sugar to sustain him for five years and Nana baking cookies on autopilot.

"Hi, Luke!" Danny yelled with a mouth of chocolate fudge.

Nana rushed past him. "Hot. Hot. Hot."

Luke backed away, knowing all too well he was in the way. He waited until she put down the tray and handed her a tree. "Merry Christmas Eve. And Danny, this one is for you."

"Wow, my very own tree?" He looked at Luke and then his aunt.

"Yes, your very own tree. I think it will look nice on your night table."

"Thanks, Luke."

Nana wiped her hands on her apron. "Thank you, Luke is very—what's that?"

"What?" Kristen looked around the kitchen. "What?"

"That." Nana held onto the tree.

Luke crouched down on the floor and pulled Kristen down with him and pointed. "See?"

She turned to her nephew. "Danny. What have I told you about that snake?"

"Sorry. I was trying to tell you he got loose."

Luke grabbed the tail popping out from under a side cart and retrieved the reptile. "Here, Bud. I think he'll be a lot safer in his tank in your room."

Danny hugged the tree with one arm and took his pet from Luke. "Thank you. Sorry, Nana."

Kristen took the potted tree from her grandmother and hugged her. "I'm sure it was an accident. I'll do better and make sure this doesn't happen again. Are you okay?"

"Sometimes that boy scares me to death."

"But he's cute, right?"

Nana smiled. "Yes, he's a keeper. You two have a date?"

Kristen tilted her head. "Why are you here? To deliver trees?"

"Actually, no." He leaned toward her. "I'd like to talk."

She was caught off guard by the glint in his eye and hesitated, but nothing got resolved if not confronted. "Nana, can—"

"I'll take care of Danny." Nana nodded and smiled.

"Thank you. Do I need anything special? Loose pet-catching supplies? Skis? Money for bail?"

"You think you're funny." He choked back a laugh.

"Sometimes. It lightens the mood, especially when it's been dark. Though my night light Christmas tree will come in handy. I hope they're not flashing lights, which can be annoying when I'm trying to sleep."

"I'm sure the tree will be fine. You can always

unplug it if it bothers you."

"True. Okay, Nana, see you soon. I have my cell on if you need me." She took a deep breath and braced herself for their pending conversation.

Chapter Twenty

Luke buckled his seat belt and adjusted the rearview mirror. "You buckled in?"

"Yes. Why? Are you taking me on a race track?"

"No, but I am pressed for time."

He placed a hand on her knee. "I'm sure you have questions, but I need answers before I can tell you everything I know. My first stop is Deborah's shop. Joan and Gladys mentioned something about me knowing something that sounded secretive. My guess is the answer lies with my sister."

"How do you know?" Her nose wrinkled and eyes narrowed.

"They said so."

"Amazing detective work. And I do enjoy a good mystery so I'll go along for the ride."

He backed out of the parking lot and pulled onto Main Street and headed for the road into Jackson Corners. "I know Deborah can be strange, but a lot was put on her when her mother died. She raised Brian, and he had issues. I guess she took it upon herself for his successes and failures. Unfortunately, the failures became more than not."

"But he was a grown-up."

"I know but, what can I say?" Snow dusted the car hood. "The self-imposed pressure of caring for him coupled with her own quirkiness was overwhelming at times. She never had anyone by her side." He realized at that moment of his attempt to convince himself he didn't want to make a mistake. He wanted Kristen in his life, so he would have to tread carefully.

"I can understand what pressure feels like, and Danny is a good kid."

"So was Brian. He was adventuresome, and it wasn't until college he started drinking. I always figured if we had been closer, maybe between me and Deborah, we could have saved him."

"From that letter Deborah held onto, it sounded like he figured out his life and attempted to make things right." She leaned back and folded her arms.

He noticed she did that when she was thinking. Now wasn't a good time to pick her brain. He wanted to get to Deborah's and tie up loose strings in one meeting so he could move on without any hidden doubt or secrets.

"Deborah never had a boyfriend?"

He shrugged his shoulders. "Not that I know of. But she's always been secretive. I figured because she was a girl. Not growing up with them kept me out of the loop. It's difficult to explain."

"I won't badger you. It's your background. If you need to talk, I'm here for you."

That gave him an immense glimmer of hope that she was realizing he didn't know Brian was Danny's father. Deborah would have no intention of taking the kid away from Kristen, but he was beginning to understand her distrust of the situation.

Something nagged in the pit of his stomach ever since he overheard Joan and his aunt at the florist shop. He wasn't leaving his sister's house until he had his answer. "I need to talk to Deborah and prefer you are there with me. But onto another subject. Are you ready to open your shop?"

Kristen plunged her hands into her jacket pockets and slid down in her seat. "I'm petrified. I never ran my own business. I decided not to open until after the holidays are over. Let my grandmother enjoy her grand opening. I need to be there to help her. Once things calm down, maybe I'll feel better equipped to take on the shop."

"Tom did a great job."

"He did, didn't he? Nice guy. I would recommend him to anyone. What do you want to know from your sister?"

With his composure on edge, he took a deep breath. "You're going to keep the conversation on me, aren't you?"

"Pretty much."

He hesitated, then glanced at her. "You said you wouldn't badger me."

"Caught like a rat in a trap." She twisted her lips.

Maybe he needed to talk in order to work through the situation. He sighed. "I feel she hasn't told me everything about my past. With my mother unable to tell me most things, I have to rely on Deborah to tell my story."

"Well, I hope she has the answer you're looking for."

"Me, too." He pulled onto Broad Street and parked in front of the store. He probably should have called and let his sister know he was coming for a visit. Then again it might be best to catch her off-guard.

"Are you sure you want me to be here when you

have your talk? I can easily walk around town and amuse myself." Kristen put a hand on the car door handle ready to exit.

"I would prefer if you stayed. As another woman, you would have a better sense of picking up on things I might miss."

"Like?" Kristen folded her arms across her chest and cocked her head.

"I don't know." He turned to her. "Doesn't your gender have intuition, or instincts that hone in on when someone is lying or telling the truth?"

"So it's been said." Kristen laughed. "I'll do my best."

He got out of the car and walked around to the passenger door and opened it.

"Thank you, kind sir."

He tipped his make-believe hat and held out his arm to guide her to the front door.

She waited.

He took a deep breath and prepared himself, for what, he didn't know. The churning in his stomach drove him to believe a secret was associated with him, and the answer lay behind that front door. "Ready?"

Kristen looked at him and tilted her head, hands in her pockets. "That's up to you. It's your conversation."

"I know. I'm stalling. She can be scary." He shuddered.

Kristen laughed. "I'm sure she's harmless, a bit odd but there's nothing wrong with that."

He opened the door.

With her hand at the small of his back, Kristen nudged him to go into the store.

"Deborah?" He stretched his neck, looking around.

Kristen pushed him all the way inside. "Deborah!"

"Maybe she's not here." He stepped farther into the store, careful not to knock anything over. *Organized hoarder.* He got anxious whenever he was in the store. Too much stuff around him made him tense. But not as anxious as the conversation he planned.

****

"She's right there," she whispered into Luke's ear as not to startle Deborah while she hung ropes of garland along the back window.

"I figured you would have been finished decorating by now," he called out.

Deborah struggled to climb down the short ladder. "Arthritis. Nothing works for it. Doctors say exercise. Lift weights, I do. But I can tell you one thing. It's going to snow, and I don't care what the weatherman says. My knees have a better accuracy rating than a questionable forecast."

Luke hurried over to help her down. He reached out his hand as she descended the last two steps. "You shouldn't be doing things like this when you're alone."

"Well, no one else is around to do it."

"Why don't you hire someone?" Luke closed the ladder and tucked it away behind a cabinet.

"Not financially viable. I've told you that already." Deborah peered over the top of her wire-rimmed glasses.

Luke held his sister's hands and looked her straight in her eyes. "Do you have some time to talk?"

"You're in luck. I was about to put up the lunch sign. Give me a minute, and we can go in the back."

Kristen held Luke's hand.

Deborah locked the front door and turned the sign

to *Closed*. She walked back to them. "This looks serious."

"It could be." Luke followed her into her apartment in the back of the store.

"Are you sure you want me here?" Kristen whispered. "She might not want to be honest with me around."

Luke squeezed her hand tight. "I want you here."

She smiled and released her hand from his grip. The tightness in her stomach intensified as the conversation drew near. She would keep her mouth shut and opinions to herself. Luke's family business was his to hash out.

Deborah pulled the small round table away from the wall to free up a chair for sitting. "Tea or coffee?"

"I'll have coffee." Kristen wasn't a fan of coffee but drank it when she was nervous or needed to focus—she was little of both.

"Coffee for me." Luke pulled out a chair and motioned for Kristen to sit.

Deborah poured water into the tank. "What brings you here? Usually you call before driving out this way."

"It's not that far." Kristen slid off her jacket making herself at home. "Well, for out here anyway."

Luke pulled out a chair for his sister. "Sit. I'll get the drinks."

Deborah accepted his offer and fanned out her dress as she took a seat, and then stood. "I'll get the cream—"

"I have it. Sit." Luke removed the hot pot from the coffee maker.

Kristen noticed Luke's hand shake a little as he poured three cups of coffee. She wanted to reach for his hand and tell him the situation would turn out okay, but she had no right to get involved in his business unless he asked.

He placed the hot cups on the table, and then the cream and sugar.

Deborah reached over to the cabinet drawer and retrieved three spoons.

Luke took his seat at the table and lowered his head as he wrapped his fingers around his coffee mug. "Thanks for giving me this time." He took a large gulp of coffee. "I overheard Joan and Aunt Gladys mention something. Would you have any idea what they are referring to?"

Deborah dropped her coffee cup, spilling it on the table. "Oh my. Where's my dish towel?"

Kristen stared at Luke with determination to inform him he hit on something. "Here you go." She pulled a towel from the oven door handle and leaned across the table, handing it to Deborah.

Luke wiped up the steaming coffee. "Are you okay? Did it get you?"

"No. No. I'm fine." Deborah's hand shook, and she tensed her fingers.

"Did I say something to upset you?" Luke poured his sister another cup of coffee. "I don't mean to if I did."

"No worries. Sit." Deborah's hands gripped her mug. She sighed, and then placed her mug on the table, then spread her palms across the front of her dress, smoothing out unseen wrinkles. "It's complicated."

Luke leaned back in the chair, pushing his cup away.

Kristen waited with bated breath, preparing herself

to referee if needed.

"I'm ready for complicated. The way they said it, the tone and secrecy, got up my hackles, and I'm curious. What should I know?"

Deborah took a deep sigh. Sweat beaded on her forehead. A gentle swipe of the back of her hand cleared away the moisture.

Kristen watched as Deborah clasped her hands and knitted her fingers together. With her eyes closed and lips barely moving, it seemed as if she was praying or mumbling some incoherent chant.

Luke rustled in his chair.

Kristen placed her hand on his arm to settle him. She was as anxious as he was, but rushing Deborah would not give him the information any sooner; in fact it might scare her off, and he wouldn't get any information.

Deborah blessed herself and opened her eyes. "Please know I am the messenger. I didn't find out myself until we were adults, and by then I figured it didn't matter but I can see it does. Especially if you have Kristen and Danny in your life."

Luke sat back with his arms folded across his chest. "More lies. I can feel it coming on."

"More like stories." Deborah smiled but her lips barely moved.

"Lies." Luke tapped a foot against the wooden floor.

"Sssssh, let her talk." Kristen moved closer, hoping her presence would calm him down.

"Brian is not your brother. Therefore, Danny is not your nephew."

Kristen's stomach fell, and her chest relaxed. A

weight of worry left her body, and her head was lighter. Not wanting to exude too much pleasure, she suppressed a smile.

His shoulders slumped. "And you?"

"Are not your sister by blood, but I have always considered you my brother."

Luke hung his head, staring at the floor. He rubbed his eyes. Without lifting his head, he asked, "And my father?"

Deborah shook her head.

"Well, wait. He has to have a father." Kristen stood and rubbed Luke's shoulders. "More coffee?"

"Please, though I'd really prefer a shot of whiskey." He stretched his legs out in front of him and crossed his arms.

"Deborah?" Kristen refilled two cups.

"No. Thank you." Deborah sunk into the chair.

"Our parents were wonderful people. I know it might not seem that way to you right now, but let me gather my words and explain it the best I can. Your mother showed up one day looking for work. At the time we were a small farm, and my mother needed help around the house with me and Brian. He was always a handful.

"Anyway, your mother was a young widow, who lost her husband in a secret intelligence mission overseas. She wanted to settle in an area where she could feel safe raising you, and so my parents hired her."

"But we didn't live here." Luke rested his chin on top of his fist.

"At first you did but you were too young to remember. You started calling my father, Dad, and we went with it. My mother didn't mind. You were so precious, and everyone felt so bad for you because of your situation. Those are the secrets of a small town. As rampant as the gossip can be, the secrets that need to be protected are held close to the heart."

"And then?" Luke loosened his grip and picked up his coffee, took a sip, and leaned back.

"And that was it. Simple. Your mother needed help, so did mine, the arrangement worked. Once Amanda grew stronger and had some money saved, she wanted to move out and have her own place. My mother helped her find an apartment."

"In Haineswood?" Luke questioned.

"Yes, and my mother helped her set up the place with furniture and was available to your mother should she need help. My parents couldn't bear to break the news to you. We were not your biological family, but you were always a brother to me."

"Is there any more?" Luke leaned forward like he was conducting an interrogation.

"Not that I know of, but your aunt Gladys might know more. All I know is your birth father's name is Andrew Baldwin, and he was an army man."

The air in the small apartment grew heavy. Unsure the ride home would prove to be unpleasant, Kristen stood, choosing to leave before the conversation turned ugly. "Thank you for the coffee and information. Luke, you ready to go?"

He nodded and stood. "Would I ever have been told if I didn't confront you?"

Deborah shook her head. "Probably not. Why upset you for no reason?"

Kristen's heart broke for Luke. How much more

upset could he take?

****

Luke opened the passenger door and waited for Kristen to get into her seat.

"Wow, that wasn't what you were expecting to hear, was it?" She wiped her brow.

He glanced at Deborah's storefront. "No, it wasn't." His mind swirled with memories he couldn't sort through quickly enough to organize. He closed the car door. *Were they true or the fabrication of a child?* In a matter of seconds, he lost the only family he knew. Chances of his mother giving him information were slim. And Aunt Gladys, how could she keep a secret for so long? He didn't know whether to be upset, angry, forgiving, understanding, or accept his lot in life, and move on. He walked around to the driver's door and got in the car.

"Are you okay?" Kristen took his hand and held it tight.

She held onto him like she was never going to let go. "I should take you home. You have a big event tonight, and I don't want to put a damper on things." He turned on the ignition and peeled away from the curb.

"I beg to differ, sir. I think you need my company. I am a delightful person, even known to be funny at times, especially when people need it the most."

"No, I—"

"No, nothing. You want to go to the falls and scream your head off? I'm your girl. You want to take this car out on the highway and press the gas pedal to the floor? Well, I'll take the wheel, and you can ride shotgun."

"I need to do something."

271

"Shopping?"

"No." The care and concern Kristen provided was more than he expected. His heart was full, and he finally understood love.

"Good, because the Christmas trees are pretty and all, but I'm at my max for indoor outdoor/shrubs."

"I want you to meet someone."

Kristen sat back in her seat and turned down the radio. "I'm up for whatever you want to do, short of anything that would get us arrested."

He slowed the car within the speed limit. His anger subsided to a comfortable level. But how was he supposed to respond when his entire life was a lie? Thankfully, Kristen seemed to forgive him and was by his side. Her calm demeanor was a grounding force. He didn't know what direction their relationship would go, but he would do his best to make *his* intentions clear. He often thought back to the day he spilled the snow cone on her new shirt. Being an awkward teenager, he didn't handle the embarrassing moment well. He knew then she was someone special and having a second chance was an opportunity he couldn't pass up.

The assisted living center loomed in front of them. He pulled into the driveway, hoping his mother was having a good day. He walked around to her side and opened the door,

Kristen looked up. "Are you sure you want me to go in here?"

"Yes. Today more than ever. I would like to introduce you to my mother." He closed the car door and rested his hand at the small of her back, and then led her up the stairs. The sun faded behind snow clouds. Unsure if introducing Kristen to his mother was a smart decision, he threw caution to the wind and decided to confront her, regardless of potential conflict.

He approached the reception desk, prepared for the inevitable conversation with his mother.

"Ah. Mr. Baldwin. Your mother will be so happy to see you. She's having a terrific day. She went on her own into the bingo parlor and played for an hour. Even sat in the lounge and made new friends."

"Thank you, Felicia." He glanced at his watch. Three-thirty. Too early for dinner. "Do you know where she is?"

"The last I saw her was in her apartment. She went to take a nap around one, but she should be awake by now. Your mom doesn't take long naps." Felicia checked the schedule.

"Thank you. I'll let myself in." He grabbed Kristen's hand.

"Ma'am? Sorry but I'll need you to sign in." Felicia handed a clipboard with a log sheet and pen.

"Oh, sure. No problem." Kristen quickly jotted her signature across the page and glanced at the clock.

"Thank you." Felicia took back the sign-in board and buzzed them into the main hallway.

"Your mother's apartment?" Kristen crinkled her nose.

"That's what it's called, so it feels more like home. I know the lobby seems a bit clinical, but the resident area is nice. My mother's unit has a kitchen, no gas, all electric, bathroom, living room, and a bedroom. It's quite nice. There is a large window—well, you'll see." He held Kristen's hand and knocked on the door at Apartment 1C. The television was playing so he knew his mother was in her residence. He waited a few seconds and then knocked again. "Mom? It's me, Luke."

The volume of the television lowered, and he heard feet shuffle toward the door. A sliver of light bled through the crack of the door. "Mom, it's me."

The door slowly opened. "Luke! It's so nice to see you."

He smiled, so far so good. "I would like you to meet my friend, Kristen. Kristen, this is my mom, Amanda. Do you mind if we come in to visit?"

"You can call me Mandy, but I don't mind either name. Come in." His mother held onto Kristen's hand and guided her into the living room.

"I see what you mean about the beautiful window. How nice to have a weeping willow tree right outside your room." Kristen retrieved her hand from Mandy's grip.

"It reminds me of when I was a little girl. I would grab an armful of branches and swing through the air. The tips of the branches brushing the ground beneath me. You can't do that anymore. Too many rules. Rules against having fun. Would you two like something to drink? No beer, that's not allowed. See another rule. But I have iced tea and lemonade."

"No, Mom. I'm fine. You?" He turned to Kristen.

"No, thank you. I'm good."

Amanda sat on the chair next to the large window, staring at a cardinal hiding in the tree. "I love this time of year. The snow makes everything seem so perfect. Shiny and new. We get much more snow here than in New Jersey. But we don't have the ocean. I miss the water. Lakes are not an adequate substitute. Well, if I can't get you a drink, is there something I can do for you?"

At the risk of overwhelming his mother but the need to satisfy his curiosity, he chose to gamble. "I do have something to ask you. And if it's too much, I understand. I don't want to put any pressure on you."

His mother leaned in. "Are you looking for money?"

He smiled at her whisper, because she always wanted to take care of him. "No, Mom. I'm fine. You've taught me well." He hesitated and buckled in for what could be an upsetting conversation but she seemed lucid and talkative.

"Well, what is it?" Amanda sat back and crossed her legs at the ankles.

She always told him a lady never crosses leg over knee—only at the ankle like a queen. "I overheard some talk today and went to Deborah for an answer. Apparently, I'm not related to the Reeves." Whew, he got it out, his chest was lighter and his head clearer, like a huge weight had been lifted from his body.

"No, you're not. Though, Mr. Reeves loved you like a son." Amanda looked out the window and traced the initials AB and AS on the window fog. "Your father is, Andrew Baldwin."

"And the AS?" He weighed the danger of pushing his mother to talk. When she became overwhelmed, she got confused and would shut down. He had gotten good at recognizing the signs but so far, she seemed okay. No confusion, and she was willing to talk.

"It's me, silly. Amanda Sofer."

He slapped his forehead. "Of course. I didn't put that together."

"So yes, Andrew was your father, he—he."

Amanda's head dropped. She fiddled with her fingers.

Luke knelt in front of her. "Mom. That's enough. I needed to know if what I was told was the truth or small-town gossip." He didn't want her to shut down.

"It was the truth." Amanda stood, shaking slightly, and made her way to her bedroom.

"Should you go after her?" Kristen's eyes grew wide.

"No, give her a moment. She's never mentioned this so I'm sure it was as much of a bombshell to her as to me." He sat on the couch next to Kristen.

She slid her fingers through his and squeezed his hand.

Amanda came back into the living room. "Here, I want you to have this. It's the only copy. The only picture of me, your dad, and you."

His hand shook as he took the picture. He had his father's nose and mouth but his mother's eyes. "Where am I?"

Amanda placed her hands on her belly. "You were right here. All five months of you and then your dad got called away—"

"Mom, don't say anymore." He stood, and then wrapped his arms around her and kissed her on the forehead. He obviously got his height from his father. "This is not the only copy." He took out his cellphone, placed the picture face-up on the couch seat, and took a picture of the only tangible item she had of her husband. He showed the picture to his mother. "Now we both have a copy."

Amanda wiped away a tear. "I'm going to miss the next bingo game."

"No, you won't. We'll walk you down to the

community room. I love you, Mom."

He slipped one hand into Kristen's and the other into his mom's. Two women in his life, completely unaware of the role each played in his life going forward. Would he be strong and sensitive enough to weather what the future had in store?

Chapter Twenty-One

In the car after bringing Amanda to be with her friends, Kristen failed at fighting back tears. She never experienced anything so moving. Her heart nearly leapt out of her chest as she witnessed the exchange between Luke and his mother. She wasn't sure but an electrical-like sensation ran through her body. She might have fallen in love with him at that moment.

He was quiet on the drive back to the inn.

Not even the radio played. She didn't want to put undue pressure on him, because he had been through enough and it wasn't even dinner time. Five o'clock and the sun was gone. Onto night with the moon hidden by the promise of more snow. Every Christmas light hung in a storefront or on a house lit the way home. Her favorite area was the middle island on Main Street in Brookside Falls dotted with black enameled steel and white frosted-globe street posts. The scene reminded her of an old black-and-white Christmas movie. She couldn't remember the title but it made her feel good when it was on TV. Maybe one day she could watch the movie with Luke.

She glanced at him as he stared straight ahead intent on focusing on the road. Every once in a while, carolers walked and sang or music piped from the speaker on a storefront added to the quaint atmosphere of her little town.

Luke pulled into the parking lot at the inn.

Danny! She had been so wrapped up in Luke's ordeal she completely forgot about her nephew. She glanced at her phone. No messages so things must be okay. Still, she didn't like to dump Danny on her grandmother because of convenience. The car came to a stop, and she waited to see what Luke's move would be. Was he staying? Going home?

He turned off the ignition.

She took it as a sign he was at least walking her into the house. Ever being the gentleman, he opened her door. "Are you coming in?" She didn't want to pressure him, but she wanted to be hospitable.

He nodded and followed her up the front steps and into the foyer.

"Luke!" Danny ran and jumped in his arms.

Luke caught him and let him hang as Danny wrapped his arms around Luke's neck.

"You missed the biggest batch of cookies. Something Nana never made before. Cinnamon, chocolate, and white frosting."

"Sounds delicious. Where are they?" Luke lowered Danny to the ground.

"Gone. The guests ate them all. You have to be in the kitchen if you want to make sure you get what's coming out of the oven." Danny ran into the kitchen.

"Um, I know you've had an unexpected day, but do you plan to hang around for bit? I could use your help with something." She tapped her lips with the tip of her finger. "It's a little work but should go fast."

"I could use a distraction." He slid his coat down his arms.

She quickly ran behind him and grabbed his coat at

the collar. "You need this."

"Back outside? I'll freeze."

"Nah, just a little outside work. Be right back." She opened the door that led to the basement, flipped on the wall light switch, and then walked down the stairs. Her breath hung in the air as she landed on the last step. "Ah, there you are." She grabbed two large plastic containers and carried them up to the foyer.

Luke closed the door behind her.

"This is our mission. I promised Mr. Parsons he could bring his horse and sleigh through the back trails. I thought it would be pretty if I strung lights along the path."

Luke took the containers and rifled through boxes of lights. "Doesn't seem like too many but did you figure out how to hang these in the woods?"

"Not a problem. The woods hold the answer." She walked to the kitchen and peeked in. Sure enough, Nana was still working. No sense getting her to stop. As long as she had people to feed, she would be cooking or baking. At least she agreed to the buffet instead of a sit-down dinner. "Danny, you okay in here?"

He nodded with a cookie hanging from his teeth.

At that rate of consumption, he could gain ten pounds by the time school started.

"I'm going to hang here. Nana is using my suggestions. I want to make sure she follows my directions."

She laughed and turned to Luke. "I'm ready."

He carried the containers and followed her to the woods behind the house and onto the beaten down trail. "It's dark back here."

"Yep, and that's why I'm hanging lights. See the

hooks slightly higher than you?"

He looked up the trunk of a maple tree. "Yes."

"The work is already done for us. My grandfather used to do this every Christmas. He would hitch up one of the horses to a hay wagon and pull me and Carly through the trails. You'll notice he has the electric strung along the hook system."

"Smart Andersons you are." He opened a container and unboxed the first string of lights. "End to end, I suppose?"

"Yep, and yes we are. This area was more rural when my great-grandparents bought the place so they had to learn to become resourceful." She watched for signs of Luke's willingness to talk. He seemed engrossed in stringing the lights in the trees so she decided to sit on her need to know.

He opened another box and stretched out the strand. "Will these be enough?"

"For this year. I figured I would light about two hundred feet starting from this edge on each side. There should be eight boxes of fifty feet. So, basically it's going to be this circle." She pointed to the layout of the trail.

"That will be nice."

"I thought so."

His lips started to move but then he stopped.

She would wait.

Hoo-hoo-hoo.

Luke looked above him. He put his finger to his lips and walked toward her.

"You see?" he whispered.

She acknowledged the great owl perched in a tree.

Luke put his arms around her shoulder and pulled

her closer. "Are you still angry with me? Do you still think Deborah and I had a scheme to take your Danny?"

She leaned in and shook her head. "No, it was crazy. Deborah's interest in Danny put me on edge, but I understand it now. What about you? How are you doing?"

"To be honest, my head is still absorbing what happened today. I guess I always figured there was more, but I never pressured my mom. By the way, what did you think of her?"

She slid her arm around his waist. "Honestly, I was surprised how clear she was."

"Yeah, she was having a good day. It comes and goes. It seems the more chaotic things are, the more confused she gets, and that's when she can't remember things. I think your presence helped her focus."

"Why so?" She leaned her head against his chest.

"I don't have a clue." He turned and kissed her.

His soft lips melted her like a snowflake landing on her nose. A rush of warmth surged through her body. Despite the thirty-degree temperature, she was hot.

****

His lips parted from hers. "You know, we have to string these lights before Mr. Parsons or Santa Claus arrives."

She let out a sigh. "Sure, whatever you say."

He held her until her body stiffened, and she was no longer enraptured in his embrace like a silk cloth.

"You took the wind right out of me." She straightened her body and flipped her hair over her shoulder.

"Is that a bad thing?" He unrolled the last of the lights and strung them together.

"Not a bad thing at all. It's a very good thing. I was caught off guard."

"Me, too. I moved to Haineswood to help my mother and got more than I bargained for. A chance meeting over a disagreement over a Christmas tree brought me the girl I met at the carnival. A woman whose concern and caring brought out the best in my mother, and a loving woman who would canvass the world to keep her nephew safe. And most of all, the woman who captured my heart, and I have no plans of ever leaving her."

A rush of excitement surged through Kristen. Her reluctance to leave New Jersey was squashed by the man who tried to steal her Christmas tree. Her heart pounded, and for the first time, she was at peace. Uncertainty faded and was replaced by love.

He glanced around the woods. "This is beautiful. I think I prefer Brookside Falls to Haineswood. I like the energy in this little pocket of semi-rural Pennsylvania."

She agreed. Moving to her grandmother's house was likely a positive decision. Her life had taken a turn she never anticipated, and only time would show if she should stay. So far, the indication was yes. "Your neighborhood isn't far. Maybe being in the woods at night with flurries landing on your nose makes this place seem magical."

"Maybe. But I think the company provides the magic." He smiled.

She cleared her throat and wasn't used to compliments so easily presented. "Are all the lights strung?"

"Yep, last one in the tree. Scared away the owl."

"He'll be back. Close your eyes."

He did what she demanded.

She flipped a switch installed on a tree. "Okay, open." White lights perfectly hung along the trail cast a wall of light to guide any horse through the woods without a problem.

"It's beautiful."

"See, I told you it would be easy. Maybe next year, I'll extend the lighting, but this works for now. Oh, I have one more thing to show you." She held out her hand to Luke.

She watched his clumsy attempt to gather the garbage and her hand at the same time.

"You wouldn't want the horse to trip over this, would you?" He picked up every last piece of cardboard box and stuffed it into one container. "What's next?"

She took his hand and pulled him toward the house. As much as she wanted to stay in the woods and take in the moment, she had to get back to help. "Come on. It's something I would do every Christmas Eve and whenever I was feeling lonely or sad."

He dropped the containers at the foot of the back steps, and then followed her.

She ran down the driveway and out to the road in front of the house.

"I don't see anything out here but empty streets."

"Open your eyes.

"They are open. What am I looking for?"

"Ah, you've been working behind a desk too long. Look overhead."

He closed his eyes and reopened them. "Again, what am I supposed to see?"

She slid an arm around his waist, and then placed

her index finger under his chin, gently nudging his face skyward. "Look at the stars. Have you ever seen such beauty?"

He hesitated. "You're right. That also means no snow."

"Funny. I thought you would enjoy seeing the stars after so many nights of snow." She sighed. "I have one more thing to show you." She slipped her arm into his and walked across the street and down a few blocks. She stopped at the vacant church.

"This?" He rubbed his chin.

"Yes, this. This was my comfort. My, where I would go when I needed to solve problems. I'd peek inside and imagine what it could be…anything."

"Kristen, it's an empty church. A very old empty church." He kissed her hand.

"You don't have any imagination. Look in the window. Try it."

He tilted his head to the side. "I feel funny."

"Just do it." She wrapped both arms around his waist and stood behind him as she pointed to the side window.

He placed a hand against the window and looked through the dirty glass. "Nothing but an empty room with a few wooden pews painted white."

"Open your mind and think," she whispered.

He squeezed his eyes shut and slowly opened them.

"Did it work? Did you see something?"

"I did." He sucked in a breath. "I—"

"Don't tell me. I know it's silly but doing this has helped me so many times. I think staring at the empty room lets your mind be free and purge the tension in your head."

"It's not silly. Thank you. So how long has this place been vacant?"

"Ever since I was a kid. I don't know why someone never bought it. I would in a heartbeat if I had the money. It comes with the little white house next door."

"What would you do with it?" He held her hand and walked back to the inn.

"I don't know, but I would own it. So the minute I think of what I'd want to do with it, I could. It's a shame to waste a building as beautiful as that one. I thought you would appreciate the structure, since you're an architect."

He stopped walking and tilted his head. "Okay, I get it. From the outside, I can guess the building has strong bones. The roof ridge was straight, and doors and windows were square. Even the stone foundation looked solid. But you really can't tell unless a thorough inspection is done."

"What's your professional opinion?"

"From an architect's view, the opinion is favorable. Of course, it's a quick summation, and I haven't seen the inside."

Kristen glanced back at the church as she crossed the street. "Maybe one day. I have something else to ask you."

"Does it involve more work?"

"Not physical, mental." She stopped walking and grabbed him by the arms. "Invite your family to Christmas tomorrow."

"What family?"

"Your mother, Aunt Gladys, and Deborah. No discussion of your past involved. Let's simply gather the families and spend the holiday together."

"Um, I don't know."

Bringing the families together was the healing she needed. What better way to weave joy into the holiday? "Please. With all the guests it will be like party anyway. No family pressure, one big celebration."

Luke sighed and frowned. "My mother might have an episode."

"Or she might not. You said it yourself, I have a calming effect on her." She squeezed his hand. "It might be what she needs. Gladys will be there to help and keep your mom company."

"I have one request."

"Go for it. I'm feeling generous tonight."

"Can I invite Joan?" He smiled.

"You have a thing for her, don't you?" Kristen laughed.

He shrugged and smiled. "She's like my best bud. I don't know if she has family, but I would still like to ask her."

"I think it will be fine. The more the merrier."

They reached the porch of the inn. "I'm going to say goodnight here."

"No hot chocolate?"

"Not tonight. I have a lot of mental processing to do."

"I understand. Goodnight." She turned toward the front door.

"Oh, no, Not that easy." He wrapped his arms around her and squeezed her.

The breath from their lips melded into the air. He hugged her like he would never let her go and sealed her desire with a kiss.

****

"It's Christmas!" Danny yelled in the hallway.

Kristen threw open her bedroom door. "Come in here. Quiet."

He ran into her room and bounced on her bed.

The jump caused the headboard to bang against the wall. "Calm down. Some guests might still be asleep."

"Nope. They're already in the dining room eating breakfast. Gladys asked me to come upstairs and see if you were awake."

"Well, if I wasn't, I would be now. You're excited, aren't you?" She grabbed him mid-air and pulled him off her bed. She shared his enthusiasm.

Their first Christmas together spent at the inn with Nana was a gift she couldn't have planned better herself. Each day, her heart was lighter.

"Can I go back downstairs?"

"Have you brushed your teeth this morning?"

"Um, no." He covered his mouth and laughed.

"Go brush first. I'll meet you downstairs." She started to close the door. "Quietly. I'll be right behind you. And don't open any presents."

He left the room in a flash.

She was sure he stuffed his face with cookies. Christmas morning was the only time sweets were allowed for breakfast, and Nana made sure she baked enough to gorge on for three days.

She smoothed out her bedding, rumpled from Danny's gymnastics. How did he have so much energy? Watching his boundless energy was exhausting, and she was concerned with ability to keep up. The aroma of maple syrup wound its way up the stairs. Her grandmother must have gotten up early, because she could smell fresh biscuits also.

The door flew open as Danny rushed inside.

Ring.

She held up her hand to caution him to be quiet. "Okay, it's fine. See you then."

"Are you coming?"

He smelled like a fresh sprig of peppermint. She hung up the phone and grabbed Danny around the waist, wrestling him onto the bed and messing up the covers she fixed. "Merry Christmas." She covered him with kisses until he laughed so hard his sides hurt. "Oh, wait—what's that? I hear bells outside."

He ran to the window and drew back the curtain. "Very cool."

"Gladys said horses were coming to take away the guests." Danny knelt on the window seat.

"I forgot. She arranged the schedule so we would have some of Christmas morning to ourselves. Put on nicer pants and meet me in the kitchen."

Danny took off down the hall.

Kristen looked in the mirror. Sleep eluded her last night, but the morning shower helped her wake up, somewhat.

She threw on her black jeans and red turtleneck. She then chose a pair of diamond earrings that reminded her of snowflakes. Carly had given them to her one year, and she wore them every Christmas. She stuck a picture of Carly in her dresser mirror. "God, I miss you. I'm giving your son the best present I can." She waited for the jingle of the sleigh bells to fade away before heading downstairs. Christmas music greeted her as she walked through the lobby.

Danny munched on cookies with Nana.

"What's this? Cookies for breakfast?" Kristen

stood with her hands on her hips.

Danny slowly lowered the cookie from his mouth. "I-I…"

Kristen laughed and held her belly. "Cookies are the traditional Christmas family breakfast. I'm not kidding you. Enjoy, but don't eat enough to get sick." She picked up a peanut butter cookie, tossed it into her mouth, and washed it down with milk.

"Morning, dear. It's fun having a house full of people again." Nana wiped her hands on her apron. "I'm glad you talked me into getting a dishwasher. I remember having to wash the dishes while your grandfather dried them."

Kristen took an oatmeal raisin cookie as her second choice, and then walked over to her grandmother and hugged her. "I know. This is a rough year."

"I've invited Gladys to spend the morning. Is that okay? She's like family to me." Nana smiled.

"It's a wonderful idea. She has been so helpful, I think having her join us makes perfect sense." She arranged a plate of cookies and handed it to Danny. "Would you please bring this into the living room? It's present time."

Gladys sat in the chair by the window as they paraded into the living room, their arms filled with goodies.

Danny took a seat on the floor next to the tree.

Nana chose the couch.

Kristen sat on the window seat. Her heart swelled with love as she watched Danny scout out the presents. "Go ahead. You can open one."

He ripped into a package, wrapped in blue paper with snowflakes. "Wow, a dump truck!" Danny tossed it aside.

"Remote control dump truck," Nana added.

"Aunt Kristen, can I open another present?"

She couldn't resist his plea. "Oh, go ahead. It's the Christmas season."

Danny lay flat on his belly, slithered under the tree, and grabbed another present. Wrapping paper flew through the air as he plowed through his bounty in less than ten minutes. Kristen thought about how much time and money she put into picking out special gifts and the fun was over within a matter of minutes.

"That's it?" He shuffled through the torn paper.

"Well, maybe not." Kristen sat next to Danny and wrapped her arms around him. She closed her eyes and willed Carly's spirit to fill the room. Her concentration was broken by a subtle knock on the door. "Come in," Kristen yelled.

Luke and Deborah walked in through the foyer to the living room.

Deborah held a present in her hand.

"Luke!" Danny jumped up.

As Luke knelt down to greet him, Danny grabbed him around the neck.

"I remember you. Hello." He held out his hand to greet Deborah.

Luke took his and Deborah's coats and hung them on the coatrack in the foyer.

"Luke, would you like cookies?" Kristen motioned to the platter of chocolate chip, oatmeal raisin, and peanut butter cookies on the hall side table.

"My mother couldn't make it this morning."

"No problem. Maybe she can come over later."

"What a nice surprise." Gladys waved them inside.

Kristen stood in the center of the living room, her stomach queasy with uncertainty. She cleared her throat. "Um, first I want to thank you, Gladys, for the amazing job you did getting this inn reopened, including the beauty shop. I was against it at first, but now Danny and I have decided to stay in Brookside Falls. The shop will be good for me to settle into work. So, feel free to come in anytime to have your hair done."

Gladys blinked back tears and waved her hands in the air, then pushed back her hair.

"Anyway, the opening of the inn has been instrumental in bringing about a few other presents that aren't under any Christmas tree." Kristen knelt to face her nephew. "I know the last few months have been difficult. Nana and I loved your mom very much and still do. I talk to your mom a lot and through her guidance have decided you should know all of your family members."

Nana knitted her brows together. "What do you mean?"

"Danny, I have recently found out Deborah is your aunt." She extended a hand toward Deborah. "She is your father's sister."

Nana sat back, her mouth agape.

Danny clung tighter to Kristen.

Deborah walked up to Danny and handed him the present she'd brought. "I'm glad to meet you, Danny. I have this little gift for you. You might not understand this now, but I'm sure it's something you will appreciate later on."

Danny relaxed and accepted the offer. He peeled away the paper, opened the box, and removed a framed picture. "I saw him before." He put down the picture and ran out of the room.

Kristen started to go after him, fearing Danny was upset by Deborah's visit.

Luke grabbed her hand and held tight. "Let him be for a minute."

"I'm sorry. I didn't mean to upset him. I thought since you said it was okay to let him know, that it was okay to give him the picture." Deborah bowed her head and crossed her arms.

Nana stood. "It's a lot for a seven-year-old to take in. Heck, it's a lot for an eighty-year-old to absorb. Brian Reeves, none of us ever knew. Poor kid has neither parent."

Danny ran back into the room, nearly out of breath from running up and down the stairs. "See. I told you I saw him before." He handed Kristen a slightly crumpled picture.

She instantly recognized Carly with Brian standing behind her, his head on hers and his arms draped upon her chest. They couldn't have been more than seventeen, and the smiles on their faces told Kristen they were happy. Her heart swelled with joy as she looked into Carly's eyes. She passed the picture to Nana. "Where did you get this?"

"Mommy. She told me to keep it safe. She said it's a picture of her and a good friend who died."

Luke knelt down beside Danny. "Well, buddy, he would be your father, Brian—Deborah's brother. Are you okay with this information? She seems like a nice lady."

Danny walked away from Luke and looked back at Deborah. He picked up a peanut butter cookie from the plate and ate it in two bites, never taking his gaze off her. He picked up two more peanut butter cookies and gave one to Luke. "I know you like these. Do you think she does?"

"I think you should ask her yourself," he whispered.

Danny handed Deborah a cookie, and without waiting for an answer, he picked up the wooden yo-yo and sat next to the Christmas tree amongst his presents and newfound family.

Kristen smiled and hugged her chest. She was proud how Danny processed the abundance of news thrown at him in a short time.

The jingle of the sleigh bells neared the house.

"Oh my, what an eventful morning." Nana wiped a tear from her eye. "Hurry. Let's clean up."

Luke walked up to Kristen. "Does this mean I can stay?"

Kristen took his hand and squeezed it. "I think we're going to be okay."

The guests returned to the inn, stamping their feet in the entry. Cheerful voices filled the room. The once-heavy air of the inn was pushed away by the gleeful spirit of Christmas.

He quietly whisked her away to the salon. He wrapped his left arm around her waist and pulled her in close.

Ever so delicately, his breath lingered on her neck. She ran her index finger along the fringe of his hair and brushed the unruly lock from his eyes.

He gazed into her eyes.

Kristen could feel his love sweep through her body. For the first time she knew what true love was, and she was willing to take a chance on embracing the future.

"I would say this has been a strange turn of events, two brothers involved with two sisters."

"Hmm, technically not." He grinned.

"I have a feeling Deborah will always consider you her brother." She tilted back her head and smiled.

"I do have a present for you." He reached into a heart-shaped, gem encrusted jewel box resting on the ledge in the salon and removed a sprig of mistletoe. Then he held the tiny branch over their heads. "I love you."

She locked the door. "I love you, too." Her heart pounded, and blood coursed through her body at a fevered pace. She found the key to her heart. What she expected to be a time of sadness turned into more love than she could wish for. His strong arms wrapped around her with a level of confidence she never experienced. She slid her arms through his and fell into his embrace—heart and soul.

A word about the author…

Lita Harris spends her time between New Jersey and the Endless Mountains region of Pennsylvania. She even lived in Alaska for a short time just for fun.

Her two rescue dogs are always close by and travel everywhere with her.

An avid crafter, unused supplies clutter her basement and attempts at making pottery, jewelry, and stained glass are scattered throughout her house. She also makes candles and homemade soap. With enough books to stock a small library, she might need to construct a building to store her literary obsession.

She writes multiple genres, women's fiction, contemporary romance, paranormal, and cozy mysteries. For more information about Lita, please visit her website at www.LitaHarris.com | Twitter | Facebook | or | Instagram |

Thank you for purchasing
this publication of The Wild Rose Press, Inc.

For questions or more information
contact us at
info@thewildrosepress.com.

The Wild Rose Press, Inc.
www.thewildrosepress.com